DRAGON OF LIFE

Book 2 Minor Gods

by

Mark Devine

ISBN 978-0-9850164-1-8

Cover photograph© Darren Baker

Book design and typeset in Bembo
by www.chandlerbookdesign.co.uk

Printed in Great Britain
by Ashford Colour Press Ltd.

In Memory of

Xing Zhi Hong, M.D.

(1902—1970)

NINETEEN SIXTY-EIGHT

1.

Winter is not Seattle's most attractive season. Deciduous trees are leafless, flowers barely a memory and Caucasian faces have become shades of gray. When first concluded, a substantial snowfall brightens the landscape, reddens fleshy cheeks and amplifies the season's scarce illumination. But while the white stuff's falling, the sun struggles for survival and headlights reach a mere foot and half, maybe two. Actually, it's far enough considering vehicles ought to be crawling and only suicidal pedestrians step in front of cars, trucks, buses and other objects on four wheels that can't stop because they're slipping and sliding.

Though evergreen trees are beautiful and prevalent, conifers don't produce light or disperse soggy clouds, so for months Seattleites wait in a wet and darkened theater for the curtain to go up and the *Rites of Spring* to begin again.

Two and half hours ago, I landed at Seattle-Tacoma International Airport to conclude a trip from Valparaiso, Chile, where the hotel we sold and financed was having serious problems, because some of the proceeds, it was eventually determined, were going into the comptroller's pocket instead of the hotel's bank account; the SOB was embezzling. I loaned the ownership group more money to pay their bills, plus some extra for a cushion. The comptroller was fired, then arrested, and procedures for handling cash were tightened. Before leaving, I calmly explained that I could and would take back the hotel, if necessary. In truth it doesn't make much sense to be supervising operations of a hotel in Valparaiso when living in Singapore.

Had not John James Scott, dear ol' JJ, suddenly needed his gall bladder removed, it would have been *his* responsibility to deal with *our* mid-December problem in Valparaiso, and *I* would not have flown from Singapore to Hong Kong to Tokyo to Hawaii to Los Angeles, etc., as the original plan had been for me to spend December in Seattle enjoying my first Christmas with a gorgeous new wife; my wife, of course.

December in Valparaiso with its Christmas spirit intact, compares nicely with Seattle in late June: blooming flowers rather than snow, sunlight rather than gloom and nary a gray face.

Presently, I'm wearing a rumpled dark-gray suit with a sat-out seat, wrinkled white button-down shirt, regimental striped tie, scuffed black brogues, and no handkerchief (lost it somewhere), with a tan camelhair overcoat across my arm, while leaning against Northwest Orient Airline's ticket counter watching an early-evening blizzard and waiting with prodigious anxiety for Martha.

We have reservations on Northwest's non-stop flight from Seattle to Tokyo, scheduled to depart at seven o'clock, twenty-nine minutes from now. From Hong Kong and Valparaiso, I've briefly talked to Martha a few times on the phone, but I haven't seen her since nine October; a long time for a gentleman who married the world's most desirable woman on twenty-seven July, last.

Oh yes, I'm holding a dozen long-stemmed roses of six different colors, wrapped in that waxy-green florist paper. They're the result of bribery (two of the roses were ready for delivery to another woman) and a frantic taxi ride to and from Burien, in the snow before it became a blizzard. The idea was purely romantic. At the time, I thought not about the obvious impracticality of taking a dozen long-stem roses aboard a 707 that would continuously (if we are so blessed) be in the air for too many hours.

Oh well, Martha will appreciate their sentimental significance and handle the situation with great aplomb; probably hold them close to her nose in hopes their fragrance will offset my gaminess until we eventually land and I get a shower.

Ah, ha! A woman who's laughing and smiling doth approach. A woman with a handsome airline pilot on either side, each carrying one of her suitcases. Perchance, they shared the Airporter from the Olympic Hotel. Perchance, I shouldn't have been gone for such a long time.

Except for a new navy-blue raincoat, her face, hair, legs, stockings and navy-blue heels are just as I expect, just as I remember. The pilots are arriving too late to be working our flight; otherwise, friendly Mrs. Martha Whitaker would spend half her time in the cockpit. She may anyway.

"Hi honey," she breezes, puts her arms round my neck and kisses me like we're in a bedroom; but not for too long, because she doesn't want to keep the principles of Pilot & Pilot, almost burro like baggage porters, waiting.

We're introduced before Martha asks if the roses are for her. I nod, she takes the flowers, exchanges more smiles with

John Wayne and Robert Stack, who walk away smiling and without a tip, leaving us alone to check her bags, the claim stub to be stapled to her ticket folder, which I extricate from my inner jacket pocket while asking if she remembered her passport. She takes the new document, with her new name, from her new over-the-shoulder navy-blue leather purse and hands it to me with a smile that's more genuine than that of any airline ticket agent in the universe; as it should be.

"Do we have time for a drink?" she grins, taking my arm as we head for the gate.

"We don't even have time for the bathroom," I gruff, and increase the length of my stride.

Nearing the gate, Martha releases my arm and veers into a river of arriving passengers. Then she stops in the path of a wheelchair being pushed by an airline employee. While I pause in wonder, Martha leans down and toward the old woman in the wheelchair, makes her a present of the roses, then gives her a peck on the cheek. As Martha backs toward me, the two women exchange nods, smiles, and little wrist-waves. Genetically flawed by gender, a young man would never give flowers, or a cigar, or even a bottle of Pepsi to an unknown older man. If not for women, men would live and die independent, alone and grumpy. So I'm thankful for Martha, the queen of spontaneous kindness with hugs for everyone – not holding a gun.

A senior stewardess shows Mr. & Mrs. Whitaker to their seats. Mr. Whitaker helps Mrs. Whitaker out of her raincoat, combines it with his overcoat, and stows both in the overhead compartment from which he removes a pillow and blanket, then latches the cover. Mr. Whitaker continues to wear his suitcoat believing it's less disreputable than his shirt, and silently approves of Mrs. Whitaker's long-sleeve, mock-turtleneck, navy-blue cashmere sweater and matching skirt with box-pleats; the sweater's not too tight and the skirt's not too short, he notes, while enjoying their ability to stimulate the imagination.

"Mr. Whitaker," Martha idles, to get my attention while passengers continue to pass us in search of their assigned seats, and rather like she's talking to the hired help.

"Yes, your ladyship," I respond, butler-like, for all who might be listening, "what can I do for you?"

"I was under the impression that we only fly First Class if there was no other choice," she critiques. "Your argument being that First Class and Tourist arrive at the same time, etc., and yet here we are, in First Class."

"I can explain, ma'am," I grovel.

"Please *do*, Mr. Whitaker."

"Well, you see, I was rather certain, after considering the extended length of this flight, that your ladyship would be more comfortable with the extra space, comfort and privacy provided by the First Class portion of this aircraft. And whereas *it did* seem more economical to ticket myself in Tourist, and I agonized, believe me I did, over the decision, I felt I could better cater to your every whim, and afford you a smidge more privacy by, well, our sitting together."

"I see. Well, I suppose there's no real harm …"

"Let me demonstrate," I interrupt, as the plane's being pushed away from the gate. "Hand me your shoes, please."

"You can't be serious," she objects. "I'll do no such thing."

"Yes'm. But I insist."

"Oh, very well," she concedes, then reaches down and removes her heels—to the nearly audible cheering of local union members belonging to the International Brotherhood of Feet & Toes—and gives them to me.

I put one shoe next to me and the other between my legs, with the toe pointing away, before taking the airline magazine from the seatback in front of me, opening it and randomly tearing out a couple of pages, which I crumble and stuff into one shoe and then the other, so the shoes will retain their shape while drying in the overhead. Martha uses the blanket I hand her, to put under and over her feet and legs. I sit down and re-buckle my seat belt before an agent of the FAA can issue a reprimand. Whining jet engines announce their readiness.

"Ladies and gentlemen …" the stewardess welcomes.

My scotch & water arrives in record time. I suspect the cabin crew would like to hurry things along, as *they* are hungry and want dinner. Martha holds a gin & tonic. Clearly, she's spent too much time in the company of JJ, probably while at the Seattle Tennis Club, perhaps taking tennis lessons. Our glasses are made of glass not plastic; the clunking-type of glass if toasting, not the good clinking-type, though there's nothing actually wrong with plastic if one's thirsty enough, and I generally am.

"Want to hear what I've been doing while you've been jetting about, living the high life, whooping it up and ignoring your wife?" Martha teases.

I nod and take a sip.

"More enthusiasm, please."

"Okay, okay! Tell me everything, I beg you. Word for word. Moment by moment. Leave nothing out. I know damn well you can do it!"

"If you insist," she giggles, takes my hand and squeezes it, and I return her squeeze, again aware of how much I've missed her.

"I insist!"

"Good, then ask me questions. That way I'll know you're paying attention, and I'm not boring you."

Martha's a clever woman. I oft wonder if I'm more attracted to her cleverness than to her … woman-ness. It doubtless has to do with aging. I'll be thirty in a few months, and Martha will be … Oh, my! She turned twenty-five on Christmas eve, and I forgot. Damn! I could ask her if she got the birthday present I sent, and when she says, "no", I can blame it on foreign postal services.

"I forgot your birthday," I moan. "As soon as we get to Tokyo, I'll make it up to you. It won't happen again."

"I should hope *not*," she whirrs. "I was waiting until we got to Hong Kong to mention it. Glad I didn't have to. But understand, dear husband, you're only breathing because you didn't forget Christmas."

"You're too kind, my love, and what would you like for your birthday?"

"I don't know. My needs are simple. Now that I have my own American Express card, well, there's not much I need that I don't have. Last summer you gave me a million dollar trust fund, and you hardly knew me."

"I still don't."

"That's because you're not supposed to," she teases, and looks at me through long eyelashes, and smiles a clever smile. "My trust fund is supposed to be in a Hong Kong bank, so when we get there, I guess we can check on that, right?"

I nod.

"Why did you do it?

"Do what?"

"The trust fund."

"Oh. Well, at that particular moment you were feeling rather homeless, insecure, a bit down in the dumps. Thought it might cheer you up a tad."

"Can you actually afford to give me a million dollars every time you think I need cheering up?" she asks, without smiling and somewhat like a mother might.

"I'll admit it's a gamble," I cajole, after a pause to consider the diceyness of her question. Our cabin attendant passes, and I hand her my empty glass along with a nod to mean more of the same, please. When portions of the world are trained to interpret my nods, it makes life so much easier, and quieter. I've not had good results in noisy countries, parts of Latin America being nearly hopeless.

"Mrs. Whitaker?" solicits the stewardess, as she delivers my glass full of ice and liquid of the proper smoky color. Martha gives up what's left of her gin & tonic in the hope of another, which magically appears.

"Of course, jewelry's always nice," Martha sighs, more to herself than me. "I wear Mei Liew's necklace all the time. I'm never without my engagement and wedding rings. I seldom wear a watch, and don't want to. Nah, nix the jewelry. I wouldn't wear most of it, so it would just sit in a vault."

I nod.

"My wants are as simple as my needs," she flashes, and takes a long enough pull on her drink to suggest the trail from downtown Seattle to the airport was hot and dusty. "There are only two things: Sex and Money!"

Apparently, the union guards assigned to watch my tongue have been skimming the scotch on its way to my stomach, otherwise I'd never be allowed to suggest, which I do, that a lot of women have developed lucrative careers in the simultaneous pursuit of those two goals—or something similar but cruder—for which I receive a threatening growl, while a hard little fist tries to imbed knuckles into my left biceps.

Just as bridges in Seattle must be raised to allow for the ingress and egress of marine traffic, so must tray tables be raised. However, unlike bridges, whoever's *not* exiting or entering must also rise and hold in their hands everything the tray tables previously held. After the trouble with my judgment-impaired tongue, it's the least I can do for Martha, though it does place me eye-to-eye with another male passenger flying in First Class, who's exercising what he assumes to be his constitutional right of standing and moving round, regardless of the fact he lacks a jacket and has loosened his tie.

"Hi," he smiles, without extending a hand for he can see both of mine are employed.

"Good afternoon," I smile in return.

"I'm Sheldon Wingate. What's your name?

"Sorry," I soulful, letting my eyes drift from his eyes to the floor, "but that's classified information."

"Gosh, what do you do?"

"That's also classified. I'm terribly sorry."

"You must work for the government," he conjectures.

"I'm afraid I can't comment on that."

"Is that your wife you're flying with?"

"Why do you ask?" I glare, changing from defense to offense.

"I don't know. Just curious I guess."

"Your question regarding the young woman could be a security problem of international proportions, Mr. Wingate. I'm afraid I must know the nature of your interest."

"No interest. Honest."

"Can I see some identification, please?"

"Are you serious?"

"Perfectly, sir. Your identification please," I serious , and he reaches for his wallet, takes out his Washington State

9

driver's license, holds it up so I can see it. "Closer, please. That's better. You live in Lake Forest Park?"

He nods five times, asks if he's dreaming, and starts putting away his ID.

"Probably," I soften. "That would explain your interest in the young lady. Neither she nor I exist, if you must know, so you might consider returning to your seat. And, just so you're correctly advised, if we have another encounter I'll have you arrested when we reach Japan."

Refreshed, Martha's back in her seat with legs and toes wrapped in the blanket. She accepts my apology for melting the ice in her drink while holding it, and for my uncalled-for smartass remark regarding sex and money. She allows that she's getting used to the latter, almost never takes it personally, occasionally finds it amusing, and believes I'll "eventually mature beyond sixth-grade behavior." I pray she's wrong. About the former, she's disappointed I wasn't more creative. After all, most of the airline magazine was still intact and, therefore, could have been wrapped round her glass to insulate it from my too hot hand. Her point's well made.

"You still haven't asked me what I've been doing," she urges.

"I *know* what you've been doing,"

"What?" she challenges, in the middle of a sip which results in a bit of coughing.

"Until JJ got sick, you continued to be a six-day-a-week volunteer RN at Children's Orthopedic Hospital, because kids don't lie, and you took the bus both ways, because you like to meet all kinds of people. When JJ was in the hospital, you were at his bedside. When he was allowed to go home, you moved into his house, slept on the sofa, and took care of him. I trust he's fully recovered."

"He is."

"Thank you for taking care of him."

"You're welcome."

"You've had dinner at Bill and Holly's seventeen times. Always brought a present for Liam, and you read to him while Holly cooked. Twice you went with JJ to visit the DC-3 at Boeing Field, and showed enthusiasm for the refurbishing that Bill supervises. Any idea when the work will be done?"

"Bill is hoping for completion by the end of this week," she says, with vicarious pride, and I'm sure she's wondering about my sources of information.

"JJ has taken you to dinner at the Tennis Club, five times, and he gave you three tennis lessons before his gall bladder attack. I'm guessing tennis doesn't light your fire."

"Good guess."

"Paul and Jenny invited you to four cocktail parties. You attended all of them. Two with JJ, and two by yourself, and you reciprocated by taking them to dinner at Canlis an equal number of times, using JJ's car for transportation, but without him, because he hates that restaurant. I take it you like Mr. and Mrs. Carlyle?"

"They're fun," she smiles. "Always cheerful, and they know *everybody*. I can tell you all kinds of stuff about the Seattle social establishment, if you want to know?"

"No, thank you," I politely decline. "Let's see … you shopped Saturday mornings, except while you were taking care of JJ, and you're on a first name basis with every sales clerk working for Frederick & Nelson."

"That's an exaggeration," she grumps.

"You've been staying in touch with Mei Liew. You've reorganized the family warehouse, spent time wandering round the waterfront, and you've become friendly with my two nurse-neighbors from Regina."

"They only said nice things about you, Luke. They obviously don't know you very well."

"I'm almost done, but this part worries me. Apparently, you have *not* been drinking by yourself, and the only things you've been cooking at home are boiled rice, and Wheaties with poached eggs on top instead of milk, no sugar. For the record, I need a confirmation or a denial. This time only, it doesn't have to be in writing."

Martha isn't responding. Perhaps because her glass no longer contains liquid, and her throat has swollen so much she can't talk. I push the overhead call button. A cabin attendant materializes and I nod. Two more drinks are served, and while Martha re-hydrates, I think of mentioning how happy I am that she's not still wallowing round on that part of the earth we're flying over—the North Pacific—but I choose silence over scratching a scab.

"You creep," she whirrs with volume, and I turn to see an unkind look. "You hired Mike Hamilton! Didn't you! To spy on me. Damn! What did I do to deserve that? I thought we trusted each other. That we were best-friends. I didn't hire anybody to spy on you, Mr. More-Or-Less. It didn't even occur to me. Of all the nerve … damn, damn, damn!"

"Is there something wrong with your drink, Mrs. Whitaker?" worries the re-materializing stewardess. "Can I get you something else?"

"My drink's fine, it's my husband," Martha glowers.

"Do you want me to get the Captain?"

"Is he single?" Martha ices, with her head cocked and one eyebrow elevated.

"He acts like he is," grins the stewardess, "but I don't think so. I'm getting ready to serve dinner if you'd like some? Or maybe some coffee?"

"Can you poach a couple of eggs and put 'em on a bowl of Wheaties?" Martha asks, with a perfectly straight face.

"Oh … gosh," exhales the lady in uniform, doubtless thumbing through the handbook in her mind, that's supposed to deal with every possible situation, "we don't have any fresh eggs … or any kinda cereal …"

"Never mind," Martha excuses, "I wasn't gunna eat it anyway. I was going to dump it in his lap. Thank you, though."

The professional smiles professionally, and leaves with something new for her collection of weird requests.

"Holly," I say, to the back of the seat in front of me.

"What about her?" Martha threatens.

"She reports to me."

"But she's *my* friend."

"But she's *my* employee, and the two are not mutually exclusive. Did she actually tell me anything that you wouldn't have?"

————◆————

2.

How many times will Almighty God bless a given person in a given day? And how do you know when you've used your daily quota? If necessary, can you borrow from tomorrow's allotment (providing you're getting one) or must you give thanks for today's blessings before God will authorize a new ration? The questions keep me awake, while Martha sleeps with the hint of an innocent smile, breathing easily, her head on a pillow resting on my shoulder.

By my calculation, a day with Martha—because she's always with me, though not always present—constitutes a daily blessing. So that's one blessing every day. This day, the fifth of January, began at midnight, as all days do, but on this *date* I've already survived a flight from Mexico City to Los Angeles and another from Los Angeles to Seattle, so that's two more blessings for a total of three, not counting the flight we're on, which began on the fifth but will end on the sixth. So I'll need at least one more blessing on this date, because I believe staying thirty-some thousand feet in the air to be more of a blessing than a scientific marvel.

And then there's the issue of our plane having enough oxygen so we arrive alive, which will be another more-of-a-blessing-than-a-scientific-marvel, since on such a long filled-to-capacity flight several unanticipated (and thus un-calculated) hyperventilating passengers can exhaust the supply. And at this altitude, there isn't more oxygen to be had by just opening a window or door. That's why the cockpit crew has oxygen masks *they* can use whenever *they* want, though the same isn't true in the passenger cabin, where the cabin attendants prefer passengers be near losing consciousness, so they can't move, talk or push the call button; sure, if the plane loses cabin pressure, little yellow masks fall from an overhead compartment (or so we're told), but just try getting at one of those yellow masks *without* the cabin losing pressure due to a big ugly hole in the fuselage, and when there's a big ugly hole in the fuselage, I don't want oxygen; I'd rather *not* be conscious, terrified, and screaming all the way down, thank you all the same and very much.

"Mr. Whitaker," the stewardess whispers, squatting next to me and smelling of cinnamon, "if you aren't hallucinating yet, I'll bring you some more coffee." I nod. "We've started our decent and should be landing in about eighteen minutes." I look at my watch. In Seattle it's five thirty-seven in the morning. "You might want to wake up your beautiful wife," she adds, "Would she like some coffee?"

I nod yet again, and a hand connected to an arm snakes from under the blanket to lovingly clamp my wrist. There will be no cuddling-with-curves upon her awakening, in spite of what she once reported to have read in a lady's room at the Reno Airport. Doubtless, there are FAA regulations that take precedence.

"Hi," Martha coos, and I twist to look at her; she's looking up through eyes hiding among long tangled eyelashes.

"Hi," I greet, and pause to enjoy the slow bloom of her come-to-me smile. "Did you pack any large amounts of alcohol, tobacco, expensive perfume, firearms or ammunition in your luggage?"

Her smile dies as she vacates the pillow and sits up to finger comb her hair, and look out the black window. "No," she thinks aloud, "no large amounts."

"Did you pack even a small amount of firearms or ammunition?"

"Of course not. Why would I do that?"

"After San Francisco …"

"*I* didn't shoot anybody. And there wasn't a gun or any ammunition around your apartment to put in a suitcase. Good grief, what's this all about?"

"We're landing in a few minutes, and we'll have to go through Japanese Customs. The things I asked about, well, they aren't allowed.

"Oh, thank you," I say to the stewardess, and take the coffee being offered in cups on saucers, then I give one to Martha.

The loud rrrr, rrrr, rrrr-ing sound of flaps being lowered earns my attention. I assume we're closer than I thought but I didn't hear the landing gear being lowered. Four jet engines are accelerating and the aircraft starts tipping from side to side. Overdosed on war movies, I initially wonder if we're being chased by an errant North Korean MiG, and our pilots are trying to avoid its cannon fire. But tracers aren't lighting the sky. I anticipate a throttle-back to be soon, and wait. It doesn't happen. We're just grinding forward with the pilots almost keeping the plane under control. Martha's out of her blanket asking for her shoes. Why, I have no idea. We're not going to get out and walk the rest of the way, nor have the fashion police announced a surprise inspection.

When I look at her, I can see she's serious. So, while making sure I keep hold of something, I get up, open the overhead, retrieve her heels, close the overhead and sink back to my seat. The grinding continues, and the rocking becomes so violent that I initiate negotiations for the current use of a future blessing. I've flown too many miles and landed too many times to consider this normal.

"Lights," Martha flashes. "I see some lights. But it's raining so hard they're blurry."

So, thinks I, we've broken out of the clouds by losing altitude over Tokyo Bay, and if she can see lights, even if they're on vessels, we can't be too far from the airport. But the grinding of the engines and rocking of the aircraft continue.

Martha reaches for my hand, and I reach for a hand I can't feel, but I know exists. Our flight from Seattle to Tokyo should last about eleven hours, and cover forty-eight hundred miles of empty Pacific. Five times the distance from Seattle to Los Angeles. And between Seattle and Los Angeles there are *dry* places to land.

Hearing the landing gear come down, I tell Martha to finish her coffee.

"I can't. I need the restroom," she counters. So I finish it for her in time to hand off cups and saucers, before returning the tray tables to their upright and locked position.

"Ladies and gentlemen …" the announcement begins, the speaker having waited until the last possible moment, due to her uncertainty about our having to ditch. Before she finishes, the engines are throttling back to a collective exhale, which puts even more carbon dioxide into the passenger cabin. Little yellow masks do not drop. They won't, I understand, if passengers are smiling, and they're smiling.

After an interminable wait for luggage, and then for our turn to make a declaration, Martha easily glides us through Customs with her flawless aplomb and patentable smiles; hugging of agents only precluded by a substantial counter. If alone and as tired as I am, I would have been garbling answers and mumbling about full-flaps and North Korea, until led away for a strip-search followed by a drug test.

Her raincoat and my overcoat go arm-in-arm toward an exit, followed by a porter carrying four suitcases. Most people believe international luggage limitations exist (no more than two bags per passenger, with a total weight not to exceed twenty kilograms, forty-four pounds) because an aircraft can only carry so much of the stuff. Whereas that's partially true, there was also crushing pressure from the International Brotherhood of Airline Baggage Porters, whose members are tipped *per bag*—not *per kilo* or pound—and there's a limit as to how much weight one porter can carry.

Out the door, and we're into rain being blown horizontally. It wakes me, and it explains the 707's rocking back and forth. The porter (whose father may have killed the father of someone I went to school with) loads our suitcases into the trunk of a taxi, while the driver (whose father may have been killed by the father of someone I went to school with) helps Martha into the backseat, and I find a pair of twenties for the wet smiling porter laboring to support a wife and kids; as Tokyo's expensive for everyone.

I push in next to Martha and slam the door. The engine's running but we aren't moving. A minute goes by. The engine continues to run. We continue to remain stationary.

"Where are we going?" I ask Martha, believing while I was mucking about in the wind and rain she told the driver the name of the hotel where she made a reservation.

"You didn't tell me."

"Of course not. You make the hotel reservations. You're in charge of living arrangements. Aren't you? Didn't you?"

"Luke," pleads the sun perpetually lighting my sky, "I'm not sure where we are, or what time it is. So how about *we* make the problem of finding a warm dry place for *us* to sleep *your* problem?"

"Just so you know, we landed about ten at night, local time. We left Seattle on Friday but now we're in Japan and it's almost midnight on Saturday. And, yes dear, I'll deal with the problem."

For triple twenties the taxi driver quickly finds us a humble but comfortable room in a facility outlined in neon that's within a mile of the airport. I know the hotel's restaurant wouldn't be serving Kobe beef, but I don't care. The bed's made, the ceiling isn't leaking and the door locks.

Patiently polite, I wait my turn to shower while trusting: Martha can't use every drop of the hotel's hot water, though she's trying; the fifth of Cutty Sark purchased in a duty free shop at the Benito Juarez International Airport, and currently being used for medicinal purposes, will last until she's finished.

Having sipped enough to reach that level of relaxation where inhibitions are off limits, I remove my necktie, doff the white button-down shirt and unceremoniously place it in a convenient trash basket, since it has become so objectionable it would permanently contaminate everything in any of our suitcases. I'm barely out of my remaining clothes and into a black silk robe, when Martha appears. She quite lovely and rather perky in semi-wet hair, a white towel and enough bare skin to justify my patience.

"Your turn," she smiles, and gives me a terry cloth hug with a kiss. "Are you sharing the scotch? Or must I get my own?"

"Come now. I share everything with you," I retort, leer and head for the steamy little bathroom.

"What's taking so long?" Martha, who's turning pages in a Japanese language fashion magazine, submits to my Executive Committee, who have never been addressed by anyone other than myself, and are now looking at each other with considerable agitation, while discussing which subcommittee should investigate and respond. Meanwhile, we sit aboard a JAL aircraft that's parked on a side-runway, it's cockpit crew doing their best to start the gyros.

"We're afraid that's classified information," I relay from the Executive Committee to Martha, attracting a bump to my ankle by a red leather heel that goes with a red-plaid pleated skirt and white blouse with gold Chinese necklace, the matching red-plaid jacket in the overhead. "Okay," I relent, "my Executive Committee has never fixed a gyroscope so they've no idea."

"That's better," she says, while reaching over to take what's left of my screwdriver. It's finished in one long swallow. "Once we are in the air, how long will it take to get to Hong Kong?"

"First we go to Taipei," I explain. "That'll consume three hours. Add an hour and a few minutes to get from there to Hong Kong."

Martha takes my wrist-with-watch, that's been corrected to local time (watch not wrist), and manipulates it (wrist not watch) for ease of reading, adds a few minutes for the gyros to get fixed, and announces we'll be in Hong Kong by noon. In time for lunch.

"Well," I sigh, signal for another screwdriver, and turn toward her. "You may be close. Did you factor in our having to get off the plane in Taipei?"

"No," she grumps. "Are we changing planes?"

"We are not, but the authorities make us get off, walk across the tarmac through a corridor of uniformed soldiers armed with machine guns, and wait in a second story holding area."

"Good grief!" she startles. "Why?"

"I'm not sure. Maybe it's because the plane's being cleaned. Who knows?" I nod at the stewardess to acknowledge receipt of my anti-scurvy medication, and the stewardess smiles in return. "From now on, Martha, not everything will make sense. Do your best to accept things as they are."

"Yes master," she says, without looking up and then reaches for my drink. Today's sharing started with her eating breakfast from my plate—though she drank coffee from her own cup—and required me to order a second, double serving of toast and marmalade.

"Then we won't get to Hong Kong by noon," she corrects.

"We might. We gain an hour."

"Oh," Martha considers, and the plane powers forward, moving through rain that's still being manipulated by the wind, but no longer in a perpendicular fashion.

Having departed Taipei and reached our cruising altitude, another meal's being severed, and Martha doesn't understand why.

"It's the custom," I expound, "for Asian airlines to serve a meal after every take off. Newly boarding passengers might be hungry, or need the proven distraction and calming influence that comes with eating, and it would be shameful, by Asian standards, to serve *only* those who have newly boarded. In addition, the price of the ticket must be justified in a way that's comprehensible to the airline's less sophisticated passengers. Though tempting when on a flight with multiple stops—as the food's good and the smiles of the servers are convincing—the inherent immobility associated with sitting for hours, suggests it's better to consume selectively rather than devouring everything in sight."

After listening carefully, Martha shrugs and eats everything. I don't understand her need for calories, but I'll be patient.

"How's Adolf?" she casuals. "I haven't talked to him for over a month. He's in Hong Kong, right? That's where I shipped everything that he wanted from Seattle. He sure didn't stay in Anchorage very long. With winter coming, I guess I wouldn't have either. Is he still carrying *the* suitcase?"

"Currently, my dear, he's somewhere round Calcutta or Bombay. And I doubt *the* suitcase, or at least its contents, are anywhere to be found. They're certainly not in Hong Kong. Hong Kong's even tougher on firearms than Japan. As you can appreciate, when you're the occupying force you want to have the only guns."

"So," she muses, "if we ever have a house and a family, *I* should be the only one with a gun?"

"You're catching on."

"What in the world, is Adolf doing in India?"

"That's classified."

"Really? Well, you know what you can do with your damn TOP SECRET stamp, don't you?"

"Okay, but this isn't for publication."

"Understood."

"He's looking for a big tug," I advise slowly and deliberately, while twisting to look at her. "A big barge. High powered water pumps. And some nozzles."

Martha's mouth gapes in surprise, but quickly closes and becomes a smile. No doubt she assumes I'm kidding, and has resolved not to become a victim. But the issue of curiosity remains. No one's more curious than Martha; smart women are that way. She's looking out the window much like a domestic cat licks its shoulder while deciding what to do next. Her window gazing will be temporary. There's nothing to look at and she'll have to know the *why* of this equipment. So she'll ask. So I'll wait.

"Have you been to Mei Liew's house near Repulse Bay?" Martha asks, subject changed.

"I have."

"Is it nice? Mei Liew wrote me that it was her dream come true."

"It was," I nonchalant and stop.

"Luke," Martha squeals in despair, "are you going to spend the day setting traps for me? Because if you are, two can play that game; though it is hard to compete with a sixth grader!"

Wounded, I require medical attention. When actually in the sixth grader, Mercurochrome or Merthiolate would've been applied. Now that I'm older, I prefer the medicinal benefits of scotch mixed with water. So I order two. If Martha doesn't want one, I'll need both.

With a properly hydrated mouth the better for speaking, and careful not to seem indulgent or condescending, and hoping that Martha has been modestly tranquilized by her own scotch & water:

"Her Repulse Bay house was spectacular. A winding staircase—to defeat evil spirits—led to seven bedrooms on the second floor and I don't know how many bathrooms. On the main floor there was a big kitchen in the back; a reception area in the front, big enough for dancing to a small orchestra; and I can't remember how she'd labeled the other rooms, but they all had marble floors. Furnishings were austere, European and likely came with the house. It was an old house, and probably needed all sorts of unseeable repairs, like a new roof. It could be her dream became a nightmare, or she tired of presuming to be royalty, without any royals to entertain. Or perhaps the idea of owning real estate that *might* appreciate, but didn't produce revenue, soured in her mouth.

"Just before I left for Valparaiso, Mei Liew invited me to a marathon dinner and told me she had accepted an offer to sell the house, and wanted to buy our old Trader hotel in Wan Chai. I was very surprised. She'd not given any sign of unhappiness with her dream house, and the Trader's ownership group had not told me they were trying to sell the hotel. Under the terms of the agreement by which we financed their purchase of the hotel, as well as providing some additional capital, the group must have my approval to sell the property or change any aspect of the ownership. The object of that clause was to keep the owners from getting snookered, and to protect me from having to deal with some, well, rascal, to be polite."

"Did she say anything about her son?" Martha queries, while continuing to ignore the subject of tugs, barges, pumps and nozzles.

"No, and I didn't ask."

"Okay," she sighs. "Are you going to approve her purchase?"

"I did. With all kinds of conditions, including one that doesn't allow her to retire my loan ahead of schedule, and another giving me an option to purchase the hotel from her, at any time, for what she paid plus an additional five percent for each year of her ownership, prorated as necessary. She agreed to everything. The deal might have closed, but I haven't heard."

"Good, then I still have a friend. Is Mei Liew meeting us at the airport?"

"No," I slowly exhale, "she doesn't know we're arriving."

Martha doesn't respond, but does finish her drink while looking out the window. "Then where are we staying?"

"I'll find something. We can always squeeze onto a sampan in Aberdeen."

As fabled, our approach to Kai-Tak excites Martha. She so loves flying over the freighters massed in a turquoise harbour and the final forty-some degree bank, that I expect her to ask the stewardess if the Captain will please do it again.

———————— o ————————

3.

"Hong Kong," I oft overheard my father say to friends, "with its sub-tropical beauty and turquoise harbour, its apparent passiveness, smiling faces and British good manners, is not exactly a gentle flower. Hong Kong is the whole damn rose bush: roots, blossoms, leaves, stems, and very sharp thorns … yes, and difficult to control infestations."

As soon as the Front Desk stops shuffle-footing and comes up with a room key, we'll be staying at the Hong Kong Hilton on Hong Kong Island, near the Bank of China and the Hong Kong Shanghai Banking Company; what more could anyone want. The former, a very tall, very austere structure the color of desert dust with snarling mythical monsters protecting its entry. The latter, a much smaller and more decorative building with a pair of handsome British lions (African males, actually) on both sides of its entrance to guard a bunch of my money and Martha's trust fund. The Hilton may also be the only hotel in Hong Kong with a swimming pool. And it's newer than most of the hotels, if less exotic. It'll be a good short-term transition-easing home for Martha. Similar to being baptized in rather tepid shallow water.

It's a tourist hotel with a cavernous lobby that's well suited for the irony of catering to Japanese tour groups, the source of current prosperity for the hospitality industry. And, given the Japanese proclivity for patiently standing in line, one must exercise caution. After all, one wouldn't want to be in the *wrong* long-line, providing there's such a thing as the *right* long-line. And for me there isn't.

Martha needs no encouragement to investigate a hotel lobby. It's something she loves to do; much like a bird dog scours a grassy field for scents. This time, I've given her five one hundred U.S. dollar bills, and asked her to change them into Hong Kong dollars.

"Have a most pleasant stay, Mr. Whitaker," smiles the British accented Chinese desk clerk as he hands my room key to a bellman. I nod in response.

If Martha's where she's supposed to be, I won't need a Lobby Page to chalk her name on a piece of black slate atop his six foot pole, then walk about twisting the pole to tinkle the little bells at the very top, to attract her attention, so she'll see her name and go to him, and he'll point at me. Altogether less disruptive than loudspeakers, and white courtesy phones.

But it's unnecessary. Mrs. Martha Perpetual-Sun Whitaker glows and dances toward me with her pleated red-plaid skirt swaying and her right hand clutching a two-inch stack of Hong Kong currency.

"Tell the bellman," she sings, and hooks my arm, "to take our stuff to the room and unpack—because I *hate* unpacking—and to bring us the key when he's done, and that we'll be in the lobby bar getting sloshed. Okay?"

I nod, and wonder why she doesn't tell him herself, but I don't ask. I also wonder why we're getting sloshed, but I don't ask. I faithfully do as desired by her Ladyship.

"Two scotch & waters, please," Martha says to the waitress, who's way, way too attractive for me to even look in her general direction, but I do.

"Two scotch on the rocks and a bottle of chilled water," I correct with a smile, and Miss Hong Kong smiles back before gliding away.

Martha frowns, perhaps at being corrected, pushes her chair away from the table and crosses her legs.

"Don't drink water in Hong Kong unless it comes out of a capped bottle," I admonish, "unless you are accustomed to the local bacteria, it can make you sick. In Singapore the water's okay, but not here."

"How about the ice?"

"Dodgy, of course. Hopefully freezing has killed most, if not all of the germs, and it's best not to drink too slowly. If you can adjust, don't use ice. The Brits don't. If you can't adjust, use cold bottled water. Or a cold bottle of soda."

"Thank you dear," Martha smiles, rather sardonically, "I can't *imagine* what I'd do without you," and re-crosses her legs.

When we're served, and the waitress departs, Martha puts both feet on the floor, pulls up to the table and says with a grin:

"Did you see that little blond boy standing in front of me waiting to change an American five-dollar bill?" I shake my head. "Well, as the man was counting those silver-dollar-sized Hong Kong dollar coins into his cupped hands, he turned and looked at me for a second with an enormous grin, his beautiful blue eyes flashing in disbelief. As he was leaving with all thirty coins cupped in his hands, he stopped and whispered, 'Wow! My mom'll go crazy.' Then he swaggered away."

"He was pretty cute, huh?"

"Yeah, he was. He *really* was. What should I do with all this money?"

"Put it in your purse," I frown, "you're not in a Macau casino. When the bellman brings the key, tip him three hundred HK. That's fifty US. The hotel's Chinese staff, as well as every friend and relative they have in the Colony, will refer to you as the young barbarian woman from the Golden Mountain (America) who tips well and wears, whatever you had the bellman un …"

"Mostly lingerie," she giggles, "Mei Liew said it would be hard to find in the right sizes."

I chuckle and shake my head: "Then your bra size will be included with the odd information that you seldom wear anything but your underwear. The men will hawk and spit, then laugh salaciously. The women will sneer and call you a slut or a whore."

"I don't believe you," Martha clangs, and finishes her scotch & bottled water before anymore ice melts. In response I shrug, and slowly blink both eyes, once.

"Don't give me that look!" she threatens. "Nobody gossips like that … and who cares, anyway."

"I assure you, *I* don't care. But Chinese do gossip. And the juicier the better. For thousands of years, gossip has been their primary source of information. Most Chinese men will think you're a whore, because that's what they wish you were, and they had the money to buy you. To them, since you're white and curvy, you're exotic and highly desirable, even though they might think you smell bad. As far as most Chinese women are concerned, you have *absolutely* everything … and they never will, and that's the best reason for one person to maliciously gossip about another."

"They're terrible!" Martha shrieks in anger and surprise, just in time for the bellman with his ingratiating smile to arrive and give her a key attached to a ten-inch long bar of plastic that won't fit in any known pocket but identifies our quarters as the Bridal Suite. Martha recovers, as Martha does, in half an eye-blink and smiles while she stands, takes money from her purse, presents it along with a hug, as if the money wasn't enough, and then blesses the astonished fellow with a peck on the cheek.

The bellman's not old, but he's no kid, his smooth skin too brown to betray a blush. Without dousing his smile, he bows and backs away after glancing in my direction for signs of mortal danger. Our waitress has been waiting to serve new drinks. With snickers barely contained, she puts our drinks on the table, and before gliding off, gives me a right-eyed wink I'm at a loss to interpret.

"What was *that* all about?" I ask, when Martha's seated and drinking. Our original reason for being in this very public place.

"Because, he will now defend my honor in the face of death," she assures. "Fight fire with fire, I say. Or at least with whatever's handy."

Martha's so self-satisfied she looks regal, almost haughty. Let her savor the moment. In this life there are too few. Clearly, it's not the time to discuss whether or not confident women prefer to improvise rather than follow some arbitrary set of rules. We finish our drinks in flirtatious silence and order more. I can't tell what thoughts dance in her mind, nor can I hear the music. Accompanied by the Lobby Page's tinkling bells, I mentally re-prioritizing a list of questions for Martha.

"Go ahead," she welcomes, somewhat reading my mind, "you've been good long enough. And I'm happy about the Bridal Suite."

Like a young Labrador Retriever, apparently I'm being trained to sit quietly, then told I'm a good dog and given a reward. Or promised one, anyway.

"I have a question going back to last summer, when we were in the Fairmont Hotel and Adolf was giving his report on the papers we spirited away from the House of James."

She nods.

"Your old passport stated you were born in New Zealand."

She nods.

"How did you get your original passport without presenting that birth certificate you seemed so surprised to hear about, when Adolf told you?"

"I didn't."

"You didn't what?"

"I didn't apply for a passport?"

"You just found it on the sidewalk?"

"Of course not. James knew all about that sort of thing. I asked him what I needed to do to get a passport. He told me to get some proper photos of myself, and he'd take care of it. So I did, and about three weeks later he presented me with a passport. What's the big deal?"

"Well, my dear, *that* passport was a fake. You must appear in person with your birth certificate. It can't be done by proxy. Do you remember everything you had to do to get your new one? Particularly since I had the old one, and I was out of the country—a damn good thing—so you couldn't use it as part of your application. Well, the process hasn't changed from what it was. Of course, now we know James knew the right people to get you a fake passport. Can't imagine why he bothered, though."

"Am I in trouble?"

"Not anymore. This one's valid. Here," I hand it to her,

"keep this with you. All the time. Even in Bed. That way I'll know who I'm sleeping with."

"Bull," she purrs, and hands it back. "You never know. And you like it that way."

I nod, and somehow manage to keep a straight face, which doesn't fool her at all. Mouth closed, I clear my throat and change the subject:

"Mei Liew has been preoccupied with her house, and now the hotel, and what else I'm not sure, but we'll eventually find out. She's from Canton, you know," – Martha shakes her head – "she left there as a little girl. Chinese families rid themselves of daughters as soon as possible, since chances are they'll marry, leave home and contribute nothing after that. In the meantime, all the food they eat and clothes they wear while growing up, become a worthless investment. Sons are the opposite. They stay with the family, get married and have children, hopefully sons, and thus expand the labor force that will eventually care for old parents, and older grandparents, and so on."

"How *dreadful*!"

"Traditional agrarian behavior, actually. Perhaps you've heard of dowries." She nods. "Nothing more than bribes to get rid of daughters. Anyway," I say and pause, waiting to regain Martha's attention. "Mei Liew isn't coming up with the people I need, so I have a question for you. What did you think of your friend Captain Mackey? He was after me to finance an oceangoing tug. Apparently, the local competition was giving him a hard time. Do you think he's married? Children? All that sort of thing?"

Martha's gazing about. Thinking, I hope.

"You know," she flashes, "if we keep drinking like this, pretty soon we're not going to be able stand or walk a straight line."

"Indeed," I agree. "It's a nice day. The sun's out, so it's warm enough to go for a swim. Did you bring a swimming suit?"

Martha shakes her head. "I doubt," she notes, "Captain Mackey speaks Chinese. The few hours we were on his boat, I wasn't thinking of dating him, so I didn't register on his marital status. The way he handled his tug seemed remarkable, but I'm not an authority. Luke, he can't be the only tugboat captain in the world."

"I know, but would you try calling him?"

"Honey, it's Sunday. I don't want to bother the poor man on a Sunday."

"I understand, but it's Saturday and that's when he'll be home."

"All right, all right," she surrenders, "I'll do it, but I don't wana be your secretary. I'm no good at that sort of thing."

"You're wonderful at *everything*," I persuade, "so why not?"

"Because I don't want to be your damn employee. Okay?"

"You're my partner. My best-friend. I can trust you," I plead, and try to think of something persuasive that isn't coercive.

"Luke," she coos, "I will *always* help you, you know that, regardless of the scheme, or the consequences, or the risk … you *are* my best-friend … and a good deal more, I'll admit. But unless it's an emergency, let *me* decide how, when, and what I'm going to contribute. And of course, I must be informed about *everything*. How else will I know …"

"You're correct. You're absolutely right, I'm sorry."

"There's nothing to be sorry about, so your apology is rejected. What you need, my dear, is Holly."

"That would be fabulous. But I don't think she'll come, and if she will, things aren't ready yet. Bill's still working on the old plane and …"

"Once again, my dear, dear husband, you are totally wrong. She and Liam will come anytime you want them. Holly believes the morning sun appears over your right shoulder. And at the end of the day, it sets over your left. It's disgusting. Sort of. But she doesn't know you as well as I do, and I'm probably exaggerating, though not much."

"We're not staying in Hong Kong, you know, that's not the plan."

"You *actually* have a plan?" Martha jabs, with a smile, and I signal for the check.

Standing and walking requires concentration. Nevertheless, I look round the room, for it seems when I'm in a foreign country with strange and interesting faces I subconsciously look for someone familiar. I'd never do it in Seattle, where I know few people, but the faces aren't particularly strange *or* interesting.

"What do you think about children?" Martha wonders, slipping her hand into mine as we leave the lounge area.

"I've seen a few I liked," I consider aloud, "but I haven't priced any. Why? Did you find some you like?"

Before she can answer, I spot WHITAKER written on a sign with tinkling bells. I turn us toward the Lobby Page. He points at the Front Desk. I tell Martha to tip him and stroll away hoping she'll watch where I'm going.

At the Front Desk, a clerk directs me toward a black telephone resting on a rosewood desk with a matching chair. Necessary pencil and notepad are present in the diminutive form. I sit, pick up the receiver and tell the operator my name. She politely informs me I have an overseas call, and that she'll make the connection, so I wait.

"Mr. Whitaker is ready," the operator says to the caller.

"Luke?" JJ asks, apparently considering the possibility there's more than one Whitaker in the Hong Kong Hilton on the seventh of January.

"The one and only," I quip, as he doesn't sound at all distressed.

"And thank heaven for that," he tries to scorn.

"It's still dark in Seattle," I note, as it's three-seventeen in the afternoon, local time, "you're up late. How did you find me?"

"Remembered your recent enthusiasm for swimming. Had the person-to-person operator work with her HK counterpart to try hotels with a swimming pool. The Hilton was her first choice. How's Martha?

"Beautiful but grumpy," I report, now that she's standing next to me. "Tired I suspect."

"Not possible! I've never known anyone with more energy. You simple bring out the worst in everyone. Let me talk to her."

"Is that why you called? To talk to Martha?"

"No, Adolf called me because he couldn't find you. Write down the number, and call him in Calcutta. He has some questions."

I write Adolf's number on the itty-bitty notepad and hand the phone to Martha, who says hello and starts to laugh, then giggles, then asks about Holly's little boy, Liam, then tells JJ that I've spent too many hours on an airplane, not enough time in bed, then giggles, and hands me the receiver.

"Have you heard whether the deal with Mei Liew closed?" I query, hoping some real news can replace all the giggling.

"Yes, it has," JJ asserts. "Considering how poorly that property was performing, I think you're rather lucky."

"We'll see. It needs to be rehabbed. I hope she has the money. Under the purchase terms she has to close down and get the work done before re-opening. I only worry about how distracted she seemed when I left here a month ago. Call me if you hear from her, since she might tell you something different than she tells me. I'm going to try and meet with her in the morning. I'll send you a telegram, Monday night. It's less expensive and I don't have to tolerate all this giggling. Now, go back to sleep."

"I will. Don't worry. And you be nicer to Martha, please. And tell her to mail me photos before deciding on a new wardrobe. And don't forget about the *thorns and insects.* By the way, I want ya to know Holly's doing a splendid job. She's very bright. I suppose you'll want her out there, so I'll be alone and miserable."

"It's being discussed. Pleasant dreams, JJ."

"Goodbye, Luke. And, well, keep in touch," he says, with uncharacteristic sadness, and then hangs up.

"So?" Martha says, eyebrows raised. "Are you going swimming, or must you do something that can't wait?"

"I need to call Adolf. But it's two hours earlier in Calcutta, so there's extra time. Doubtless, he has questions about tugboats and barges, and I haven't any answers. Captain Mackey would, though. I'm sure he'd rather hear your voice than mine."

"Do I have to?"

"Afraid so. Sunday doesn't qualify as a day of rest in Calcutta. If Mackey's friendly, *I'll* talk to him."

"You'll have to, Luke," she dismays, "because I have *no* idea what this is really about. In fact, give me the gist of what you want me to say, providing he answers the phone, so I'm not just a dumb broad calling him at an unreasonable hour. I bet he won't even know who I am."

"You're on," I say, and put my arm round her shoulders as we finish walking to the elevators. "A thousand, and you pick the currency."

4.

Last night and without my participation, it was determined I would meet Mei Liew on the Star Ferry leaving for Kowloon at six-thirty this morning. Without breakfast, and while Miss Cuddles remains in a warm bed, Mr. Limited Patience stands in detested fluorescent light and watches people, cars, and lorries coming from Kowloon as they disembark into what's left of a Hong Kong night. Thirty-five minutes from now the sun will officially, though cautiously, peek over some local mountain that's immediately east of Victoria. At this latitude twilights are brief; today's will last for eleven minutes.

I've unsuccessfully searched for Mei Liew dressed as a Chinese lady in western clothing. Zero women of any race, and only fifteen men are waiting to board the ferry. Except for a whiff of cloak-'n-dagger, the air usually dominated by diesel fumes smells surprisingly fresh.

Stepping lively, I hurry to get aboard. It's about an eight-minute crossing and Star Ferries are as impatient as I am.

In January, Hong Kong averages a high temperature of sixty-five degrees Fahrenheit. Mornings are cool enough to justify my dark-gray suit, button-down white shirt, rather bright tie of the Malaya Regiment (slanting half-inch strips of gold bisected by an eighth-inch strip of ruby, repeating on a background of Jungle-green), black brogues plus camel hair overcoat. There's little chance of me being mistaken for a secret agent of any nation; regrettably, it's a bit of an issue these days.

Stiff upper lip assertions, treaties, and a few war ships notwithstanding, Hong Kong's a part of China. When the Cultural Revolution, using gangs of kids called Red Guards, began in the late summer of nineteen sixty-five, Hong Kong cast more than a casual eye to the north. With the Red Guards terrorizing the countryside, the flow of refugees (somehow escaping across the supposedly closed Chinese/Hong Kong border) increased dramatically. Today, regardless of fences and watchtowers, the Revolution disrupts the Colony's normal optimism, and has Hong Kong's government more than just *glancing* in every direction.

Shortly before the communist's nationwide victory in nineteen forty-nine, Mao, a peasant himself, publicly spoke to the economic challenges ahead: "We shall have to master what we do not know. We must learn to do economic work from all who know how, no matter who they are … We must acknowledge our ignorance, and not pretend to know what we do not know."

Mao ignored the economic prosperity of Capitalist Hong Kong and turned to the Soviets, whom he had never liked. Throughout the nineteen fifties, the People's Republic of China built Soviet-style bureaucracies and peasants starved to death, by the millions. The Cultural Revolution was supposed to be for the purpose of disassembling these bureaucracies, among other goals, by illogically torturing and murdering teachers and professors, among others.

A rather popular beginning, to be sure, as almost every kid everywhere has at least one teacher or professor he or she would like to maim and/or kill.

The recent back and forth business of revolution in China, has gone on for decades. Always a nasty affair. It's reported that in December of nineteen twenty-seven, just up the Pearl River from Hong Kong, in Canton (now Guangzhou), twelve hundred military cadets and their officers (apparently communists) got out of hand and were punished by the non-communist revolutionaries then in charge. To save ammunition, sizable groups were roped together, taken out to sea on barges and thrown overboard. A little later, five officials of the Soviet consulate were put up against a wall and shot. All Soviet missions in China were soon ordered closed, for a while.

Like most ferries, the Star Ferries are double-enders. Vehicles and drivers on the bottom deck, passengers on the upper deck, where bench-style seating runs fore-to-aft. There are no Chinese women on the end I enter. It's possible that Mei Liew's still below with her car and driver; could be why I didn't see her waiting to board. I but pause, as the trip is brief, before walking forward to check seating at the other end. If she's not there I'll come back. The ferry slides through a perpendicular steam of fishing junks and sampans, also starting their day.

Fifteen men scattered round the forward seating area does not make for a crowded condition. So why are three people, with their backs to me and dressed in black quilted jackets, jammed together like a book between bookends? Two brothers and a sister? Mom with large protective sons?

I wheel round and go back the way I came; relatively sure Mei Liew will have materialized from below and be waiting.

I don't like to be wrong. No one does, I suppose. But I really *hate* being wrong before breakfast. Mei Liew's not sitting or standing or walking nor hiding under the seats, which are of wooden slats and I can see through them. Fuse ignited and burning with the help of *anger*, for sleep has been lost and time wasted, I sadly lack a victim other than myself. And berating *me* won't make *me* feel any better.

My Pacifist Committee quickly convenes, and immediately pass a resolution—with the representative from the union representing my adrenal glands, abstaining—suggesting I *again* check the forward area, and if Mei Liew isn't there, further suggesting she might meet me when we dock in Kowloon. A bit strange, all in all, but I've nothing to lose, and I don't want a general strike, though all strikes require the approval of my easily influenced Executive Committee.

There's no Mei Liew – anywhere. With our arrival in Kowloon eminent, I don't sit but amble round the perimeter, intent on discovering something of the book and bookends. My covert-as-possible glances reveal the three are doing nothing but staring straight ahead. Emboldened by their lack of attention to almost everything, I look at the their faces … and discover Mei Liew dressed like a black & white amah, accompanied by two young rather scruffy men with overfed bodies and, given their glazed eyes, underfed minds.

Wanting an explanation, I step close and lean forward. Mei Liew looks up without recognition, so I extend my left hand. Her eyes flash, she takes the hand and yanks herself erect. Thug on left doesn't react. Thug on right jumps up and takes a swing that misses, then he steps into the first jab I've thrown since high school. I'm the luckier and he's the shorter; his crumpled nose gushes blood, and my fist hurts.

Sore fist jams itself into my overcoat pocket and the thugs freeze in awe of the bulging pocket. Lacking a real weapon, I glare back with threatening disdain, while Mei Liew takes refuge behind me.

Nose Gushing Blood and his brother, retreat from each other, and from me, until they're apparently satisfied the distances between them won't allow me to kill both with a single bullet. Encouraged by the ferry hooting our arrival, they back toward the exit and disappear. *Anger* and *Adrenaline* want a chase, but I'm restrained by a majority of the Pacifist Committee, as well as by Mei Liew's arms round my waist and the throbbing gunless fist in my pocket.

"Shall we get off?" I ask, not sure what to do next.

"*Ayeeyah!*" she shrieks in Cantonese. "You crazy?"

I shrug; neither confirming nor denying her question, and keep silent, for she's too excited to answer questions. With my right hand on medical leave and afraid to leave its pocket, I put my left arm round her shoulders to steady her slow, wobbly, progress as we shuffle toward the ferry's other end.

A reign of silence nurtures consideration for the power and primitiveness of adrenaline, and a realization my adrenal glands surely came from my father along with a thousand years of Shoshone survival: fight or flight, scalp or be scalped. Goodness knows what would have happened moments ago if I'd had a knife: probably a pursuit and the first scalping in the Colony; doubtless the first on a Star Ferry. I look down at my rather aggressive necktie and wonder if it could have been a party to scaring away the thugs. Regimental ties are military in origin. Henceforth, I'll see them for the modern war paint they are.

In its own language, the ferry announces our impending arrival at Victoria, ending the silence.

"You okay?" she asks, her trembling almost gone.

"Yeah," I mumble

"Where your hand?" her English impaired by trauma.

"Hiding."

"Oh," she whispers, suppressing a giggle. "You not beat Martha, yeah?"

"Not often enough, I guess."

"Good. And thank you for help."

"Did they hurt you?"

"No," she sighs, after some consideration, "but I need a drink. Then we can talk."

"Tea?"

"*No!*" she scolds. "Booze."

By taxi to a joint in Wan Chai, maybe a block from her currently closed Trader Hotel. I'll bet a round-eye hasn't brought a black & white amah here since time began—amahs being respectable Chinese ladies in baggy black pants and starched white jackets that run your home, any children, and your life.

Burning incense dominates. An improvement over other possible odors. Chinese lanterns of red paper and gold tassels hide incandescent bulbs and glow in each corner; all the better for the less than attractive B-girls to hustle lonely guys of every race. The girl drinks tea in a clear glass; the customer drinks what he ordered and pays for both, as if both are the best scotch. But the customer's not alone, and the girl will attentively listen to what he says without arguing, and she'll smile often, as her understanding of what he's saying isn't important. I suspect there are worse ways to spend an afternoon or an evening.

As Mei Liew and I are the only human occupants, except for the bartender, who might actually be the cleanup man, early mornings obviously don't qualify as times of *loneliness*.

Mister Undershirted Sourpuss makes his way to our table while loudly slapping his backless slippers against the floor as he walks. He doesn't smile, bow or ask if he can help me out of my overcoat. He says nothing. If I were to order *anything* in English, he would shake his head as a sign he doesn't understand, and then point at the door. As soon as I figure out what I'm willing to drink without ice or water, and without using an unwashed glass, I'll …

In testy Cantonese, Mei Liew orders for both of us. After all, she has lived in San Francisco for so many years it's her inalienable right. I think the bartender's objecting, because he's shaking his head and Cantonese-ing in a high key. Mei Liew turns up her volume, and seems to place the order again. Then she points at me and says something quite adamantly—"tai-pan" being the only word I recognize— before uttering disparaging sounds to the accompaniment of equally disparaging facial expressions and gestures, probably regarding the miserable nature of this man's ancestors, and what will become of him if he keeps wasting our valuable time. He departs with mumbles and slippers slapping.

By looking at her with raised eyebrows, I ask what we're having.

"Bourbon and cold beer," she wroths, as if I should know, because we drink it every morning, "Cold beer will come in a capped bottle. We must open and drink some beer before pouring in bourbon from the unopened bottle of bourbon that he will leave on the table. We will pay for the entire bottle of bourbon, whether we drink it all or not. Be sure and wipe off the beer bottle where your mouth will touch it."

I nod.

"I suppose," she saddens, after two uncapped bottles of beer and a sealed bottle of bourbon have been ungraciously

43

dropped onto the table, "you want me to tell you about … about a while ago?"

I nod, swallow some beer because there's nowhere to spit it out, and we take turns carefully pouring bourbon into our beer bottle's empty space. I sip. The bourbon's ruined, but the beer's improved, and I label the concoction as suitable for desperate alcoholics and middle-aged Chinese women without prescriptions for tranquilizers.

"I knew I was being followed," she moans, and looks at me with eyes seeking sympathy. "That was why I told Martha to have you meet me so early, and on the Star Ferry. My excuse to her was that I had errands in Kowloon, and that if you and I met early, I would have time to lunch with her. It was a lie. I thought they would not expect me to be out before dawn. But just in case, I caught an earlier ferry and walked to the Peninsula Hotel, where I changed into this amah costume I had hidden. It isn't me, is it?"

I shake my head, twice.

"That's what I thought. But *they* must have recognized me when I got on the ferry back to Victoria, where I was planning to meet you when you boarded for Kowloon. *They* came from two sides, held my arms and threatened great bodily harm, pain and death if I did anything but go with them."

"Where were they taking you?"

"Somewhere in Kowloon," she says, and then takes several sips. "Their headquarters, I guess."

"What the hell have you done? What kind of trouble are you in?" I drill, with the realization I had more than just freed her from some random mugging.

"Conditions are very bad in China, but I'm sure you know that. When I got to Hong Kong, I managed to contact my two younger brothers in Guangzhou (Canton).

They're married and have children. My parents are dead." She takes two more sips from her beer bottle, then adds more bourbon. "They are the only family I have," she pleads. "I wanted to help them; get them out of China."

"What about your son?"

"Not now, please."

"Sure, I'm sorry. How did you make contact with your brothers?"

"There are people here, who are in the business of finding family members in China. Particularly in Guangzhou, home to so many in Hong Kong, and in San Francisco."

"They're reliable?"

"Oh, yes," she enthuses. "I received a short letter from my oldest younger brother, with family information that could not have been fabricated. Yes, yes, he is who he says he is."

"What did you do after getting the letter?"

"Finally, through a friend of the now retired general manager of the Trader Hotel, I was introduced to a man who smuggles people out of China; for a fee. So I paid the fee and held my breath. Much time went by. Again and again I was assured arrangements were being made, but I dared not push too hard; I was afraid they'd be scared away. Smuggling people out of China is illegal and very dangerous. If caught in China, everyone is executed; those being smuggled and those doing the smuggling. If caught in Hong Kong, those from China are returned to China, and those who are not from China go to prison in Hong Kong, for many years."

"I'm not surprised," I think aloud. "Was your smuggling deal made before or after you bought the Trader?"

"Before," she scorns, and takes a swig, and I join her because I'm getting hungry. "The hotel will support my family when they get here."

"Was the fee large?"

"*Ayeeyah!*" she quietly shrieks, with a brief waving of both arms. "Yes, very large, and getting much larger. They are here, I am told, my two brothers their wives and children. And there were *unexpected* expenses. The smugglers insist I pay more, before they will tell me where relatives are being kept. But they give me no proof family is here. Or even alive. So I have not paid. And the smugglers are very angry. We exchange harsh words. I believe they are the ones following me."

I'm sipping more than I should, while listening and trying to understand something I know little about. If Martha gets a whiff of my breath, she'll think I've been frequenting a previously unknown Jack Daniel's *brewery* somewhere in Kowloon.

"Who are they?" I ask, more relaxed and patient than when we sat down, as my hand no longer throbs. "Some kind of tong?"

"Yes, I think so. If we were in San Francisco, I would be sure."

"If you had this problem in San Francisco, what would you do?"

"Get a gun and shoot them!"

I've had too much bourbon and beer to fully suppress my laugh, and Mei Liew has had more than enough not to get angry with me for finding humor in what she said with such seriousness.

"Well," I idle, when I can command a straight face, "we're not in San Francisco. And neither of us has a gun. And a fist in a pocket won't work twice. You're not broke are you?"

"I not broke," she grumps, "yet."

"Why not pay them?"

"Because, I think they have done nothing. I believe my brothers and their families are still in Guangzhou. I have given them a hundred thousand Hong Kong dollars, and they have only wasted time. My brothers could be dead by now," she groans, and bows her head toward the table. I see what I think are tears falling to the table and mixing with dust to become tiny mud puddles, though it's possible she's only drooling.

"You can't blame yourself," I comfort, and pat her hand. "There are rogues, scoundrels, and blackguards everywhere."

When she looks up, I present her with a handkerchief. She dries her eyes, and I silently swear a pox on all human predators, larger or small, rich or poor; without regard to gender, race or religion.

Attempting to lighten the atmosphere, I tell her about Martha having the bellman unpack her underwear, and how she tipped him, and hugged him, and pecked his cheek. Then I relate Martha's thoughts on "fighting fire with fire". Altogether, it coaxes a tiny bit of nodding along with a pitiful smile, there's no laughter. Not even a grin. Apparently, nothing will amuse her at the moment … but the business about *fighting fire with fire* gives me an idea.

"I'll wager there's more than one Tong in Hong Kong," I conjecture, rather cheerfully. After some hesitation Mei Liew nods. "Okay," I continue, "in a couple hours I'm meeting with a local lawyer. By then I'll find a way of approaching him about hiring a Tong to investigate the Tong you hired. I'm sure you're right about your brothers not being here, but we need to know for certain. And we need to know damn fast, right? Because if they're not in Hong Kong we need to get 'em here; so you can GET-BACK-TO-WORK!"

She looks at me in shock, then nods several times. But she isn't crying, and she isn't sipping; which I find encouraging.

"Good. Now then, even though it's closed, I'm sure you're living at the Trader, and that simply won't do. I'll go with you to pick up what you need, and then I'll put you up at the Hilton, as my guest. You'll be safer there, and we can keep an eye on you. From now on, please dress as if you were in San Francisco. You'll get more respect, and you'll be much more attractive."

Mei Liew nods. I pay Mister Sourpuss in U.S. dollars. He actually looks at me, but he doesn't smile. On our way to Mei Liew's hotel she buys two big navel oranges, and peels one as we walk. When she hands me half, she tells me I should never buy anything from a street vendor that can't be peeled before being eaten. We pass an old man roasting chestnuts in a pan over charcoal. I'm not particularly keen for the smell, but Mei Liew buys a sack full, peels one, and gives it to me; roasted chestnuts and fresh orange slices make a tasty breakfast that will never be found on a restaurant menu.

5.

"Captain!" I greet, as if I'm thrilled to see him enter the room, which he figuratively did when Martha handed me the telephone after finding him at home in San Francisco, "it's ten o'clock tomorrow morning, here. You're talking to the future … Yes, yes. I've always wanted to as well. Listen Captain, I'm in need of a tugboat and someone to drive it round Southeast Asia … Tow a barge … Mostly in the Straits of Malacca … Yes, and it could be very dangerous … That's the spirit … It wasn't repossessed, was it? … Sorry. Just a guess. Last summer you told me business was awful … If you're interested in a new command, I'll buy the right tug. Something bigger than you had, with a longer range and some firefighting capacity … I'll explain everything another time … It should be able to make it from Dutch Harbor to somewhere near Sapporo, Japan, without refueling … About twenty-four hundred miles … Adolf, you might remember him, he was the big guy with a suitcase … Right, right. Well, he's looking for a barge in India … No, it's too far. You'd use too much fuel towing a barge from

North America to Singapore … Nope, you pick the crew. You'll need 'em to get here, and then for later. Find some guys you like, who'll stay with you for at least six months … When you find the tug, we'll work out who's getting paid what … For years, I hope. Will that be a problem with your family? … You're kidding. She really served you with divorce papers the day after they took your boat? … I guess so … I have to run, Captain, so I'm handing you back to Martha. Give her your address, and we'll get you a check for expenses. I'll be in and out, so if I'm not here, tell Martha what you've found … Don't worry about that, she has a mind like a tape recorder … Sometimes, but it can also be a pain in the ass. It might be easier for you to call Holly Stuart in Seattle. Martha will give you some phone numbers. Holly can call us and we'll call you back … Why, you? Well, to be honest, Martha liked your style … Come on Cap'n, don't be getting emotional. There's always somewhere the sun's shining … You're welcome. Happy hunting, and all that rot. Here's Martha. Bye, for now."

Hotel car and driver to high-rise on Connaught Road. Address befits a lawyer with the status of Sir Gordon Beasley. Pure British, fourth generation Hong Kong. The Governor's his good friend. Chairman of the Hong Kong Safety Committee, etc., etc. Terribly affable. Terribly expensive. Gorgeous Chinese secretary. Gorgeous blond wife. Perfectly mannered twin daughters headed to Cambridge with straight 'A's.

It's rumored that colonial life produces closets full of skeletons, and I'd be surprised if the combined generations of Sir Gordon's family in Hong Kong haven't at least one skeleton for every million HK dollars in his bank account, or in the stock market, whichever's more. He's exactly six feet tall without shoes, I'm told, and played college rugby. Still looks like a rugby player, and he's addicted to navy-blue wool blazers, even during the rather warm and sticky summers; doubtless, he has a different one for each day of the year. Always a neatly folded Chinese-red handkerchief in his breast pocket that occasionally clashes with the redness of his nose. His eyes are blue and a bit watery. A strong chin. Hair that's saltier than peppery. When I'm shown into his office, he'll greet me with: "Young Whitaker".

Just like the building and this elevator, his offices are austere-modern with teak and chrome, and a fascinating, though very distracting, view of the channel between Hong Kong Island and Kowloon. With nary a piece of paper in sight, I've concluded he has a perfect memory, or hidden cameras and tape recorders.

Am I envious? I'll covet his peanut butter and jam sandwich, if he's eating one, but not his hours inhabiting an office, and not the hours given to committee meetings, receptions and social affairs requiring brilliance, sincerity, politeness and good manners.

The homely (because legions of higher ranking secretaries don't wish to be upstaged) receptionist looks up, as I push through the heavy glass door and welcomes me by name along with a show of concern for my level of hydration. Without frowning, I shake my head to decline all liquids. Her smile never changes as she pushes a button and announces my presence to Judy Chen, secretary to Sir Gordon. Judy arrives, welcomes me effusively and, with Martha in the Colony, looks somewhat less gorgeous than I remember. She knows the way to her boss's office, as do I, and opens the door with the flourish of a headwaiter.

"Young Whitaker! What a pleasure," Sir Gordon booms, as though I've unexpectedly chosen his office for my unscheduled return from outer space. He's standing behind his desk, smiling broadly with hand extended and frozen in place, while I take the twelve required paces to get from closed door to his empty desk.

"You seem to be aging well," I frown in seriousness, as we shake hands, for he's twenty years older than I.

"Yes. Well. Have you ever considered spending a bit more time in Singapore?" he grumps, and I'm pleased to have finally found a tender spot.

"In the future, perhaps. I understand it's more relaxed than Hong Kong."

"*Quite*," he reproves. "Judy has the closing papers. We could have mailed them, and saved you the time and expense of coming for them."

"I'll pick them up on the way out …"

"Very well, then. Good to see you," he dismisses. "Oh, I do have one question, if you don't mind. Why were you so heavy handed with Miss Mei Liew? I believe she's been with your family a longtime."

"I've little tolerance for failure," I shrug, and I can see he doesn't understand. "Would you send either of your daughters into court, this very afternoon, to represent a client?"

"No! Of course not," he rebuts emphatically, and pauses. "Yes. Now I see. She's never owned a hotel, and probably hasn't managed one, either."

"Correct. Now sir, I have a question for you." He nods. "Could you put me onto the leader of a good local Tong?"

Sir Gordon laughs while motioning me to a chair.

"Are you serious?" he chides. "And it's likely you mean Triad, by the way.

"I am extremely serious. I need information about a couple of men and their families. The men might be in

Hong Kong or in Canton. It's a matter of some urgency. Of course, I'm willing to pay for the information."

"Proper channels won't do?"

"They're not Americans. They're Chinese. I'm not sure there *are* proper channels."

"Not on the mainland. Not currently. Hmmm," he says, and swivels to look out the window. "I do know someone," he mumbles, with his back to me, "who might know the right person. If you wish," he offers, while swiveling back to face me. "I'll make some inquiries."

"Good," I nod and smile. "I'll meet with anyone who can help. I'll need you to assure the party of the other part, that I'm not with the police, or a secret agent of any kind."

"These are unsavory people, you understand," Sir Gordon scowls, while nodding that he'll give me an endorsement, "I wouldn't want to lose a client. Especially one so young; who has so much to learn about good manners."

I nod several times, my grin irrepressible. When I stand, I put out my hand, and he takes it so firmly that its union issues a formal protest referencing this morning's combat.

"I'm staying at the Hilton," I advise. "Martha might answer the phone. But we're married, so you can tell her whatever you would tell me. And thank you. I'm grateful for your help, and I owe you a favor."

"Congratulations! ol' chap. We'd love to meet your bride. I imagine she is very attractive. Men like you always snag beautiful women."

"What do you mean, 'men like you'?"

"You know: tall, dark, not handsome but ruggedly interesting and eternally casual as if nothing bad has ever happened to them. Rich, of course, almost well dressed with an aura of power …"

"I hate to disappoint you, Sir Gordon, but she fell for

my neckties. Martha *loves* my neckties; everything else was subject to negotiation."

He comes from behind the desk, puts a comforting arm round my shoulder, and we start for the door. "Well," he frowns, feigning sympathy, "she certainly has good taste in some things then, doesn't she?"

It's past noon when I read a note Martha left in our charming suite telling me to call Adolf. A second note says that she and Mei Liew will be lunching downstairs. A third note claims she loves me and suggests I should join them. Lacking a fourth note, or an exotically lounging female, I order a cheddar cheese sandwich and chocolate cookies.

Gentle knocking announces the floor manager. A medieval despot to his staff, he knows *everything* that happens on *his* hotel floor, and controls most of it. If he doesn't have what you want or can't get it, it either doesn't exist or it's much too illegal. He's delivering six cold bottles of water to restock the baby refrigerator. I thank him, before hijacking one for cooling and diluting the scotch (Cutty Sark, as *Mr.* Walker became too solicitous) that'll be needed to properly consume the sandwich that's inevitably on slightly dry white bread, mayonnaise notwithstanding.

Before the long-distance operator can reach Adolf, lunch arrives on a tray and I accidentally smack my sore hand against the back of a chair getting to the door. It's so grumpy that I put it in the sink and run cold water over it. Predictably, the phone rings. Dripping, I dash to pick it up.

"Adolf, good morning! … We're well. Yourself? … You must be more careful what you eat … How big's the barge? … That's almost perfect. I was thinking three hundred feet long by a hundred wide, but I'll settle for two-ninety by ninety, if it's steel and rides at least eight feet above the water, unloaded … That's a foot higher and even better … Rusty, I suppose … British company? … Good. If a thousand US will hold it for sixty days subject to an independent survey, they have a deal. I can have Hong Kong Shanghai wire funds to their bank … Okay. Put the paperwork on a flight to Hong Kong. Send me a telegram telling me when it will arrival and I'll pick it up … You can forget about finding a tug. Remember Captain Mackey? … Yes, the same. I've got him looking for a tug. If he finds one, and I'll bet he does, he'll drive it out here and work for us. But keep looking for diesel powered centrifugal pumps, with a combined capacity that'll deliver at least twenty thousand gallons of water per minute … Well, maybe the British company can help … If nothing's for sale inquire about having some built … Yeah … Don't forget nozzles … Okay. Goodbye, and take care."

Cheddar mates well with scotch & cold bottled water sans ice. A few bites, a few sips, and the phone rings.

"Bill Stuart! Wow, what a surprise! How's the plane coming? … That's good news, but isn't this the wrong time of year for flying to Dutch Harbor, then flying non-stop to Sapporo? … Don't misunderstand, I'm excited you can get the plane here so easily. I was afraid it would have to travel as deck freight with the wings off … Wait a minute! Do you have your pilot's license back? … Congratulation! Have you found a good co-pilot? … That's up to you … When all the work on the plane's finished, we'll talk about Holly and Liam coming out. Current conditions are a bit temporary … Martha's made that clear … Bill, please, please, please take time to do test-flights … That's right. Let me grab something to write with, I want to double-check your calculation. Okay, I'm ready. Distance from Seattle to Anchorage? … One thousand four hundred and fourteen miles. From Seattle to Dutch Harbor? … One thousand nine hundred and fifty miles … What's the plane's normal range? … Two thousand one hundred and twenty five miles. Aren't you cutting it a bit close, if the weather won't let you land at Dutch? … I *understand* you're putting an extra three hundred gallons in the cabin. Six fifty-gallon drums, I suppose … It sounds silly, but what's your mileage? … Wow! Two and a half miles to the gallon at a hundred eighty miles an hour … Yes, of course, without headwinds. Still, it's better than a tug burning seventy-five gallons of diesel an hour … Humor me. Fly to Anchorage and get some sleep. Fly to Dutch and get some sleep. If, and only if, the weather looks good, you can continue to Sapporo the next day. That's two thousand four hundred and forty-four miles; about a fourteen hour flight from takeoff to landing … It's another twenty-one hundred and fifteen miles from Sapporo to Hong Kong … Good. I'll arrange for you to land and park the plane at Kai-Tak … Yeah. Do the test flights and keep your damn blood pressure down … Yes sir. Goodbye, for now."

I put the receiver down and stare at the phone. Telephones know when they're being stared at, and it's a proven way to keep them from ringing. Careful not to let my eyes drift, I back to the refrigerator. By touch alone, I open the door and take out a bottle of water. Using only peripheral vision, I get to the scotch and start unscrewing the cap when unexpected knocking on the door causes me to drop the cap. As my eyes follow its decent the phone rings, of course, and someone's still knocking on the bloody door.

I answer the phone and ask Judy Chen to wait a second. I open the door so M & ML can enter, and I don't take the time to ask why Martha's room key doesn't work in the lock. Judy asks me to wait for Sir Gordon, which I do. He gives me a name; advises the gentleman speaks English; adds an address and the meeting time, which I write down, then hangs up before I can say "thank you" or "goodbye". Apparently, he's not one to linger when dealing with the distasteful.

ML looks much better in a medium–gray straight skirt, black heels, white blouse, red wool-blazer and makeup. Martha's wearing more cloths than when last I saw her. Black slacks, brown penny loafers and a dark–green V-neck cashmere sweater with long sleeves. The ladies stand together and stare at me. Not quite like I'm a hairy fish from the deep, rather it's with disdain, as if I might deliver bad or unwanted news. Their posture thwarts all thoughts of a reprimand regarding how to use a room key.

"Did you have a nice lunch," I smile.

"Why are you trying so hard to look innocent?" Martha seems to interrogate, moving one hand to a perfect hip. ML doesn't move hand to hip, but the women's facial expressions are identical.

"I'm not *trying* to look innocent or any other way," I insist. "Look under the bed if you want. Check with the floor manager, and don't forget the shower and closet."

"I'm not accusing you of anything," Martha lies. "Why are you being so defensive?"

"Damn good question," I glower. "It might have something to do with my being busy … and not being sure you'll approve of not having one hundred percent of my attention."

"Busy doing what?"

"I'm sure you've heard about this morning." Martha nods. "Well, since I last left the hotel I've been sitting on one toilet after another, all over the Island. Sometimes just squatting over a trench with running water. For a guy my size, squatting ain't easy. Came out of our bathroom just before you knocked."

"You're lying," she scowls, adding her other hand to her other perfect hip, "You've been eating sandwiches, I can see the crumbs, and drinking scotch, haven't you?"

"Yes, if you must know. And I'd sooner eat contaminated broccoli than sit on a public toilet or squat over a trench."

"So what *have* you been doing?"

"Talking to Adolf. Talking to Bill Stuart. Talking to Sir Gordon."

"Really?"

"Yes, mostly on the telephone, for heaves sake, and whatever you had for lunch, never have it again."

"We had perfectly *awful* hamburgers," ML injects, and makes a face. "Coffee with *dreadful* cream. Right here in the hotel's cafe by the street. We thought you wouldn't want us to leave the building."

"What," I quiz, looking at ML, "have you been eating for the past almost five months that you've been in Hong Kong?"

"Until I moved into the house on Repulse Bay," ML flutters, "I stayed at the Trader, ate Chinese and drank tea. Then I had my own cook; Chinese, and drank tea or something stronger, but no coffee, just as I did in San Francisco."

"I see. Well then, let me explain. The beef in your hamburgers came from Australia. Great country. Wonderful people. I don't know if they eat what they export, if they do they're a patient lot, since they have to chew each bite for an hour before swallowing and, therefore, have jaw muscles that could fell a tree. As for the cream in your coffee, it was condensed canned milk. British, I imagine."

Their facial expression changes to indefinite. Martha's arms drop. She takes two steps and gives me a quick wifely smooch.

"Pour us some scotch & cold water," she repents, "and tell us what's next."

"Or?" I taunt.

"Or … I'll hug you into submission."

"Mei Liew," I say over my shoulder as I pour, "please write down the names of your brothers, where in Canton they live, and their occupations. Add the names of the men you paid to smuggle your brothers out of China, and anything else about them that comes to mind."

"*Ayeeyah*," she squeals, loud enough that Martha jumps, "you have a meeting?"

"Just write," I shuffle.

"You have a *meeting*?" Martha echoes, in a tone to suggest it must be a salacious rendezvous.

"At three o'clock."

"With whom?"

"Someone Sir Gordon dug up. Who might possibly help."

"A man?"

"Unless it's a woman in disguise."

"You're not funny!"

"Yes, ma'am."

"I'm going with you."

"That's a bad idea. You should stay here and paint your toenails."

"Be as nasty as you want, but I'm going with you. You've already gotten into one scuffle today. And with a sore hand, you won't do well in another. Besides, I have a calming gentle way with people that nurtures trust, and I almost never lose my temper. I know you're thinking I'll just be a worry," – which indeed I am – "but *you* are the one who espouses four eyes are superior to two, four ears better than two, and I don't think you've ever mentioned noses or …"

I wave for silence, and there's momentary silence.

59

"I must be the one to go with Luke," ML volunteers, "I speak Chinese."

I wave again, and again there's silence, so I vow, as soon as it's practical, to try waving for silence in a crowded room. If that works, I'll take it to the streets. With my imagination airborne, I consider the ways Martha could be an asset at the meeting. Indeed, she might be of more value than she thinks.

"Okay," I announce, "you can come. On one condition. That *you* do all the talking, because two tongues are *not* better than one. I'll sort of brief you, and I'll be there, but you'll have to wing it on your own."

"OH, YES!" Martha enthuses, with seismic vigor.

ML first looks at me in shock, then looks at Martha with a measure of horror, but she finishes writing down the information. I assure Martha she's dressed appropriately, and excuse myself to put on a clean shirt and a different tie. The ladies are finishing their scotch & cold waters, as I leave the room and I'm betting they'll be into seconds by the time I return.

It wouldn't do to wear the same *war paint* as worn this morning. So I select the most smashing regimental tie in my small collection, that of the Fife and Forfar Yeomanry, Scotland's senior Yeomanry Cavalry Regiment. A background of new-red divided into one-inch diagonal stripes by a three-quarter inch stripe of navy, bordered on either side by quarter inch stripes of saffron. The Forfar troop was originally raised in seventeen ninety-three and the Fifeshure Light Dragoons, about seventeen ninety-eight. The FFY regiment saw its first action of World War One at Gallipoli, and has been dismounted ever since. Currently, I believe they're a tank unit; a tough bunch of guys who dislike walking.

6.

"For the year nineteen sixty-four, Hong Kong officially estimated its population at three million six hundred and seventy-five thousand—excluding ghosts, minor gods and evil spirits. All of which, by the way, the Chinese know are here, but they take up little space and are difficult to count.

"Though no one knows for sure, by now the population could be four million, with non-Chinese comprising less than three percent. Seven out of ten people live in Kowloon, on the mainland side of the bay, and at least two of the remaining three live in, or near, the Central District of Hong Kong Island," I lecture Martha, as we ride to our meeting in Aberdeen, in the backseat of the hotel's largest Mercedes and while she's probably wishing she'd never said something about so many people being in one place.

"The citizens of Seattle and San Francisco," I continue, "are under the impression they have congestion issues. By Hong Kong standards, Seattle and San Francisco still have room for buffalo to roam; the bison type, of course."

"Before you talk me to death," Martha sighs, "you'd best give me that briefing you mentioned."

"What if it's boring?"

She replies by sliding close, and looking at me with her head turned perfectly for peeking up and through a tangle of eyelashes. The look's but a tease, considering where we are and where we're going on this bright afternoon with a very polite Chinese driver in command of the rearview mirror, and driving on the left side of the road; the wrong side as far as I'm concerned.

"All right, then," I succumb. "The following information is historical hearsay. I have not witnessed the events, nor have I been able to cross-examine anyone who has."

Martha nods, perhaps with interest.

"Originally, Triads were Chinese revolutionary organizations. In the 1760s, a society called the Tian Di Hui (Heaven and Earth Society) was formed in China to overthrow the Manchu-led Qing Dynasty and restore Han Chinese rule. As the Tian Di Hui spread through different parts of China, it branched off into different groups, known by different names. One group called itself the Three Harmonies Society, referring to the unity between heaven, earth and man. It was a catchy name and other groups adopted similar triangle-type imagery.

"Following the overthrow of the Manchus in 1911, the revolutionary Hung clan suddenly found themselves without a seat at the table, so to speak, and without donations or support from the general public, because the revolt was over.

Having missed out on government positions that would produce income from graft and corruption, many in the clan were angry and depressed. Worse, they were unable to adjust to civilian life after so many years as outlaws and extremely violent killers, though no one thinks they tried very hard. In a short time, the ex-rebels reunited as a criminal cult to extort money from a public that no longer was willing to support them. The new venture, using their old triangular name, was successful. Since success breeds imitation, other ex-rebel organizations founded similar criminal societies, using similar triangle-type names.

"When the Communist Party took over mainland China in 1949 they made life rather difficult for the Triads, causing even more migration to Hong Kong, where—through bribes and *relationships*—they were already well established. The label "Triad' (for triangular imagery) was invented by a Hong Kong official, who once worked on Fleet Street, to describe this particular type of Chinese criminal enterprises. I'm told there are more than fifty Triads in Hong Kong, but many are just neighborhood gangs.

"The large traditional Triads have individual origins that can be traced back several hundred years. They're headquartered in Hong Kong, Macau, Taiwan, and mainland China. All use binding rituals and oaths. Most of their senior members are quasi-legitimate businessmen; leaders are either influential individuals or cliques of individuals. The traditional Triads have branches in, or connections within, every Chinese community of any size in the entire world: Seattle, Portland, Sacramento, San Francisco, LA, San Diego, New York City, Philadelphia, Boston, Washington DC, London, Paris, and so on. They join forces to conduct various types of specific *business* ventures in various locations. And then they dis-associate to reconfigure at another time and place. Unlike Mafia godfathers, the significance or importance of a leading Triad crime figure relates to the size of his profits, from both legal *and* illegal business activities. The latter includes smuggling—drugs, people, and anything else of value—illegal gambling, prostitution, car theft, financial fraud, and counterfeiting, etc."

"Our kinda guys, right?" Martha surges.

"Goodness me. Are you serious?"

"Hey, don't misunderstand. I don't want 'em living next door and dating my daughter—should I ever have one—but if you need something done, and you have the money, well, it seems to me, these are the guys … if they can be trusted."

"Maybe," I consider aloud, and pause, as Martha can be unexpectedly provocative. "They certainly aren't in the Yellow Pages. They aren't the fellows you call to get your cat out of a tree … unless your cat's a leopard that you smuggled into the country and it just ate your neighbor."

"See, that's what I mean," she thrusts. "Little normal things you can do yourself. These guys are perfect for *unusual* problems that can't be solved, well … routinely."

"Like what?" I probe.

"Like a neighbor who's driving you crazy, but isn't doing anything against the law, and won't listen to reason."

"So you'd have your Triad friends bump off an irritating neighbor?"

"Of course not! How *they* solve the problem is up to *them*."

"But if the neighbor disappeared, you wouldn't care how it happened, right?"

"You're just being picky," she sighs.

"You won't think I'm being picky when Cleaver-for-Hire gets caught and tells the police why you hired him."

"In medicine," she ices, "I saw it all the time …"

"Doctors killing pesky neighbors?"

"No. The best doctors would go beyond conventional treatments to save a patient that would otherwise die. The doctors who were mediocre, or worse, would go by the book and let patients suffer to death."

"Then," I sigh, with dismay, "you recommend sending sick pesky neighbors to mediocre doctors?"

"That's a thought," she giggles. "But what I meant is, that you can't always play by the rules. Sometimes breaking the rules doesn't work, but sometimes it does … if you know what you're doing. The trick, I suppose, is knowing when to do what … and who should do it."

"In its purest form, that's an issue of management. Making a decision based on existing circumstances and known facts. Not letting the decision be made for you, because you did nothing. And, most importantly, you must be willing to change your mind if the facts or circumstances change."

"I do that all the time," Martha breezes, and wiggles a hip into mine."

"I know you do. Because you like to fly by the seat of your pants."

"You noticed!"

"I notice everything regarding the seat of your pants," I admit, glance at the rearview mirror and see a grinning driver.

"I'm glad," she coos, and squeezes my thigh, then instantly becomes serious and asks about *face*. She wants to know what's this *face* I keep mentioning.

"I'm not sure any westerner has a complete answer," I ponder aloud, and think of asking the driver to explain but I don't, because if I disagreed with him in front of Martha he would lose *face*. "May I start with losing face?" I plead, "It's rather the long way round, but …"

"Okay, though do shorten the trip, dear. We haven't all day."

"In that case, never mind. Just be sensitive to feelings. Chinese are awash in feelings. Few things are more important to them than how they believe other people are

65

perceiving them, or might perceive them. They hunger for importance, though status might be a better word. When they believe they have some status, they'll kill to keep it. So be damn careful about *who*, and *when*, and *how*, you even slightly embarrass or insult a Chinese person. And if you must embarrass or insult a Chinese person, don't do it in public unless you're ready for the consequence."

We stop at the gangway to one of Aberdeen's huge floating restaurants. I've only been in the area at night, when thousands of lights outline long, fluted Chinese roofs and bring to life the sculpted gods, dragons, and assorted mythical monsters. In the sun of this lovely afternoon, surfaces painted in green or Chinese red are backgrounds for giant Chinese symbols covered by a thin layer of shimmering gold leaf.

While the driver helps Martha to exit, I open my own door, walk round to her side and tell the driver we won't be long. Martha takes my arm, which is a smart move, as she's so busy rubbernecking she pays no attention to where she's walking.

"Luke," she squeals, "imagine the money we could make with one of these floating off Fisherman's Wharf, in San Francisco?"

"Yes, dear, until there's a storm."

"Damn, you're picky," she grumps, and we're at the door that's opening for us because we're on time; it's too early for regular customers.

"Mr. Tommy T, please," I smile, to the mature Chinese gentleman dressed in black, who's looking at me with suspicion. Without smiling, he bows at the neck then motions us inside.

Empty but for a man seated in the furthest corner with his back to us, the behemoth establishment easily seats a thousand guests. We follow our greeter through a time consuming labyrinth comprised of tables and chairs. If one believed his ultimate destination was the possible displeasure of the man in the corner, such an excursion might generate considerable anxiety.

About ten feet from the man, we're stopped, so our greeter can approach him and whisper in privacy. Martha holds my hand, and her hand's dry, so she's calm.

Mr. T unfolds to an unexpected height of about six-five, and walks toward us with a smile. He's Chinese, and pushing forty. Long arms, big hands and black hair in the style of a nineteen fifty's duck's ass crew cut. Suit of Thai silk: iridescent gray that changes to black with his movements and varied lighting. Black loafers, white silk shirt with spread collar and a black knit tie, one inch in width. His smile certainly seems genuine. Eyes narrow and sure. His body moves with the relaxed confidence of an athlete.

I take his offered hand and bow slightly for no other reason than to accept his gracious manner and uniquely tasteful appearance, while wondering if 'T' stands for 'Tall'. Martha also accepts his offered hand in a ladylike fashion, and smiles, but doesn't hug. Still in silence, he leads us to his table. As he helps Martha to be seated, a pot of tea and three Chinese cups are placed in the center of the table. During the time it takes for Mr. T to fold himself back onto his chair, Martha does a proper job of pouring tea, then carefully points the spout at the window, not at any person sitting at the table. Bravo!

Introductions seem superfluous. Nevertheless, I indulge in the formality and delight in how well Tommy speaks English, but I'm disappointed that 'T' stands for 'Tang', a name best remembered for Tang Xiangming, who, after the Xinhai Revolution of nineteen-eleven, carried out such a brutal anti Kuomintang reign of terror in Hunan Province, that he was nickname 'Butcher' Tang. Not one of his gene-pool contributors, I'm hoping.

Martha compliments the dining establishment and asks if it's his. He says, "Not entirely." Modesty becomes him. He asks her if she's from San Francisco, and she flutters, "Yes," in honest surprise, then asks how he knew.

"The Japanese started invading China," says he, and a swirling dark cloud furrows the small space between his heavy eyebrows, "on the seventh of July, nineteen thirty-seven. By October of thirty-eight, the Japs had captured the Canton-Kowloon Railway and Churchill made it clear that Britain couldn't protect Hong Kong, and I turned eight. With a plane ticket and a small suitcase, I kissed my parents goodbye and cried most of the way to San Francisco, where I was sent to live with my mother's brother and his family, in a small apartment over their store on Grant Avenue. Except for summer visits after the war, I stayed in San Francisco until I finished school. University of San Francisco, class of fifty-two.

"How about you?" he brightens.

"Burke's" she breezes, "then UC San Francisco School of Nursing. But I was a child prodigy … I turned twenty-one in December … last month."

Tommy smiles and nods, probably flattered that she wants to lie about her age. I'm having a difficult time keeping a straight face, until I realize she could have answered with her mother's New Zealand story followed by a sailing odyssey, with some espionage covered in Sauce à la Tina for dessert.

"How can I be of service?" Tommy solicits, his hard face still friendly.

"My mother died when I was young," Martha saddens, and pulls closer to the table, the better to refill our teacups while talking. "I was raised by a wonderful Cantonese amah … who moved to Hong Kong a few months ago. Mei Liew, that's her name, has been trying to organize a dinner party for her brothers and their families. The arrangements have not gone well. Frankly, I think she's been taken advantage of, so I'm stepping in to help. I'd like to have the party in this magnificent restaurant. If that's all right? And if you can provide transportation … for her brothers, their wives and children."

Tommy watches Martha and withholds his response. Doubtless he's as confused as I, yet his eyes have a wee sparkle. Maybe he likes puzzles, or he's endowed with extraordinary patience, or both. Perhaps the predator has identified a prey. Maybe I should intervene.

"If her two families," Martha bullies, a bit arrogantly, "are in Hong Kong, as Mei Liew has been told, I'm sure you can find them. *Certain people* say they are keeping them safe, until she reimburses them for some stupid expenses they didn't expect, and they won't even provide evidence her families are actually in Hong Kong. They're being very unprofessional, in my opinion. And I'm sure you agree, that such behavior shouldn't be tolerated. It's upsetting to everyone."

"You're right," Tommy states. "Why are these *certain people* keeping these families *safe*, as you put it?"

"Because they brought them from Canton to Hong Kong."

"And how much were they paid for … for arranging a dinner party with transportation?" Tommy quizzes.

"One hundred thousand Hong Kong dollars."

"Ah, then your wonderful amah got a bargain. Or she threw her money away. Too bad, of course, but it happens. Being paid for doing nothing is always profitable;

whether in Hong Kong, or San Francisco, or anywhere else. I suppose she didn't know any better, or trusted someone she should not have trusted," he sighs, then shrugs, and finally smiles in condolence.

"She trusted the General Manager of the Trader Hotel in Wan Chai," Martha specifically accuses, and I cringe.

"Why him, of all people?"

"I imagine it was because she was buying his hotel."

"I'll be damned," Tommy flashes, "I knew it was for sale. But I was told the current lender had to approve any new purchaser, and that he'd never approve of me as the purchaser. How did she pull it off?"

"Mei Liew knows the lender," Martha casuals, and hooks her thumb in my direction. Tommy's eyes shift to me, and I nod once, as confirmation.

"Would you have approved?" he challenges.

I shake my head. For half a minute he stares at me. When the stare becomes a knowing grin, he speaks in Cantonese to our greeter, who has remained ten feet away, and who acknowledges whatever he was told by an exaggerated nod-type of bow and then scurries off, no doubt for a meat cleaver.

Tommy turns and looks out the window, apparently not wanting to view his intended victim: me, of course, as Martha will be spared for pleasure and because she lied about her age. If I run, I'll gain the lead while he's unfolding. But my flight will be slowed by hundreds of tables, and a thousand chairs, and the door will be locked and require a key. Knowing the US Cavalry won't be riding to my rescue, I'm keen to hear the whooping of a well-armed Shoshone war party in feathers and paint.

Disliking unexpected silence as much as I, Martha pushes away from the table and crosses her legs.

With overwhelming luck, I might wrestle control of the cleaver, and if I do, I'll toss it to Martha. Of the two of us, she's the more hardened combat sergeant. If provoked, she could hack anyone into small pieces and walk away whistling.

I'm rather disappointed when a young Chinese man dressed in black removes the tea service, before our greeter places a tray on the table … with three bottles of cold beer, a sealed bottle of bourbon and no meat cleaver. Surely, we're not going to toast my impending execution. That would be in dreadfully bad taste.

"I realize," Tommy idles, and turns from the window with the smugness of a cat cornering a mouse, "that it's late in the day for these beverages, as you prefer them for breakfast. But if you will demonstrate the correct technique, Martha and I will join you."

"As you wish," I jolly, and reach for a beer, remove the cap with a bottle opener and take a swig, then swallow and look at Martha. She's understandably aghast, and remains so as she watches me open the bourbon and pour as much as I can into my beer bottle. When I take a sip of Mei Liew's boilermaker, my wife's nose wrinkles and her brows knit.

"Not bad if you're desperate," I rumble. "Mei Liew was. Her morning had gotten off to a bad start. That was your bar, I suppose?"

"One of many," Tommy puffs, but not too much.

"I suppose your profits come with eyes and ears?"

"The best of all three," he grins, quite widely. "You wouldn't believe what men tell my girls. I'm sorry it took me so long to make the connection, between yourself and the 'tai-pan' wearing an aggressive tie, early this morning, and who was buying drinks for an excited amah, and paid with American money. I'd ask how much you gave the cleaning man, just to make sure his profit was not too great, but this time it isn't important."

"Well, old chap," I grin, "given your current level of delight, I think however the profits were split, it was fair. And anyway, I can't possibly remember how much I gave him."

Meanwhile, curious Martha has been pouring her own boilermaker-in-a-bottle. She sips. "Ugh," she utters. "That's the last time I let you and Mei Liew go anywhere, together."

Tommy laughs, and stoically begins to make one of his own. "So," he seriouses, "you're a tai-pan?"

"Hardly," I dismay. "This morning, the lady was desperate to get your fellow's cooperation. I'm not the tai-pan type. I mostly hang out with Martha, watch television and read newspapers."

"Me too, except for the part about Martha," he grumps, and takes a long swig. "Not bad stuff, really. I wish I'd thought of this concoction when I was in high school, stateside. I could have sold it to my entire graduating class and driven a new car instead of taking buses and riding cable cars."

"Would you two good ol' boys mind if we got back to business," Martha exasperates.

"No, not at all," Tommy humbles, with feigned subservience. "What's you pleasure, Mrs. Whitaker? Your every wish is my command … as long as you can pay for it. Whoops," he chagrins, "that's not quite true. We don't overthrow governments. The expenses are far too difficult to project."

"Will *you* be serious," Martha mothers.

"I'm more serious than you can imagine," he scowls. "What can you tell me about the families you're looking for?"

Martha elects the opening of her purse to trusting her perfect memory; briefly roots therein, pulls out the sheet of paper prepared by Mei Liew, and slides it across the table. "This is all we know."

There's silence, while the leader of a major Triad gives professional attention to the information.

"Anything else?" he asks Martha, as if she's ordered a meal that will fail to properly feed a child, let alone an adult; then waits for her response with eyebrows raised expectantly, his head cocked a bit like a salesman, sans pad and pencil.

"As a matter of fact," Martha smiles, then pauses, during which I'd like to kick her under the table, but we're sitting next to each other, and she's backed away from the table with her legs and arms crossed. I stare at her with a look that's supposed to suggest I might put a hand over her mouth, but she won't look at me; much like a two-year-old who's intent on doing what's forbidden won't make eye contact with any potentially disapproving adult.

"I think," she whirrs, and Tommy takes a proper pen— in Hong Kong that's a fountain pen, since a signature made with a ball point pen can be transferred to another document by cleverly using the heal of a hand as a blotter, if the day's heat and humidity are favorable—from his shirt pocket, removes the cap and turns Mei Liew's paper face-down, so he can take notes, "the people who have taken advantage of Mei Liew should be punished. The Trader Hotel is going to be remodeled. Perhaps you can recommend a good architect along with some good contractors and suppliers. Your help may be needed to get the required permits … and with union issues … finding a good staff … and, of course, keeping the project free from vandalism."

She pauses again while Tommy writes. I'm looking down at the white tablecloth that's covered by a piece of glass much too thick for me to break off a corner and use on my wrists. Hoping she knows what she's doing, while remembering her natural luck and how much I love her, I raise my head to look at Tommy, and grimace.

"Around the end of the month," Martha continues, "our plane should arrive. We'll need to clear it through Customs and have a place to park it at Kai-Tak. Then there's the tugboat. I don't know whether it's coming from the States or India, but we'll need moorage. And we'll be working on a barge conversion, so we'll need an architect and contractors for that. We'd like to hire a car and driver, if that's not an imposition, and the driver should speak English, and be able to provide us with … well, security since my body guard is currently in India. And, while I think of it, how're your connections in Singapore?" she queries, as casually as if this was a meeting of some community organization that she alone endows.

Tommy stops writing. He stares at her. Briefly looks at me. Then looks out the window again, before giving his attention to pouring more bourbon into his beer bottle and swigging until the beer bottle's empty. I just smile, dumbly, as one might after being hit on the head with a cast iron frying pan.

"What kind of a plane?" he eventually asks.

"A DC-3," I answer, believing Martha might not know. "And a marine architect has drawn plans for the barge conversion. And I've already contracted with a shipyard in Singapore to do the work."

"Interesting," he reflects. "You have an aircraft capable of using almost any airfield, even a small one, with a fairly large cargo. And a tugboat that I'll presume has an extended range, a barge that I'll guess needs a superstructure … and you desire a car with an armed driver. If you weren't so young and appear so innocent, I might think you were planning one hell of a smuggling operation. And," he enthuses, "we should be discussing some sort of *cooperation*."

"Shrimp," I frown, "if you must know. And I'd appreciate your keeping that to yourself."

"Sure, sure. Stealing or catching?"

"Buying and processing. Straits of Malacca."

"Those are pirate waters, Mr. Whitaker."

"I know. Hope you don't have friends in the area."

"Hell no!" he wroths, loudly. "Hate the bastards. I hope you'll sink them all, and they will be eaten by sharks."

Surprised at his vehemence, I glance at Martha, who's smiling and nodding cheerfully. He asks where we're staying, and Martha tells him.

"Good," he booms, "I don't do business with the Peninsula Hotel, or anyone staying there. Silly," he scorns, "but it was Japanese Army headquarters during the occupation. And that's where the Governor of Hong Kong surrendered on Christmas Day of nineteen forty-one. By April of forty-two it was renamed the Matsumoto Hotel. To me, even though I wasn't here, it will always be the Matsumoto Hotel. The Japanese occupation of Hong Kong was very ugly for my family … and for many others.

"By morning, you'll have a car, and the kind of driver you are wishing for," he states, with unchallengeable authority. "Cost is five hundred Hong Kong a day; payable weekly. The driver will send a note to your room telling you how to recognize the car.

"About the families that are perhaps in Guangzhou. Because they seem the most pressing issue, I'll find out where they are. If they're still in Guangzhou, I'll give you a price for … for their transport to Hong Kong. In a day or two we can have dinner and discuss the matter. Since you're now friends of mine, from the old days in San Francisco, we needn't be afraid of being seen together in public. But that is not true of the amah. For me to be seen with a Chinese woman at a social occasion, who's not an employee, will create an unwanted typhoon of whispers."

"Perfect," Martha smiles, and stands. Then she helps me to my feet, for I'm a bit overwhelmed.

7.

Worldwide, over twenty million telegrams were sent in the year nineteen twenty-nine. Giddy speculation had ended with a crashing stock market, a depression was beginning, unemployment was rising, and Germany was bankrupt.

Prior to the implementation of our modern phone system, telegrams were the most common means of fast long-distance communications, providing one discounts smoke signals and beating drums due to their limited range and being easily disrupted by unexpected changes in weather, etc. Interestingly, all three systems (smoke signals, drums, and telegrams) rely on some sort of code.

Transatlantic and transpacific phone calls are expensive, and inconvenient if the communicating parties are in vastly different time zones. Two reasons why I told JJ I'd send him a telegram on Monday night. But I didn't do as promised.

Before retiring on Monday night, as happens so often, the day's activities had yet to be reviewed by my Executive Committee and granted formal approval prior to being filed. Unless I'm traveling alone, *after* retiring I'd rather *sleep* than jump from bed in the wee hours and sit at a desk.

To properly compose a telegram, one mustn't ramble. One must strive for a balance of clarity and brevity. The longer the message the greater the cost. What the recipient physically receives, will be in capital letters and without punctuation marks. If required, punctuation must be written as a word, i.e. *comma* (not c-o-m-a, which's a much longer if not fatal pause), *semicolon*, *colon*, *apostrophe*, *exclamation point*, *question mark*, *open quote*, *close quote*, and so on. The exception being the word *period*. In a telegram it's replaced by the word *stop*. Being cryptic may also be advisable, as privacy doesn't exist. Telegrams are read by the persons taking them over the counter or over the phone; by the persons transmitting them; by the persons receiving the transmission; and (these days) by the persons phoning them to the actual recipient before putting them in envelopes for delivery—no longer by a man on a bicycle.

Obviously, sending a telegram when one is groggy and/ or disorganized isn't the best of ideas, and that's my excuse; though I don't need an excuse for *not* sending one to JJ on Monday night.

To JJ (his address and phone number at the top) dated January ninth, nineteen sixty-eight:

WE ARE WELL STOP MARTHA HELPING ML BY PLAYING WITH THORNS STOP ADOLPH SECURED BARGE PENDING INSPECTION STOP CAPT MACKEY LOOKING FOR TUG STOP OKAY HOLLY ADVANCE HIM FUNDS FOR EXPENSES STOP TRY A TEST FLIGHT WITH BILL AND URGE PATIENCE STOP CONSIDER CONVERTING ALL MORTGAGES TO OWNING DIRT AND LEASING TO OWNERSHIP GROUPS STOP DEFINITELY WORTH DOING HERE STOP HOW ARE YOU FEELING QUESTION MARK WOULD LIKE YOU TO

PARTICIPATE IN PLANNING HK REMODEL STOP EVERYTHING BUT MARTHA UNDER CONTROL.

Well that wasn't so hard. And most exquisitely, there's no conversation, so there's no bickering, questioning, screaming, yelling, sighing, or moaning. Cold but true, as far as the sender's concerned. I nod to the young Chinese lady and sign a chit charging it to the suite.

"Come on, come on," urges Martha, who eleven minutes ago I'd left alone in our suite. She grabs my left elbow and propels me in the direction of the Hilton's main entrance. "Tommy called," she excites, "he has an emergency. The car's waiting."

"What happened?" I mumble, not wanting to draw additional attention nor disclose my disappointment at missing breakfast for the second time in two days. "Has the spirit of some dead ancestor fallen to earth?"

"I don't know," Martha hisses, "and this is no time to be silly. At least *you're* fully dressed," – I look at her. She's wearing yesterday's slacks and a white blouse from the day before – "I just grabbed what was handy. No lipstick. I haven't even brushed my teeth."

A young Chinese man with a worried face holds open the back door of a nineteen fifty-five black Cadillac. Martha piles in and pulls me after her. The door closes. The young man gets behind the wheel. The engine revs and we're off. To where and why, I've no idea. But I have just learned to whom American funeral homes sell their used limousines.

We're speeding, if that's possible in this congestion, toward the harbour. The circuitousness of our path seems somewhat reminiscent of a taxi running up the meter. The aggressiveness of our driver requires a flashing red light on top of the car and resembles taxi rides I've had from LAX to the Sunset Boulevard, during which the taxi driver pretends he's at the wheel of an Indy car on its final lap. I twist round to look through the rear window. That's how one checks one's back-trail. A procedure recommended by characters of western novelist Louis L'Amour for finding one's way home after riding at full gallop into strange desolation. Indeed, things *do* look different if going the opposite direction.

We stop with a jolt that throws us against the back of the front seat. The driver quickly opens my door and says: "Luke, Martha, follow me," in such a familiar way that he might have said, "Uncle Luke," and it would have seemed normal.

He jogs, so I do too. When I turn, expecting to see Martha lagging behind due to her attractive but shorter legs, she reaches out and touches my right-shoulder so I'll move left and let her pass. Martha will never succeed as a sauntering fireman. She will, however, quickly rise to the top of any corporation *managed by crisis*.

We round the corner of a decrepit godown and see a Chinese junk, made of teak that's so highly varnished it glares; about seventy feet in length; two bamboo masts; sails lowered; an engine or two rumbling their impatience. Our leader zips up the gangway with Martha all but pushing him. Even I don't stop to check mooring lines to be sure the gangway won't accidentally fall in the water if the junk drifts from the dock before I'm boarded.

The bow's to my left, pointing seaward. Tommy hurries Martha toward the big poop deck astern, but before they start climbing they turn left, then left again and disappear down stairs to somewhere below. Junks look clunky and primitive compared to modern vessels, though they're delightfully spacious, and supposedly designed to withstand typhoons. Their design has survived for over a thousand years, so the Chinese have had ample time to make needed refinements.

We're unceremoniously underway. When I reach the mystery stairs, the driver of our car stands at their entrance holding up his hand with its palm in my face; the international signal for halt.

"Hospital." he grunts.

"I'm okay!" I roar, and shake my head to disagree with him then renew my advance.

"No!" he trumpets, pointing down the stairs. "Hospital! You wait here!"

It's perfectly ridiculous, of course, for there to actually be a hospital in the vessel's main saloon, but so are thoughts of Tommy declaring an emergency just so he can get Martha aboard his beautiful junk and spirit her below for a round of early morning molestations; I wait as requested.

Shortly, I see Tommy climbing the companionway to the main deck. He nods, but doesn't smile, and beckons me to follow him as he climbs a ladder to the poop deck.

Behind the helmsman, six deck chairs surround a permanent looking circular table of teak, the surface inlayed with random pieces of oval shaped jade and tiny gold bars. The restaurant-greeter, or his identical twin, materializes wearing black pants and a starched white jacket. He carries a tray with a teapot of ornate silver and two white-porcelain cups sporting some unidentifiable British Coat of Arms. Each cup has an ear for picking it up and a matching white-porcelain saucer. There's cream (probably condensed canned milk) and sugar in little silver containers similar to the teapot. There are no lemon slices, but there are biscuits, likely ginger, on a plate that matches the cups and saucers. Rather too grand, all in all, for morning aboard a Chinese junk slowly weaving through Hong Kong Harbour traffic with an emergency of some sort going on below. Nevertheless, the tea pours as British-black not China-green.

I presume Tommy isn't trying to impress anyone; it's just his life; the way he lives. Why else would hidden speakers be delivering a somewhat muted Elvis Presley bemoaning something about life instead of a respectful silence, or a bit of Mozart.

"He's one of my favorites," Tommy says, as much to himself as to me, while staring into his tea cup, "I would hate to lose him."

His reference to Elvis leaves me without a reply.

"One of my protection clients," he scorns, after looking up and somewhat in my direction, "has been having trouble with a communist labor union. Earlier this morning, the union was trying to keep non-union workers off the job. The union members were getting rough, and Chen Yee started showing them how wrong they were, when one of the union bastards shoved a knife in his stomach. That fellow and five of his friends have joined their ancestors, but Chen Yee needed surgery."

"Martha's operating on Chen Yee?"

"No, she's helping the doctor who's operating on Chen Yee."

"Oh," I mutter, trying to understand. "Where?"

"Below," Tommy disparages. "I have an operating room down below. It's fully equipped; with only the best. Most of it was involuntarily donated."

"Stolen?"

"Of course. An operating table, overhead lights, air-conditioning, anesthesia equipment and gases that have the potential for blowing us up like we've been hit by a torpedo. An autoclave and too many surgical instruments to count or name; everything the doctor wanted.

"We even have a blood bank. Members give blood on a regular basis, and it's refrigerated or frozen, hopefully never to be used. There's a compact laboratory, recovery space for six patients. A kitchen, bathroom, two showers, and so on.

"Would you have guessed," he grins, "from looking at this boat, even after you boarded, that it was anything but a rich man's toy?"

I frown and shake my head.

"Good."

"What do you do when the weather's bad. And where in the hell do you get surgeons?"

"There's just one surgeon," he gloats. "He's onboard day and night, every day. He doesn't wager as well as he cuts and sews. Poor fellow couldn't pick a winning stock any better than he could pick a winning horse. If he works for me two centuries, he'll still owe me money. He can't leave the boat or be on deck when the boat's within a thousand meters of land. But I take care of him. Food, a little alcohol, a soft bed and a few friendly nurses. The weather," he shrugs, "is simply the joss of the wounded. Their personal luck. If it isn't blowing too much, there are the typhoon shelters near Aberdeen. Otherwise …"

"I see. Well, if you have nurses, why do you need Martha? And I certainly hope your resident surgeon doesn't think she's one of his playthings."

"He *is* a letch," Tommy sneers, "but I told him Martha was a nurse from San Francisco, and that she's married to a friend of mine, so I'm sure he'll behave himself. If not," he chuckles, "I'm betting she'll make him wish that he had. As for the regular nurses, two are sick. One is missing. The other didn't answer her telephone. I pay them handsomely … but not everything can be scheduled. Would you like another plate of biscuits?"

I shake my head, smile and pour myself more tea. For stimulation, a quart of tea equals a cup of coffee.

"I realize there hasn't been much time," I casual, "but have you heard anything about Mei Liew's family?"

"It's more what I *haven't* heard," he navigates, while leaning into the canvas-backed chair, the movement causing his iridescent suit to shimmer from dark to light-blue. "No rumors or boasting of holding people for ransom were reported by girls working my bars. Last night, I'd even offered a bonus for any information about a kidnapping. Sometime today, I should get a report from my spies in the other Triads. If there's nothing from them, the families are likely still in Guangzhou ... or dead. Tomorrow, I'll get a report from Guangzhou." Tommy leans forward and finishes the tea in his cup, then leans back. "However, I do have a number for rescuing the families if they're in Guangzhou. But I can wait for Martha to finish ..."

"Give it to me," I ice, in preparation for negotiating.

"There's considerable risk, as I'm sure you can appreciate, to everybody: my people; the family members; me, of course; you, even Martha and her amah. One simply never knows. It must be mentioned that I cannot guarantee the outcome. The mainland is supposed to be controlled mayhem, but it's absolute chaos. If I didn't believe you and I might do business in the future, nothing would make it worth the risk. Good men, you see, are hard to find, and I pay death benefits ..."

"I don't understand," I inject, "why there's so much contingent risk?"

Tommy smiles rather knowingly. Then he inhales and reaches up with both hands, using their palms to smooth his oiled-into-submission swept-back side-hair. Such narcissistic preening may demonstrate his confidence that I'm ready to accept the highest possible price, or soon will be.

"You never know," he exhales, and stares at the sky's only cloud. "If a Guangzhou person gets hurt, his or her father, uncle or cousin might be an important Communist official. Or, if by some misfortune, one of my men is recognized, later captured and tortured into telling what he knows, and that information leads to me; and by association to you and Martha; and by association to Martha's amah. Well, you and Martha and her amah might be kicked out of Hong Kong, and I'll have problems with our police that I don't need. You just never know …"

"Nothing else? Just diplomatic bull?"

"Not quite. The British aren't letting the mainland regime push 'em around, officially, but they're not going to get all huffy to protect the likes of us. I would not be surprised if your State Department didn't pull your passports and send you home, to stay."

I shrug to cover the giant pain such an event would cause.

"Even if that doesn't bother you," he hisses, misinterpreting my gesture, "some hothead can retaliate more directly: as in killing for the sake of his family's honor."

"I imagine you have a solution," I idle, as if becoming bored.

"Are you sure you wouldn't like more biscuits or something else to drink," he offers, with the kindness of a victor relishing the moment of victory.

"Sure. How about something cool and alcoholic with no ice."

He waves for the white jacket, who's never far away, and gives instructions in Cantonese.

"Luke," he says, while insisting upon looking me in the eye, "you're giving me the impression you feel as though you're being manipulated."

"*Tommy*," I retort, mimicking his use of first names. "I'll admit the possibility has been considered. I've even wondered if you stabbed the poor man down below just to *need* Martha, and have me alone. But my imagination has been called a plague … as well as a blessing."

He laughs, and it seems genuine. He gets up and comes round the table to offer his hand, nodding the whole time. I take it, and he claps on his other hand to insure sincerity. The nodding stops as the hands start pumping, and when that's finished, he returns to his chair with an enormous smile.

"*Imagination*, my dear young friend, is *not* a plague. It may not be the Butterfly of Happiness, but neither can a butterfly soar to the height of an eagle. A butterfly is a worm that becomes a bug with pretty wings for playing among flowers and being driven by the wind. *Imagination*, well, it's the Eagle of Opportunity; though with few admirers and a lonely existence."

Tommy seems happy with his eloquence, which he created rather well, or read somewhere and remembered. Everyone has an imagination, I want to tell him, but then I would have to add how paranoid some imaginations can be, and that would reflect on me, and it's all better unsaid.

The man I now think of as *the ever present*, returns with a tray bearing two open bottles of Coca-Cola, a straw in each. I'm served first, and whereas it isn't alcoholic, I take the offering, then wait for my host to take his. We nod to each other in a silent toast before sucking on our respective straws. It's ice cold and not what it appears to be. Until now, I've only heard of rum & Coca-Cola. It beats the hell out of bourbon and beer.

"The number?" I wonder.

"There are two."

"Wanta bet I can add 'em together?"

"Just suck on your straw," he booms, loud enough to startle me but when I look at him, he's grinning. "And don't talk until I tell you to."

I chuckle and nod with a straw in my mouth.

"There is what might be called the economy package, and it's the most risky. You give me a deposit and I send most of it to some associates in Guangzhou. They find the families and smuggle them into Hong Kong waters where my men take over. F.O.B. Kowloon dock. You pay me the balance, and I give most of it to the associates in Guangzhou. Even the economy package will be three times what the amah wasted.

"If they were my family," he sighs, "I'd go myself. But I cannot recommend Martha's amah doing the same. If for some reason I couldn't go myself, I'd want people I trusted going to Guangzhou and *personally* escorting the families back to Hong Kong. I wouldn't trust unknown associates to do the job. Or to keep their tongues still if they were caught.

"I needn't tell you," he glowers, "but I will, so you and I understand the situation in exactly the same way, that it is more trouble to get my people *into* Red China and *out again*, safely and with the families, than to have associates in Guangzhou put the families on a boat, cover them with vegetables and send 'em down the Pearl River."

I nod. In principle, his point's well made.

"That *number*," he asserts, "is one million Hong Kong dollars."

"Are you serious?" I scoff. "Hong Kong's annual per capita income hovers at five hundred US bucks. I can hire an *army* for that kinda money."

I wait as passively as possible. He waits as passively as possible.

I have no leverage other than his wanting the project to impress me, and to gain him favor and face, and to get him closer to the airplane, and the tug, and the barge, improvidently mentioned by Martha.

Will he gamble on the future and lower the number? Does he think I'm waiting until Elvis finishes *Jailhouse Rock*, so I can compliment him on his choice of music, agree to the amount and offer a nooner with my wife?

I could insult him by slapping a twenty on the table, thank him for the refreshments, and ask for the junk to be turned round; except I like him. And he has access to a network of people that might be helpful in the future.

"Half a million," I smile, "and a hug from Martha."

He laughs, which may be a good sign.

"Half a million," he smiles in return, "*two* hugs from Martha, a ride in your airplane, and you will consider my helping you with your business ventures, at least in this part of the world."

"When the job's done," I condition.

"When the job's done," he clangs, and extends his hand, which I take (or rather he takes mine as his hands are extra-large), while he's waving with the other for *the ever present*.

With negotiations momentarily concluded, Elvis rewards us with a pleasant silence and I stand for a better view of this infamous though beautiful harbour. The color of the water's not as purely turquoise as from an airplane. It's a murky green-blue, thanks to the Pearl River down which everything floats including many species of dead bodies. All manner of lighters are slowly hauling cargoes to and from anchored freighters, most of them coastals. A primitive process that produces pluperfect results from a population of professional participants, or something like that. Unlike a Tuesday morning on Seattle's Lake Washington, there's no shortage of activity, and it's easy to understand why smuggling can't be controlled, for the system of moving commodities defies inspection by anything less than armies of inspectors, most of whom would be underpaid and accepting bribes.

When a tray emerges with four new coke bottles, I return to the table and my chair, though Tommy continues standing near the helmsman and looking down at the deck. He turns, catches my attention, and motions me over to see Martha at the top of the companionway. She's dressed in scrubs, shoe covers, and an ugly little hat; round her neck dangles a surgical mask. Her body language suggests a distracting displeasure. It could be anything, but I elect to descend and investigate, via the table to pick up a pair of rum & cokes.

"Did the patient die?" I probe, with my best guess.

"Worse," Martha spits, figuratively, of course, her eyes searing with anger.

"What could possibly be worse?"

She doesn't answer until her bottle's half empty, which doesn't take long. "My sponge count is off. I lost track of the damn sponges. I haven't done this for a long time. To start with, I was so rusty you wouldn't believe it. I've never worked with this doctor, obviously, and we really needed one more nurse or another surgeon. Naturally, the boat's constantly moving in every damn direction, which takes some getting used to. He's good, by the way. I'll tell you more about that later. Right now, I have to go back and re-count the sponges for the umpteenth time. If I'm still short, we'll have to open him up, again, and fish around till we find the missing sponge, or it'll kill him. I hope to hell we have enough blood," she moans, "or we'll need some of yours." Handing me her empty bottle, she starts down the stairs.

Relieved that we've finished our negotiation, I explain the situation to Tommy. He's not the least upset. So much for losing good men.

Hearing or seeing something that I don't, Tommy moves to his right and hits a big freestanding gong—that I hadn't noticed but I'd love to have for future company meetings—and a deck hand quickly appears, as a speedboat, a Garwood I think because of its throaty exhaust, pulls alongside. Amidships, the deck hand lowers a substantial looking rope ladder. A Chinese lady, attractive from a distance, blithely climbs aboard, waves to Tommy and disappears down the stairs.

"The missing nurse!" he gladdens. "The speedboat will take you back when Martha's ready."

We make polite conversation while waiting for Martha. He's not sure where I can buy a gong, but we agree on dinner tomorrow night above the Hoover Theater. Because I ask, he passes word to the boat driver that it's okay for Martha to take the wheel. I'd like to give it a go myself but I don't ask fearing protracted negotiations.

On a nice day like today, his junk's a pleasant place to do business. Sunshine, a light breeze, a pretty woman arriving by speedboat, endless rum & cokes, no telephones, a crew taking care of menial tasks, the *potential* for good music, and an operating room in the event of an acute appendicitis.

———————o———————

8.

While Martha takes an after-lunch post-surgery nap, I'm walking crowded streets near the hotel. Every narrow alley throbs with industry, Chinese industry. In one, two young men squat and rewind the armatures of old electric motors while their kids play close by. In another, three fellows with their wives and children wrap apples in purple tissue paper, then carefully place the wrapped apples into cardboard boxes printed with the official Diamond brand and touting the contents as being *Washington State Apples*. The apples originated deep in China and came down the Pearl River to Hong Kong. I'm guessing they're being prepared for shipment to India, the Philippines or Australia; wherever *Washington State Apples* sell for a premium. A fraud? Certainly! But the humble packers are no more guilty than are the men rewinding the electric motors that will receive a coat of paint and be sold as new.

The alley-families are mainland refugees, who have escaped the ravages of the Cultural Revolution. And though for the moment they're at the bottom of the economic pyramid, they seem genuinely happy to be in Hong Kong. Happy to have a job, food to eat and some awful place to sleep that isn't going to receive a mid-night visit from a blood thirsty gang of twelve-year-olds. I've noticed all plants and animals strive to achieve their expectations, with success and happiness most often going to those with the humblest of goals – unlike me and mine.

"When the Whitakers," I mumble, for the company my voice provides, "were in shipping, I'm sure people accepted what we did at face-value. Though from the beginning, in the late eighteen-eighties, how and why we split profits with Chinese agents, who arranged for cargoes, was never revealed.

"When the Whitakers owned and operated hotels, people had no problem nodding to demonstrate their understanding when they were told what we did for a living. Everyone thinks they know what it means to be in 'the hotel business'. They never equate it with a twenty-four-hour-a-day, seven-day-a-week operation that requires excellent management, staff, food, liquor and beds, every second of every day.

"Tell someone you've sold the family hotels and now live off interest being paid by the new owners of those hotels, and they nod—sarcastically thinking 'Tough life!'—never giving a moment's consideration to the fragility of a mortgage, as their understanding of such matters equals the clarity of a gray smudge.

"Tell someone you're getting into the shrimp business, and they think you're going to grow shrimp, catch shrimp, or cook 'em and put 'em on their plate so they can eat 'em. In Seattle and San Francisco, they envision teeny-weeny shrimp that are used for salads ordered by customers too cheap to order a Louis with Dungeness crab. The listener has no idea how a beautiful big shrimp gets from Indonesia to New York City, and they don't care."

Telegram from JJ, waiting in the suite upon my return:

FEELING GREAT AND WILL COME FOR REMODEL ON PAA WEDNESDAY NEXT STOP LIKE TRADING FOR DIRT IDEA STOP GOING ON TEST FLIGHTS THIS WEEKEND STOP BILL WORKING VERY HARD STOP I CANNOT IMAGINE MY LIVING WITHOUT HOLLY AND LIAM STOP MACKEY SAYS HE FOUND THE RIGHT BOAT AND WILL CALL YOU STOP WINTER STILL IN SEATTLE

Telegram from Adolf, waiting in the suite upon my return:

FOUND TWO DIESEL PUMPS EACH PRODUCING EIGHTEEN THOUSAND GALLONS PER MINUTE AND ONE STEAM DRIVEN PUMP PRODUCING TWENTY FOUR THOUSAND GALLONS PER MINUTE STOP DEMO TOMORROW STOP ALL THREE FOR TWENTY-FIVE GRAND US DOLLARS FOB CALCUTTA STOP COULD BE LOADED ON BARGE IF FRIDAY SURVEY IS OKAY STOP STILL LOOKING FOR NOZZLES STOP ADVISE PLEASE

The hotel's long-distance operator gets Adolf on her first attempt. He gives me payment instructions for the pumps, and the flight number with the arrival time for the barge paperwork he airfreighted this morning. He's optimistic about finding nozzles, maybe even the firefighting monitors I really want, and he wants to know if he should stay in India until Mackey gets there to tow the barge. I tell him if the barge and pumps check out, and if he comes up with monitors, everything can be loaded onto the barge, and I'll pay the British firm we're buying the barge from to put a round-the-clock guard on the barge. I also tell him to hire guards to watch the guards, and then to fly back to Hong Kong for a rest in Hilton-style-comfort until Mackey shows up, and the two of them chug back to Calcutta via Singapore. He's happy with the proposal, so I hang up and go downstairs to give our Tommy-driver directions for getting the package from the airport, which will actually be coming from New Delhi, since there are no direct flights between Calcutta and Hong Kong.

When I get back up to the suite, Martha's awake, talking on the phone and laughing. She's so elegantly un-attired I immediately close the drapes.

"Captain Mackey's on the phone," she tells me, and offers the receiver. I barely notice her smile.

"Thanks," I whisper, but she misunderstands and gives me a right-eyed wink.

"Captain," I grin, "rumor has it you've gotten lucky … No, no, I haven't heard anything about *that*, I'm referring to finding a suitable tugboat … Yes, I believe a hundred and nine feet should be long enough … Wow, a range of thirty-eight hundred miles will do very nicely. How about fuel consumption? … My, that's only about six and a half gallons an hour … Sixteen knots top speed. What's that in miles per hour … At eighteen and a half miles per hour, the tug could pull a dozen water-skiers … Okay, two dozen. Is the seller making any claims about the boat's condition? … How long will it take to find a crew? … Excellent. Have you included a navigator? … A five-man crew plus yourself means … I don't think long watches are terribly safe … That's better. And once you're in Southeast Asia, and everything's operating, the boat'll be on station for a week at a time … If you say so. And yes, wages of five thousand a month are in the budget, but you can't hog the money and treat your

94

crew like slaves. They're going to be a long way from home … You're right, they *can* live better and cheaper out here than in San Francisco, or Seattle, but so can you … I'll come up with bonus money based on profits. Where's the boat? … Do you know a good survey firm in Anchorage? … No, no. I want a survey for insurance purposes and my peace of mind … I'm salivating. Test 'em to make sure they work, but having two firefighting monitors on top of the main cabin, one on each side, well, that's pretty close to perfect. I suspect the main engine powers the firefighting pump but check, please … Make sure all the electronics and everything else actually work … Yeah … And make sure each crewmember knows how to work everything … No! Teaching them while you're cruising out here might be efficient, but you're literally in deep trouble if there's an early problem, and early's *exactly* when and where the weather'll be the worst. Terrible in fact. And if something goes wrong with the boat, that's when it'll happen … Yes, captain, *you are* working for an old woman … If the tug's priced under a hundred thousand just make the deal … Well, sir, you can complain about how much you hate the monitors, and if that lowers the price, fine. But understand, I want those monitors! … I'll tell you why, when you get here … Holly has you covered … She knows how to reach me … Call if you make a deal. And line up a crew just in case … Yes, sir, me too. Congratulations and goodbye for now."

Martha's dressed, so we may be going out. The time it takes for Martha to put on clothes varies from seconds to hours.

The lift opens at the lobby level, where there's a mob of Japanese tourists waiting to go up. Mei Liew stands to one side, wearing a medium-gray suit with large gold buttons and a tight short skirt, white blouse, black leather heels, a new short haircut and makeup that quite nicely makes her oriental eyes rather exotic. She looks to be in her late thirties, not early fifties, but I'm forever misjudging the age of a woman. She prefers to smile as a greeting, versus joining the crush, and when she knows we've seen her, she turns and walks slowly away. We follow her to a space that's so sparsely populated I can actually see a floor of polished white granite.

"Where shall we go?" she sings. "It's early, only half past four. The bars are empty."

"First," I glower, and note their dismay, "you must do something. Use the hotel florist and send a very expensive flower arrangement to Sir Gordon. Have it delivered to his office, *today*. Both of you sign a thank-you card using your first and last names. Next, speak to someone in authority, and have any phone calls for us, forwarded to the Victoria Room. That's where I'm going. And that's where I expect you might join me."

M and ML both nod several times, but their feet seem stuck to the polished white granite. "Chop, chop," I insult, and walk away, believing if I don't, they'll do nothing.

Evidence suggests that in the early nineteen sixties, encouraged by an evil foreign power, perhaps Mao himself, Hong Kong was silently invaded by a coalition composed of Denmark, Sweden and Norway, who dispatched an army of salesmen under the command of a few architects and interior designers. Their mission: to rid Hong Kong of all *form* that does not follow *function*. One needs to look no further than the nearest office to realize the extent of their victory. Even the skyline hasn't been spared. Before long the Hilton's Victoria Room will be stripped of its precious period pieces, items I find psychologically soothing.

As much as I truly abhor bad taste, it's better than no-taste-at-all.

"Sir," says a Chinese waiter costumed as a pre-eighteen fifty-seven Indian sepoy in British Khaki, standing at stiff attention next to my table, eyes straight ahead, chin pressed to his chest.

"I'm being joined by two ladies …"

"Yes, sir," he interrupts.

"Do you have coffee made with boiling water?"

"I'll check, sir," he snaps, and before I can give him complete instruction, à la James Prindle, he marches off with an exaggerated high step.

"No, sir," he scorns, back in less than a minute.

"Well then, if you will keep your mouth shut, pay attention, and write down my instructions, I'll tell you what I want.

"Yes, sir. Sorry, sir."

"Find some instant coffee," I instruct, "freeze-dried if possible. Into each of three tall clear-glass cups, or heavyweight highball glasses, if you haven't the cups, put one level teaspoon of instant coffee. Add boiling water until each container is three quarters filled, stir to thoroughly dissolve the crystals, then put the containers in the refrigerator for seventeen minutes, or until the coffee reaches room temperature. When they're ready to serve, add one and a half ounces of Bushmills. If you have proper, somewhat sweetened whipped cream, I would like a dollop on top of each, but that isn't life or death."

"Yes, sir. Anything else, sir."

"We'll probably have several rounds, providing the drinks are any good, so you may wish to prepare and refrigerate some extras."

"Yes, sir. Are you certain the ladies want Irish coffee?"

"Damn your impudent eyes," I exasperate, for the smirking fellow could have been more forthcoming. "I'll simply tell them it was your idea. That you were born and raised in Hong Kong; that'll be that. Trust me."

"As you say, sir," grins the imitation soldier, before he performs a smart military-style about-face and marches off leaving me in my campaign chair of leather stretched over a frame of dark mahogany, sitting in front of a low campaign table of hammered brass, surrounded by three more chairs of the same stretched-leather construction.

Nothing so well represents the reign of Queen Victoria as the British domination of India. Here in the Victoria Room, British India lives on in magnificent detail, but nothing's more amazing than waiters dressed like sepoys, and behaving as the native enlisted did toward British officers, except, of course, during their Mutiny of eighteen fifty seven, fifty eight. After the rebellion, there were several thousand sepoys in Hong Kong (Kowloon, actually) during the summer of eighteen sixty, prior to their sailing north and eventually marching on Beijing. Notwithstanding such colonial difficulties, I'll wager the Victoria Room dishes a smashing variety of curries, none with less than seven boys, each in its own little bowl. My favorites being: chutney, toasted coconut, lime wedges, raisins, chopped unsalted peanuts, crumbled crisp bacon, and diced hard-boiled eggs.

As M and ML are shown to my table, before drinks arrive, I stand to greet them as imperially as possible; the act's hindered by my blue blazer, white shirt and tie that aren't a real uniform, and I'm without a proper hat sporting gold braid, and I've no swagger stick at all. Americans usually fail at pretending to be imperial, though Martha's not bad, on occasion.

"Hi, honey," M breezes, as I seat her. "How did you ever find this … this movie set?"

"It is, isn't it," echoes ML, seating herself. "What fun."

"Now ladies," I sigh, as I return to my chair, "it's time we get serious. There are several important …"

"I *love* getting serious," M grins, "but I'm not sure this is the right place," – she quickly looks at ML, then back at me – "and I doubt you can handle both of us."

ML blushes, and pats Martha's hand with feigned disapproval. At the same time the Irish coffees are presented; the ladies unconsciously furrow their brows and flare their nostrils.

"It's January," I growl. "Irish coffee is perfectly appropriate. Drink up or I'll have you taken away and flogged."

By golly, they set about carefully stirring in the whipped cream, and seem delighted with their first sip.

"Martha," ML says to me, after her tongue has cleaned some foam from her upper lip, "has told me all about this morning's surgery. Each scalpel cut, cautery, blood spurting artery, suture and retraction of tissue was described in horrific detail. Now then, I believe you talked to Mr. Tang while Martha was laboring, and I'd appreciate your telling me if he has news of my family."

"Tommy doesn't think they're in Hong Kong. But he considered his reports to be incomplete. After a bit of negotiating, we agreed on a fee for his men to rescue your family, and it's more expensive than having some *associates* in Canton put them on a vegetable boat going down the Pearl. But he and I believe it's much safer for everyone concerned."

Her face's clouding over. "Don't worry about the money," I cheery, "it's a Chinese New Year's present from Martha."

"That's too much," ML scowls, while shaking her head and looking at M, who shrugs, though neither one knows the actual terms of the agreement. "How much?" she demands, with the intense curiosity of a cat's paw searching a dark little hole. "And what happened to the money I paid?"

"That's gone," I dismiss. "It appears you were swindled. And I suggest all those people who worked for the Trader's old General Manager can't be trusted … and I'd sack the lot of 'em, if you haven't already."

"I have," ML sighs. "The hotel is closed, as you know. I won't pay people for doing nothing. But … but I want to go to Guangzhou with Mr. Tang's men. I …"

"Out of the question!" I state with authority, and reach for my Irish coffee. "Too dangerous. And Tommy will charge extra. *I* sure as hell would."

"Luke," she pleads, "the *worry* … it's like swatting cockroaches, it never goes away."

Knowing I'm right, I shake my head and stare at her with a frozen face to demonstrate my complete implacability.

"Me too," surges Martha, "in case someone gets hurt. I'll take a few things in a bag. I can help, you know."

"Good grief," I bellow. "Why not wait for Mackey and the tug? We'll pack a picnic and go for a little cruise up the Pearl River into Communist China. They won't shoot at us or lob artillery shells or arrest us, confiscate the tug, and throw us in prison … because we'll be smiling and waving."

"Luke," Martha ices, "you needn't be sarcastic."

"Really?"

"No," she says, with her usual self-assurance, and crosses her legs. "Mei Liew feels very strongly about this, and so do I."

"Fine. It's not up to me anyway. It's Tommy's decision. *You* can deal with him … and *you* can pay for it yourselves."

I finish my drink, while the ladies watch me with maternal patience; certain the evil-tempered adolescent male will relent.

"How much?" ML eventually asks, again.

"Half a million Hong Kong, two hugs from Martha and a ride in my airplane. When it gets here."

New Irish coffees are delivered. I ask for a plate of ginger biscuits instead of the bowl of peanuts being offered. I'm yes-sired by the waiter standing at attention with gut sucked in, one arm rigidly at his side, eyes front, and he has earned an extra thirty percent of the bill for not alternatively offering a bowl of salt-dried anchovy filets.

ML crosses her short shapely legs and says, "I will pay him … and anything extra he wants for taking me."

"Two hugs," chimes M, "is fine. I might even agree to four."

"How about the airplane?" I needle.

"When it gets here," M states, "he can have his silly ride."

"Says who?"

M looks a ML, then at me.

"That's right, dear. Only if *I* say so. And if you continue with your lunatic need to be Florence Nightingale, *I* ain't sayin' so. Which means Tommy's price goes back to the original one million Hong Kong. And even if he'll take Mei Liew, and he won't, he will never, ever, ever take you, Martha. With y*ou* along, his worst case scenario almost becomes a reality."

"I should go alone," ML solemns to M. "Thank you for offering. But you are not Chinese, and that is too obvious."

"All right, then," I say, quickly, hoping to end the discussion. "I'll raise the issue of your going at the first opportunity. By then Tommy will be certain where your brothers are." ML nods. M glares. "At the risk of seeming morbid," I tweak, "and only because of our mutual interest in the hotel, I must ask if you have a will?"

ML nods, and though I don't believe her, I don't press. The point's made. Silence shrouds the room, removing all glamour and let's-pretend, dulling the wallpaper and staining the chandeliers, slumping the waiters, and would have totally spoil the mood if not for the timely arrival of ginger biscuits and another round of Irish coffees. It's my fault, of course, so it's up to me to improve the atmosphere.

"JJ will be here next Wednesday," I announce, putting on my best smile. "He's excited about remodeling the hotel. Do you lovely ladies have any thoughts on the subject?"

There's no response. Neither a glint in an eye, nor the partial opening of a mouth with nothing coming out, or a raised eyebrow, or flaring of nostrils; not even one nostril.

"I talked to Captain Mackey," I continue, undaunted, "and he thinks he found a tugboat in Anchorage. It's not too old. Built in nineteen fifty-three. It has two firefighting monitors. He's already lining up a crew. If it passes its survey, he could start for Hong Kong in a week. The trip will take nineteen to twenty days. Either of you want to fly to Anchorage and come back on the boat?"

Both women shake their heads.

"Adolf telegraphed from Calcutta. He found three pumps. Tomorrow, he'll see a demonstration. I called and talked to him. If they pass the test, he'll have 'em loaded on the barge, providing the barge passes its inspection. But he hasn't found any monitors or nozzles. After Mackey and crew have a few days of rest in Hong Kong, they will be cruising to Singapore, about a six-day trip, and then on to Calcutta to tow the barge and pumps back to Singapore. That will be a two weeks in the beautiful Bay of Bengal, Andaman Sea and Straits of Malacca. Would you like to go?

On any leg? Either one of you? All expenses paid?"

The women look at each other, then they look at me, their expression signaling their disdain.

"This weekend, JJ's going on test flights with Bill Stuart. When the plane's ready, Bill's going to wend his way to Dutch Harbor, that's in Alaska, then fly to Hong Kong via Sapporo, that's in Japan. A little over twenty-four hours total flying time. I don't suppose either of you want to go on the plane's maiden crossing of the North Pacific."

They don't.

"Martha, Mei Liew," I growl, without a smile and loud enough for them to jump, "Do either of you have a real understanding of why we're in Southeast Asia? Because if you don't, stop sulking and pay attention! We're not on a bloody holiday!"

They're offended—thank heaven—but the room seems to be throwing off its shroud. Our waiter marches toward us, perfectly erect and carrying a telephone with a long cord that's unwinding behind him. He places it before me, announce that I have a call, and that I'm to pick up the receiver, and the operator will make the connection. Toe-to-heel, he about-faces and marches off.

"Yes, Judy Chen, Luke Whitaker, here … Informal, I hope … What time? … You don't have to send a car, but at the moment I've nothing to write with. My wife … Yes, Martha, will call you tomorrow and get the address … They are but humble flowers … You are too kind. I will convey your appreciation … Yes, goodbye."

"It seems," I gladden to M and ML, who are now paying rapt attention, "that your flowers arrived in record time, and the recipient was duly impressed, as was his secretary. Congratulations for remembering we're in the land of understated elegance versus stems by the dozen.

Sir Gordon and his wife are having a few friends in for dinner, tomorrow night. And we," – I hold up three fingers – "have been invited. But you two" – I fold one finger down – "will have to attend without me. I've already agreed to dinner with Tommy, and that's too important to cancel."

"What's the name," Martha beams, "of the lady I'm calling for an address, and what time …"

"Judy Chen. Cocktails at six. Dinner at eight. And by the way, informal doesn't mean …"

"Thank you dear, but I *know* what informal means. And don't worry, Mei Liew and I will have oodles of fun without you," M assures, and looks at ML, who appears less certain. "You haven't forgotten how good my memory is, have you?" – I shake my head, once. – "I'm glad, because while I was sitting around Seattle, by myself, I memorized a charming poem, a Rudyard Kipling poem, that I'd like to share. It's something for you to consider as you dismiss our possible contributions to the Canton rescue mission:

"'When the Himalayan peasant meets the he-bear in his pride, he shouts to scare the monster, who will often turn aside. But the she-bear thus accosted rends the peasant tooth and nail, for the female of the species, is more deadly than the male.

"When Nag, the wayside cobra, hears the careless foot of man, he will sometimes wriggle sideways and avoid it if he can, but his mate makes no such motion where she camps beside the trail – for the female of the species is more deadly than the male.

"When the early Jesuit fathers preached to Hurons and Choctaws, they prayed to be delivered from the vengeance of the squaws – 'twas the women, not the warriors, turned those stark enthusiasts pale – for the female of the species is more deadly than the male.

"Man's timid heart is bursting with the things he must not say, for the woman that God gave him isn't his to give away; but when hunter meets with husband, each confirms the others tale – the female of the species is more deadly than the male.

"Man, a bear in most relations, worm and savage otherwise, man propounds negotiations, man accepts the compromise; very rarely will he squarely push the logic of a fact to its ultimate conclusion in unmitigated act. Fear, or foolishness, impels him, ere he lay the wicked low, to concede some form of trial even to his fiercest foe. *Mirth* obscene diverts his anger; *doubt* and *pity* oft perplex him in dealing with an issue – to the scandal of the Sex! But the woman that God gave him, every fiber of her frame proves her launched for one sole issue, armed and engined for the same, and to serve that single issue, lest the generations fail, the female of the species must be deadlier than the male.

"She who faces *death* by torture for each life beneath her breast may not deal in doubt or pity – must not swerve for fact or jest. These be purely male diversions – not in these her honor dwells – she, the *other law* we live by, is that *law* and nothing else!

"She can bring no more to living than the powers that make her great as them, mother of the infant and the mistress of the mate; and when babe and man are lacking and she strides unclaimed to claim her right as femme (and baron), her equipment is the same.

"She is wedded to convictions – in default of grosser ties; her contentions are her children, heaven help him, who denies! He will meet no cool discussion, but the instant, white-hot wild wakened female of the species warring as for spouse and child.

"Unprovoked and awful charges – even so the she-bear fights; speech that drips, corrodes and poisons – even so the cobra bites; scientific vivisection of one nerve till it is raw, and the victim writhes with anguish – like the Jesuit with the squaw!

"So it comes that man, the coward, when he gathers to confer with his fellow-braves in council, dare not leave a place for her where, at war with *life* and *conscience*, he uplifts his erring hands to some God of abstract justice – which no woman understands.

"And man knows it! Knows, moreover, that the woman that God gave him must command but may not govern; shall enthrall but not enslave him. And she knows, because she warns him and her instincts never fail, that the female of her species is more deadly than the male!'"

"Luke," ML chimes, after a long sailboat-type silence, "since I may die soon, I'd be pleased to know your plans if you don't mind."

"Sure. Let me start with the shrimp part. Big shrimp. Tasty tender Tigers. In the area we'll be operating in, they're the most important, though we'll have to take all but the smallest sizes."

She nods. Martha stares, or glares.

"There's a strong and growing demand for shrimp in Japan, and the United States. The only natural shrimping grounds under American control are in the Gulf of Mexico. Japan has no shrimping grounds under its control. Australia has some shrimping grounds, but they're an importer of shrimp not an exporter. Europe gets shrimp from the Mediterranean, and imports some from Pakistan. The industry's developing in parts of South America, mostly Brazil, but they're only exporting smallish and mid-sized shrimp, and even those are not yet in big quantities. Mexico has a shrimp industry, and exports to the United States. But currently, political and economic conditions are wrong for its immediate development. The Philippines, Malaysia and Indonesia could all be major exporters … but it's not happening. The shrimping they do is mostly local, for local consumption.

"To process shrimp for export, all kinds of things are required. Most important: large quantities of uncontaminated water, a steady supply of shrimp and, of course, the means of freezing 'em. Once they're headless, peeled and de-veined—with or without tails, cooked or uncooked—they're arranged in what will become a block of ice containing a net product weight of five pounds. The freezing equipment requires investment capital that's generally unavailable in the Philippines, Malaysia, and Indonesia. Presently, in those countries, *oil*, ladies, *oil* has the attention of investors, not shrimp."

M and ML have finished their drinks. I swallow the rest of mine, not because my throat's dry or because I enjoy the influence of alcohol or because I enjoy the taste of an Irish coffee, only so Mr. Semi-Subservient-Pretend-Military will bring us more, and, thereby, we can support the local economy, which eventually helps the unwashed; though I've been watching groups of Chinese ladies enter the Victoria Room in full-length fur coats, and I am developing serious doubts that much money finds its way from the tills of Hong Kong merchants to the alleys I passed a few hours ago.

"Singapore," I enthuse, "has the large quantity of un-contaminated water needed for processing. We could build a plant in Singapore, and go out to the terminal-of-stinking-fish every day before dawn with the hope of buying shrimp that are not rotten; sometimes there are a few. Sadly, none of the shrimp catching boats have any refrigeration, not even crushed ice.

"All day in the sun, the fishermen drag cone-shaped nets. If their skill and luck are good, and their harvest big enough, the fishermen put-put from the northeast coast of Sumatra over to Singapore. Fifty to a hundred miles across the Straits of Malacca, in average nighttime temperatures ranging between seventy-three and seventy-five degrees Fahrenheit. Such conditions are *not* conducive to shrimp *not* rotting. And that's very bad for land-based shrimp processing plants.

"Back to the importance of good water for processing. When frozen shrimp arrive at any US port of entry, they are randomly tested by the USDA. If the samples are found to be contaminated—usually with e-coli or coliform—the whole load's rejected. So, it's prohibitively expensive to insure against that potential loss *unless* the insurance underwriters know you're using *un*contaminated water, which confines the risk of rejection to something happening aboard the freighter, for which the shipping company is liable. *We* will be shipping from Singapore. Singapore does random testing *before* allowing food products to be export. A fact that will keep our insurance premiums nice and low."

I pause for the delivery of more Irish coffees by a Chinese waiter dressed like an India sepoy in a Hong Kong hotel with an American name. I say, "Thank you," and give him a U.S. hundred-dollar bill. He says, "You're welcome, sir. Thank you, sir." I ask if he can seat us for dinner in half an hour and he says he can. And when I inquire regarding *him* serving our dinner, he says it can be arranged. Hating to break in a new waitperson, I'm pleased. He about-faces, and I wonder if these fellows ever crash into customers standing unseen, and too closely behind them.

"So, then. Oh, yes. We're going to construct a two-story building on top of the barge Adolf found in Calcutta. The top story will be eight feet smaller, in length and width, than the first story. The entire structure will resemble a Chinese pagoda, though it will be a twenty-five thousand square foot processing plant with freezers, generators, sleeping accommodations, kitchen, dining hall, showers, bathrooms, sorting area, etc., etc. Unloaded, the barge rides nine feet above the water. With the superstructure, that'll be reduced to less than seven feet. Take away another foot or so for the week's supply of fresh uncontaminated Singapore water, which as it's used, will be more or less replaced by the blocks of ice containing frozen shrimp.

"Beginning two feet from the top of the barge's hull, we're going to cut holes in the hull that are eighteen inch in diameter every six feet on center. They will be covered with heavy watertight Plexiglas. Behind the Plexiglas will be high-powered lights to help the fishing boats find us at night, and to illuminate their unloading.

Just for fun, we're painting the area round the lights so they appear to be the eyes of a dragon.

"Working in shifts, the processing plant will operate twenty-four hours a day, Monday through Friday, while our tug tows the barge up and down the Straits of Malacca. In international waters. Keeping a schedule yet to be determined.

"Every Saturday morning, the tug and barge will return to Singapore, unload the frozen processed shrimp, along with the barge and tugboat crews. We'll take on fresh water; diesel for the tug, generators and pumps; food for the crews and everything else that might be needed, like medical supplies and Singapore currency. Every Monday morning, tug and barge will leave Singapore and be on station, ready to work, by Monday afternoon.

"For our investment, and all the trouble we'll undoubtedly have, we get a constant supply of big shrimp, the bigger the better, in excellent condition, that are quickly processed using good water, to eventually be shipped from the creditable port for Singapore to New York City. The fishing boats from Sumatra will save time and fuel. More importantly, they'll get paid for what they catch instead of having a high percentage of their catch discarded because it rotted before reaching its destination."

I take a few swallows, strictly to give M and ML an opportunity for questions. None are noted.

"There are similar operations in other parts of the world, involving fish and crabs, where the weather's too foul for barges towed by tugs, and where armed pirates don't prowl and attack unarmed commercial shipping whenever they feel like it, as they do, and historically have done, in the Straits of Malacca.

"Mei Liew," I sigh, looking at her, "I'm sure you heard the stories of Rose Line freighters being attacked."

"Yes, Luke, I did. You may not remember your father's first office, but it was on a small barge moored to a San Francisco pier. It was paneled with the wooden wreckage of Malaccan pirate boats that had been run down by Rose Line freighters. Some of the floating wood was salvaged. The pirates were left to drown, because those were the captain's orders."

"It's still a problem," I casual, not wanting to alarm the ladies. "They come from the same Indonesian coastline as the fisherman, and the government's given squeeze to do nothing. Some law says commercial vessels are not allowed guns bigger than rifles and pistols, which aren't much use when the crew's surprised in the middle of the night, and crew members aren't marksmen to begin with. If the pirates get aboard, they murder the crew and take the vessel; sell the cargo on the black market, and eventually sell the ship to its insurers for less than the insurers would have to pay the legal owners. They are a dangerous and bloodthirsty bunch of cutthroats – scum of the earth..

"That's why we're putting firefighting monitors on the barge. Think of them as water cannons. One at each corner atop the first story, and one on a small tower mounted in the middle, on top of the second story. Five in all. Each having a metal covering in the form of a dragon's head to protect the operator, and to make it appear the giant stream of water is coming from a dragon's mouth. The tugboat Mackey found, has two monitors, or water cannons, on top of its cabin, one on either side. I don't know their capacity, and I have no immediate plans for painting the tug or its water cannons to look like dragons, though it might be fun.

"Both of you lived in San Francisco for a longtime. You've seen fireboats perform: welcoming the Navy or just showing off," – they nod – "those huge plumes of water come from firefighting monitors, and the water was going as far as a football field. The top most of the barge's water cannons will shoot water that far, and perhaps farther, because it will be piped to a pump that pushes out four hundred gallons of salt water *per second*, through a nozzle, which creates a tremendous force. The other four water cannons on the barge, will each shoot a hundred fifty gallons *per second*.

"If we are attacked, some of the pirates will immediately be blown into the water. If any pirate accidentally opens his mouth, he'll be drowned. The rest of the pirates, unless they retreat within seconds, will go down with their speedy little open boats that quickly fill with water and capsize, or sink. Tommy thinks the sharks will love us. And, best of all, it's perfectly legal."

"What about the fisherman?" M worries. "Won't the pirates steal their money? The money you pay them for their shrimp?"

"You have a point," I squirm, "but the fisherman have the same problem returning from Singapore, which is even further from home."

"What's the airplane for?" M wonders.

"To fly supplies and passengers to a resort we're going to build on an island in the Andaman Sea, off Malaysia."

"When?" ML startles, but her eyes are sparkling.

"As soon as possible. As soon as the plane gets here and we're settled in Singapore and find a good location."

"Why are you taking these risks," ML suddenly disparages, with a motherly frown.

"I promised Martha adventures, and I need accomplishments. Some of the profits can go to good causes, like building and staffing small hospitals in remote places; training the natives …"

"At last. Now, that's a *real* adventure," Martha interrupts and enthuses, with a fresh smile.

9.

Hong Kong successfully mixes everything with everything else. Within its cosmopolitan atmosphere, to drink Greek ouzo during a dinner of delicious India curry seems perfectly appropriate. As an added benefit, ouzo instantly betrays even the smallest amount of water, contaminated or not, by turning from clear to a whitish opaque; no doubt an ancient Grecian alarm system developed by the original Brotherhood of Digestive Components. My ouzo arrives well chilled and perfectly clear.

The little ouzo glass never remains empty for long, though I sip liberally with the assumption to over-consume anything from a tiny glass, that doesn't burn your throat, must be impossible.

After a period of pleasant dinning, a fiendish Martha begins taking advantage of my dulled senses: challenges my business ideas, calls them non-adventures on a scale too small to warrant attention, etc., etc. Mei Liew does her best to intervene, but reminiscent of a hungry trout, I rise to the bait and slur stuporous remarks about building a railroad along the coast from Hong Kong to Singapore; through mainland China, North Vietnam, South Vietnam, Cambodia, Thailand and Malaysia; providing that would impress Martha, who only scoffs and replies that nothing less than a railroad along the coast from Hong Kong through mainland China, the Soviet Union, across the Bering Straits, transiting Alaska, Canada and continuing all the way to San Francisco – would impress her.

Whereas her malicious taunting can no longer be tolerated, I'm forced to retreat rather slowly because I can't stand without help from two waiters.

Morning arrives with Mother-Mei-Liew graciously taking Martha to tailoring shops, as Martha needs an expanded wardrobe. Last night she wore the same outfit she did while flying from Tokyo to Hong Kong, and since the clothing Martha wears influences her persona, I'm hoping for an improvement.

During the coolish month of January, there's no quieter place in Hong Kong than the area surrounding the swimming pool at the local Hilton. I've done fifty laps and feel better, nearly alive. A bottle of Coca-Cola has helped. So too, has the cloudy sky that causes me to shiver while wearing a bathrobe and reclining on a chaise lounge.

I share this sizable area with one small boy, age about seven or eight, who's undaunted by the weather. He's out of the pool, onto the diving board and back into the pool as if he's training to be *the Apprentice* in a new production of *The Sorcerer's Apprentice*. I'm keeping an eye on him and occasionally wondering where his parents are. I'm also thinking that if I want challenges (and according to Martha, nothing *I do* will ever be generally applauded) I might as well raise a child or two. After all, children are fascinating, and I'll bet they're easy to impress; at least for a while.

Through a glass door leading from hotel to pool area, comes a jacketless man in dark slacks, white shirt and tie; he's accompanied by a woman with a significant mass of someone's brown hair twisted into a bun and perching atop her head. She's wearing a black, very business-like suit whose skirt unstylishly stops just below her knees. Her heavy black low-heeled shoes fail to enhance her appearance. The boy, apparently sensing their presence, aborts the execution of his nine hundred and ninety-seventh cannonball—his preferred way of entering the water—walks off the diving board, towels himself, then pulls on a pair of baggy blue shorts before wriggling into a yellow T-shirt. With their hands in his, and chatting quietly, they walk to the door, where a young overfed Chinese fellow politely holds it open for them to enter the hotel. As they pass by him, he's joined by another young overfed Chinese fellow with a sizable bandage over his nose.

The pair loiter and look round as if searching for items needing maintenance, but they neither point at anything nor speak to each other. Having two men doing the work of one seems a waste of wages. Mentally, I begin questioning the Hilton's staffing policies until I'm reminded by my Pacifist Committee that this is not my hotel.

Swinging my legs over the side, because it's time to go, I sit up so feet can find and enter old loafers. Strangely, the inspectors are walking toward me in a rather accusative manner. Perhaps they believe I've been urinating on *their* aggregate.

About thirty feet away, they stop. Each pulls something from his coat. They hunch over as close to the walking surface as possible, which seems peculiar unless they're trying to sneak a look under my bathrobe. In unison, as if they've been practicing, their right hands snap at the wrist. Two metal blades appear. I almost laugh. Guests simply aren't mugged in the pool area of the Hong Kong Hilton, not with thousands of people behind glass walls that rise for hundreds of feet, and a wait staff that's omnipresent. Then again, if they actually believe I've been inappropriately relieving myself, they might have orders to cut off the offending anatomy.

It's hard for me to recognize people out of context, but now I do. They aren't inspectors or maintenance men, they're the bloody ferryboat-twins wanting a rematch. *Anger* adjourns the Pacifist Committee, trips *Fear* and *Caution* as they walk past her (of course, *Anger*'s a her) and yells: "Imagine the nerve! Cinch up thy bathrobe belt, wrap a towel round thy left arm, and with thy right hand pick up the empty coke bottle by its neck."

Waiting to see their next move, I think of Seattle's Lakeside, my small all-boys high school. If you weren't on crutches, weighed more than a hundred pounds, and had been alive for at least fifteen years you played varsity football. Having no choice, and forgetting we rarely made a first down, I had volunteered to be the kicker in hopes of spending most of my time sitting on the bench. Well, after a while I got used to bulked-up bastards coming at me. And these two remind me of the Italian twins, who'd played for Seattle Prep and reveled in knocking me on my ass, *after* I kicked the ball.

Anger advises that attacking will be to my advantage, and she notes *the bandage* isn't breathing well. So I stand up straight, eyeball the distance, estimate the steps, and start jogging at the brother without a bandage. Left arm with towel extended defensively; right hand waves the coke bottle in wild circles at arm's length. Perhaps excited about stabbing me to death, my opponent stops hunching and menacingly moves the knife back and forth. *The bandage* has disappeared somewhere out of sight to my right.

I slow and skip twice prior to shifting my weight to my left foot, planting it and swing my right leg as hard as I can. The kick lands ankle-to-crotch, not toe-to-crotch as intended, but with enough force to lift him off the ground and send the knife flying into the pool. Dismissing shrieks of pain, I whirl to face *the bandage*.

"YES!" *Anger* yells. "Now *the bandage* believes you're a barbarian. Offal on two legs. So kill him! *I* don't want any witnesses."

He's slowly circling out of kicking range, and he seems distracted by the on-going tragedy of his brother. I can't spend all day chasing him, for soon this tawdry scene will attract attention. The police will be called. The police will be Chinese and the barbarian, me, will go to jail.

Trusting to the innate sneakiness of *the bandage*, I drop both arms to my sides. Turn my back on him. Watch his reflection in the windows, and start for the door. After seven steps not eight, as I'm not Chinese, I bring the coke bottle from my side to my stomach. Fiercely gripping the neck, I start a wild backward swing. Momentum pulls me round – to see the bottle bounce off his cheek bone. I watch him drop to the concrete and note the knife bouncing away, and that he isn't moving.

An ugly sound: the bottom of a heavy-glass coke bottle makes when smashing into the side of someone's face, if you're close enough to hear it. With *Anger* losing support from *Adrenaline*, I slip the bottle into a bathrobe pocket, open the door, and saunter into the hotel.

Showered, dressed and waiting for Martha. Dark-gray vested suit, white button-down shirt, black brogues, feet-first white handkerchief installed and wearing a necktie of the Ninth Queen's Royal Lancers—alternating five-eighth inch stripes of gold and Kenya-red. Too much for lunch but fine for dinner. And I have a new personal rule: I'm not dressing twice during any day that begins with combat.

The Ninth Queen's Royal Lancers began their existence as a dragoon regiment in seventeen fifteen. Switched to a lancer-type cavalry in eighteen sixteen and later helped to put down India's Sepoy Mutiny. Considering the amount of ouzo that make-believe sepoy poured last night, a bit of symbolic retaliation seems justified.

My impeccably accurate watch reads almost three minutes past noon, local time, and the phone's ringing.

It's Martha announcing they won't be coming back to the hotel for lunch. She tells me where they *are* going, if I wish to join them, and I decline. She sounds very happy and expresses her enthusiasm for her morning's activities. She has seen some beautiful fabrics and hopes to have a dress made in time to wear to Sir Gordon's. I wish her luck, remind her of our four o'clock meeting at the bank, and idle: "I love you, of course." In response to which she breezes: "Of course you do, dear." and we hang up.

A Room Service order-taker promises to send two cheddar cheese sandwiches with extra mayonnaise and a pair of Coca-Colas. In Seattle it's slightly past nine at night, yesterday. Not too late I decide, and place a call to Holly and Bill Stuart. After a short delay the operator makes the connection.

"Luke! How wonderful!" Holly effervesces. "I'm just putting Liam to bed, would you like to say goodnight?"

"Hi, Uncle Luke," greets the next ruler of the world.

"Hi, Liam. Where I am, it's about noon tomorrow."

"It is? Then you're in the future. Wow! What's gunna happen at my school tomorrow? And when can we come and visit you?"

"Tomorrow at school, you are going to know the answer to every question. But only if you get plenty of sleep. Okay?"

"Yeah. How about the visit?"

"Soon, my friend. Right now things aren't ready."

"Thanks, Uncle Luke. I love you. Goodnight. Here's the phone, dad," I hear him say, as the receiver passes from one Stuart to another.

"Luke," Bill booms, "you all right?"

"Yeah, sure. Though I could use an old airplane with an even older pilot."

"That combination is scarce. Everybody wants it. But just for you, I'll see what I can find."

"JJ said you're ready to start test flights this weekend."

"Those are the *final* test flights, if they go well. So far, everything's working perfectly, including the two co-pilots and the two navigators. The new electronics are phenomenal. Powerful radios, new gauges, navigation stuff, independent forward and ground directional radar, a waterproof microphone we can drag in the water to listen for submarines or anything else. There're some other goodies I'll show you when I get there. The navigators are young, single, and really jazzed about electronics. They prefer working with transistors, resistors, color-coded wires and other stuff I know nothing about – to sleeping."

"Wow! It sounds exciting," I resonate. "Have you put enough hours on the new engines that you're comfortable?"

"Absolutely!"

"Bill, I've been thinking about the issue of weight and

extra fuel. What have you done about the plane's interior; the seats and all that?"

"Ah, glad you asked," he seems to celebrate. "The last time I asked you about *how* we were going to use the plane, you mumbled 'some of this, some of that'. So, after considering how much cheaper labor and most materials are in your part of the world, I've left the cabin empty. For the trip, we'll take folding cots and chairs. We'll eat sandwiches and drink coffee from thermoses. As you wanted, the head has been expanded to include a shower.

"However, and this is the exciting part," – I can hear it in his voice – "some guys at Boeing, friends of a friend, showed me how we could put a fuel tank where there once was room in the belly for baggage. They even introduced me to one of their subcontractors, who makes fuel tanks for Boeing, and another guy, who knew about installation, plumbing and pumps.

"Full of fuel, our payload is reduced by about two thousand four hundred pounds. But we can carry four hundred extra gallons of fuel. That gives us five and a half more hours of flying time and increases our range by a thousand miles. Damn cool, if ya ask me. And no more gasoline drums in the main cabin."

"So, you can fly almost thirty-one hundred miles without refueling?"

"More or less," he boasts, "depending on weather conditions."

"You'll call me before you leave Seattle?"

"Yes, sir. Holly's back. Do you want to talk to her?"

"If you don't mind."

"Hi, Luke," Holly excites, and I've a mental picture of her smiling, without makeup, in a house dress and wearing flats; standing tall and perfectly straight, ready to solve any and every problem from stopping a nuclear attack to getting someone a drink of water.

"How's your Mandarin?" I tease.

"Oh my, I didn't know you wanted me to learn Mandarin. Should it be a family affair, with Bill and Liam? By the way, I wired five thousand dollars to Captain Mackey."

"That's perfect, Holly. And the family affair's an excellent idea. But sometime in the future, not right now. Has JJ made you a signer on every account?"

"Every account in Seattle, and currently that's everything except the Hong Kong accounts. The nineteen sixty-seven financials are ready. Do you want a copy? JJ has approved them."

"Yes, thank you, and I have a couple of questions. How long will it take you to get everything arranged so you can be functioning in Hong Kong for a while, and then in Singapore? And how do you feel about Liam not going to school until we get to Singapore on a permanent basis? I'll hire a tutor for a few months, if you want. And do you mind living rather temporary? Does Liam have a passport? Canadian, I suppose, or do you have to get him one?"

"Liam's on my passport," she rather shines, in a pleased and pleasing way, "and yes, it is Canadian. Liam would be thrilled with a tutor as long as there's some playtime and some kids to play with. We don't mind living temporary. We're doing that now. Liam and I will get on an airplane tomorrow, if you want us to."

"I could use you, tomorrow. I needed you yesterday and the day before, but I don't want you to come until your husband gets to Hong Kong, and you've made all the arrangements you feel are necessary. Write a list of to-dos and slip it in with the financials. Martha and I'll help where we can. Okay?"

"Yes!" she says, "that's very okay. And it will *have* to be soon. Liam's super excited about visiting the future, and seeing Uncle Luke. Thanks to *you*, I'll be getting questioned for days. He's convinced the future's magic, and you're the magician."

"Don't I wish."

"Truth is," she gentles, "Bill and I agree with Liam. We're so happy, and having so much fun, it seems we weren't really alive until we met you and Martha."

"Nonsense! If not for you, I'd still be nearly naked wandering about the Empress Hotel. And if not for Bill, well, Martha might be a lounge lizard trudging from bar to bar in Neah Bay. Seems to me, those who are rescued should become rescuers.

"Call me in a few days, or when you hear from Captain Mackey. I'd tell you to hug your husband for me, but in our family Martha does all the hugging. Goodbye."

"Don't worry, I hug him all the time. Goodbye, Luke, and say, 'Hi,' to Martha."

When first in the British Crown Colony of Hong Kong, westerners notice how *western* it seems by comparison to their preconceived ideas of China and Chinese. Sure the smells are exotic (except for the diesel), and the street language (Cantonese, should you be able to hear it over the din of vehicles) must be labeled non-western in tone, pronunciation, pattern and vocal animation. But there are no conical straw hats or women with bound feet hobbling along with children strapped on their backs; nor are there any rice paddies. Additionally, the westerner must overcome his or her ego to accept the Hong Kong of three million Chinese does not exist for him or her, regardless how important he or she presumes to be. If Hong Kong were a living entity, as some suggest, its beating heart would be pushing *Chinese blood*.

Perhaps the neon signs best tell the story. On every street they are so profuse, so copious, and so close together they transform themselves into a kaleidoscopic blur of red, yellow, and green, with bits of blue and white. That's through western eyes, of course, that can't decipher the symbols and are not looking for anything specific. My point: the uncountable signs are not meant for me; *I* am not the market.

Certainly, the older multi-story buildings have a touch of something foreign: sewer pipes running down outside walls—because it never freezes here—and the upper floors of Kowloon apartment buildings with garments of the occupants' immodestly threaded on poles protruding from windows so the hand washed laundry can dry.

In time, *foreign* becomes *familiar*, and *beauty* hold-hands with *ugly* until both become *normal*. I make an exception, however, for the woman currently departing a funereal limousine that's double-parked in front of the Hong Kong Shanghai Banking Company's main office. Martha will never be *normal*, if normal is average, as she will forever be beautiful.

———————•———————

10.

"Confucius say," Tommy asserts—as he starts to answer my question about recruiting men for his organization, just before his mouth succumbs to chopsticks loaded with some of our heavenly Peking Duck, that's best during the dry winter months, and has yet to be renamed Beijing Duck by Mao, though these specially bred foul are raised on ponds close to Beijing until age sixty-five days, when they are force-fed and not allowed to stand during their last twenty-one days, for the sake of tenderness—"'Good government obtains when those who are near are made happy, and those who are far off are attracted.'"

We both nod several times to show our agreement with Confucius. Tommy's too busy chewing to speak, as are his two lieutenants, who were summoned to consume Martha's portion of succulent food ordered in advance and being relished beyond description in the unpretentious confines of a private room in this prize restaurant above the Hoover Theater.

The not-so-young-lieutenants are as trim as Tommy. Unlike Tommy they're of average height for male Chinese, about five-six or seven, and dressed in suits of black/gray iridescent Thai-silk that are not as well tailored as Tommy's, and without a folded white handkerchief. Their shirts are black and open at the neck. Tommy wears a white shirt with a narrow black tie, as he did in Aberdeen. A subtle distinction of rank, perhaps.

A moment ago, my local Brotherhood of Digestive Components issued a stop-eating order and banned the intake of tea for twenty-four hours. So I'm gently sipping unadulterated Coca-Cola through a straw, while watching chopsticks being manipulated by masters.

Rather than invite his lieutenants to this wonderful dinner, Tommy could have ordered leftovers put in paper containers with wire handles and given them to these two men. But leftovers are leftovers. Sharing a meal honors all guests. Especially when one of the guests might be an important American, or a friend of the boss. Such a dinner becomes an event to be discussed, declared, and remembered. An excellent example of "*when those who are near are made happy, and those who are far off are attracted.*"

"There are a few matters to discuss," I invite, "but if you prefer privacy, they can wait."

"I understand," smiles Tommy, placing his chopsticks on their holder. "Would you care for tea, or something stronger?"

"Thank you, no," I shake my head. "John Barleycorn wrestled me to the floor …"

"*Ayeeyah*, you are a fan of Jack London," he erupts with a gleeful cry. "Wonderful man. Afraid of nothing and worked very hard. A great talent. California's best writer, ever. A terrible shame he died so young. He was even faithful to his wife. Can you imagine?"

"Actually I can," I enthuse, and return his smile. "And I

agree with you, about Jack London."

"You agree with me about more than Jack London," he taunts. "How about some walking or a short cruise, or both. On a night like tonight, Hong Kong is spectacular from the harbour. We cannot go far. I never know when my hospital will be needed," he says, with an obliging wink of his left eye.

"Providing Elvis has retired," I idle, as I stand to get my backside off the hard little chair that I've perched on for over an hour, "otherwise, just a walk will be fine."

"Then we'll walk to the boat, it is not far, and I'll let Elvis slumber, though I doubt he ever does."

There's no dinner check to wrangle over. Either it's been pre-paid or has fallen victim to an *arrangement* of sorts.

We ambulate in silence until Tommy asks if Martha has a sister: preferably single, widowed or divorced; he isn't picky. I tell him she's an only child, and he bemoans the injustice of the gods. When I pointed out there's only one of him, he laughs, and says that shows their wisdom. From then until we reach his junk, whose lights will be on with engines asthmatically idling, I consider whether or not my great-grandmother, Summer Moon, would like him. I suspect she would, but I can't be certain.

We stand together at the poop deck's port rail, watching the city lights. At first, they're strong and distinct. As the distance increases to several miles, some lights begin to twinkle like stars in their own universe.

"Mei Liew's brothers are still in Guangzhou," Tommy states. "The wife of her youngest brother, Mei Foo, is recently dead. Poor health. Natural causes, we're told. His two children are well, so far, but they suffer from their father not being allowed to work. They have little to eat."

Tommy pauses and the celebratory beauty of an illuminated Hong Kong becomes dull, thanks to the nearness of China and Guangzhou, and a single tragedy that can easily be multiplied by a number in the millions.

"The older of her younger brothers, Mei Han, is also being punished," Tommy eventually adds. "He has been placed on a watch list. And because he cannot work, his family is being fed, more or less, by his wife's family, at considerable risk to them."

"She wants to go," I mumble, "Mei Liew wants to go with your men … to get her brothers."

"That's crazy," he groans, then hawks before spiting into the harbour and turning from the lights to look at a fleet of unrelated freighters tethered to buoys. "I understand about family. But still it's crazy. We're going to have trouble enough with the wife of Mei Han. If she and her husband and their children escape, disappear, *her* parents, brothers, sisters, aunts, uncles, and cousins could be punished. Severely. The wife may not want to go because of that … and she'll be right in the middle of our operation. If she makes a fuss, everyone's in danger; probably dead.

"Add the unexpected appearance of a strange meddling sister-in-law," he groans, loudly, "who has lived most of her life in very bourgeois San Francisco, and what da ya have? Nitro-family, that's what ya have. A *family* explosion; my men are captured, killed, or left bleeding to death … and nothing is accomplished. Like your Bay of Pigs."

A tense silence on a Chinese junk with a big unarmed man isn't nearly as bad as a tense sailboat-silence shared with a new wife and her crazy girlfriend holding an ugly revolver. Nevertheless, there's something about being afloat, surround by water and darkness, that doesn't allow for the subject to be changed. Besides, he's right. And that's far more serious than his being adamant.

"Obviously, you recommend scrubbing the whole operation."

"I'm glad you find that obvious," Tommy grunts.

"It's not a matter of money …" I start to say, seeking a reassurance that we're not re-negotiating.

"Absolutely not!"

"Good. I thought not, but I abhor assumptions when they're unnecessary. I didn't mean to be offensive."

"You weren't."

"Thank you," I say, and pause. "How long can they stay alive? As conditions are, of course."

"Luke," he frustrates, "my crystal was broken many years ago. Weeks, I guess. And that's only a guess. If the fickle powers want them to live longer, they will live longer. Or they could be dead by morning."

"I'm sure you've given considerable thought to *all* the various issues," I humble, "but will you indulge me? So we can understand each other, for the future."

"Only if we're both drinking," he goads, with surprisingly good humor. "Unfortunately, you're on the wagon. Besides, I'm sure you want to get back to Martha and hear about Sir Gordon's party."

I'm quietly chuckling because it's not what I expected him to say. And besides, I think he meant to be funny. Cutting, of course, but funny.

"Actually," I smirk, hoping not to be seen, "we don't have to go back. Anticipating this cruise, and because her report on the dinner party has such a high priority, I've arranged for the lights of one floor of an entire office building, to flash on and off as necessary. I'll get the report by Mores Code. Providing I can recognize the building. In the meantime,

I'll drink with you. You're good company, sir, and that's rare. Yes, a scotch & water would be delightful, since your ice and water must be pure enough for medical purposes, and I should have thought of that yesterday morning."

"Shall we sit?" he suggests, after checking the skyline.

"Only in chairs," I quip, and he waves for *the ever present*, to whom he gives instructions before directing me to the round table behind the helm, which he does by extending a lengthy right arm, and nodding once.

Tommy and I choose un-opposing deck chairs. We're both looking forward. There's one chair between us. I'm to port. He's to starboard.

"I'm reminded of a football game," I sigh, "an American football game …"

"Yes," Tommy joins. "Cal Berkeley and Stanford. I went to three of those games. Stanford lost 'em all. Myself, I was not a jock. But go on, I shouldn't have interrupted."

"Football isn't a game at all; it's a complicated contest with two teams playing to win. Otherwise, eleven guys would walk on the field, step on a scale and the team with the highest total weight would cheer and go home. But that isn't what happens. Nor's the contest only about which team can run the fastest, or throw the farthest, or stand on their heads for the longest time. The best games are about cunning; as well as ability."

"*Ayeeyah*," he roars. "You are suggesting our attack on Guangzhou should be cunning! I do cunning all day long! Cunning doesn't replace the need for a battleship!"

"There's no need for a battleship, and we're not *attacking* Canton, damn it! Once I'm in the game, I wana win not quit before it starts."

"Even if your Mei Liew stays in Hong Kong," he says, and hunches forward to protect his vital organs from my insistence, "Mei Han, her oldest brother, is on a watch list. That means he is being watched, and anybody trying to help him will be seen. An alarm will be sounded. Death will come running."

"Dear Tommy, you've been such a big fish in your own pond for so long I wouldn't be surprised if the police send you flowers as an apology for arresting one of your men. If opposition to you arises, it soon disappears. You're the bloody Manchu mandarin of Hong Kong, and before you take that as a complement, remember what happened to those conceited fellows."

"Should we turn around and take you back to shore?" he challenges, and sits straight to show off his height.

Drinks are served. He lifts his and takes a long swallow. As much as I want to do the same, I leave mine on the table.

"I suppose so," I exhale, slowly. "I'm glad we had this chat. I want to thank you. It has saved me from having expectations that would never have been fulfilled. When choosing associates, you of all people, appreciate the importance of reliability *and* resourcefulness. Plans never go as planned. Some call it Murphy's Law, and it operates in this part of the world as well as everywhere else. Indeed, Confucius say: 'The man of virtue makes the difficulty to be overcome his first business, and success only a subsequent consideration.' But you knew that. Perhaps you also remember what our old friend Mao Zedong said in nineteen thirty-eight: 'Weapons are an important factor in war, but not the decisive one; it's man and not materials that counts.'"

There's silence.

Almost everyone in this part of world smokes cigarettes. If I did, it would give my hands something to do now they're being forbidden to hold a glass of cold smoky colored liquid of an acquired taste, that I've cultivated so well and for so long that it has become a bit more than desirable.

"The police have never sent me flowers … and you shouldn't call Hong Kong my pond."

"It's about five one-thousandths the population of China," I manage to enunciate because I'm sober.

"Yes, but Honk Kong is a tiger."

"No, *you* are the tiger, not Hong Kong. And *you* are the only tiger in the colony; emperor of the jungle, tolerant of monkeys, cobras, and noisy birds. Only those police you haven't bribed, the *white hunters* of Hong Kong, provide opposition to you; but you keep them distracted with monkeys, cobras, and noisy birds. Besides, you and the *white hunters* walk different roads. And that's the way *you* like it. And that's the way *they* like it."

Tommy finishes his drink with a third prolonged swallow. Then he reaches for mine, as waste is a terrible thing. The junk isn't turning, though it will, or the boat'll be too far from shore for its primary purpose.

"What makes you think there are any police I haven't bribed," he tries to cajole. "And you should be congratulating me, not ridiculing me."

"Gee-whiz. What a jolly idea. Congratulating you would solve everything, wouldn't it? Then we can get drunk, go below, ride the duty nurse; go home, get some sleep, eventually wake up and make bloody damn sure the *new* day doesn't have any *new* difficulties. I think not, actually, because *you*, old man—and I mean that as an endearment— are not so *venerable* that your future has nothing more grand … than death."

With my feet incited to restlessness by empty hands, I stand and begin to pace. Three slow steps and turn; three slow steps and turn. If I pace too far from the table I'll have to shout, and that won't do at all.

"More money," I drill, "may not be something you need—I certainly don't—so if life isn't about more money, but rather it's about getting fat and growing long fingernails, we'd best change our ways. Dismiss everyone and hire the best two chefs on the planet."

"I'd hate that!" he grumps, "but it would be an improvement over being harangued by you all night."

"Would it, now?" I say, and chuckle none too kindly.

"Damn you!" he explodes. "What the hell do you want?"

Two more scotch & waters are placed on the table, and before *the ever present* can remove the empty glasses, Tommy takes one in each hand and tosses them over his shoulders, over the stern rail, and into the harbour. Thus, making my point.

I stop pacing, lean forward so he's looking at me. "Do you know what you just did?"

"I'm angry. And I'm very frustrated."

"Yes, of course. But look deeper."

"So I threw away two empty glasses, so what? "

"Tommy, Tommy, Tommy. It's much more," I counter, dramatically shaking my head. "Ordinarily, you'd have waited for your servant to remove the *difficulty*. But you took it upon yourself and did it in such a way that a greater *difficulty* wasn't created. You didn't smash 'em on the deck, as would a petulant child, with broken glass flying everywhere, even though that would have better displayed your *anger* and *frustration*. You harmlessly tossed 'em into the harbour, and by doing so, you showed me your ability to successfully contend with *difficulties*, without regard to tradition, sentiment, or cost. *You*, Mr. Tang, would rather solve your own problems, deal with your own *difficulties* than have others doing it for you.

"But, Tommy, you are crippled by tradition. You are too

important and too successful for dealing with *difficulties*. You are supposed to have mechanisms and minions to do that. And, if *they* can't deal with a given *difficulty* you abort the project so the *difficulty* vanishes along with any potential loss of face." The junk turns to starboard, creating a conversational time-out, and reverses our direction.

I'm figuring: so what if he chooses not to understand, but the possibility that he will understand provides me with patience. And a drink would provide even more patience.

"In *your* mind," Tommy says, while pushing his empty scotch aside and taking mine, "how do you … deal with *difficulties*? And remind me, please, to never, ever quote Confucius when you're present."

"I've a confession to make …"

"*Ayeeyah*," he roars, and I snap round expecting him to be on his feet. But he's hunched over *my* now half empty glass in a huge hand. "Alert the world! Mr. Golden Mountain may not be perfect after all."

"Yes I am," I grin. "That was the confession."

"Rubbish, with putrid rats and dying snakes and all manner of maggots devouring the lot. Try again!"

"If you insist."

"I insist. And why aren't you drinking?"

"How can I?" I feign complaining, "you keep grabbing my glass."

"Oh, indeed. So I do. Your confession, please," he orders, as one does who's accustomed to issuing orders.

"Very well, if I must."

"You're the one who volunteered."

"So I did. Well then—you'll love this—I have a tough time focusing on *difficulties* that are not somehow connected with profits. And, generally speaking, *difficulties* that are nothing more than one-time events rather bore me." I stop

133

pacing and sit in my chair. "Take the case at hand: getting a few people out of Canton. An excellent solution won't have casualties or uncontrollable costs and, very importantly, should be repeatable; able to be done over and over again. At a profit, of course. The first question isn't how to do it. The first question should be about market size. How many people outside of Hong Kong will pay handsomely to have family members extracted from Canton? Any idea?"

It's a dicey question justifying thought. *The ever present* delivers two new scotch & waters and whisks the empties away before Tommy can toss 'em in the harbour. Most of the time, Hong Kong's humidity condenses on a cold glass and runs down the outside to make a puddle, but not on this dry January night.

"Just like I said," Tommy gladdens, "we *are* alike, aren't we?

"Certainly not!" I blast, as indignantly as possible, "I'm much younger, not Chinese and far, far better looking."

"Too bad you're not Chinese," he smiles, "if you were, you could work for me."

"Funny you should say that. *I* was actually thinking *you* should go to work for *me*. Race, since I'm a colonialist at heart, being a non-issue."

"Novel idea," he mumbles to himself, or to his glass as it's getting intimate with his mouth. "You give orders. I take orders. I solve *difficulties*. Or we solve 'em together. Maybe. Yes, maybe." The mumbling stops when Tommy and his glass share a kiss. And then they kiss again.

"The market is large," he idles, "in Hong Kong and around the world. But we cannot advertise. Other than to whisper. And even that would have to be done carefully. And deniably. If you promise not to get any better looking or poison my drink while I'm gone, I'll go below and bring up some papers you should see."

I nod. Tommy unfolds from his chair, pauses to say something to the helmsman, and then descends into the darkness of the main deck. I assume he continues down the companionway. After a few minutes the junk again turns to starboard. One hundred and eighty degrees later we're headed away from the city.

Tommy climbs the ladder using only one hand. The other hand and arm clutch two bulging three-ring-style notebooks.

"I'm sorry," he says, while putting the notebooks on the table, "everything is written in Mandarin. I don't suppose …"

While I'm shaking my head, *the ever present* materializes with a Coleman lantern, which he pumps, and then lights to illuminate Tommy and his notebooks. A long arm and big hand motion me closer to the table, and while I remove the chair from between us and scoot forward, Tommy takes the scotches and places them to his right; out of his way, out of my reach.

"I'll read to you if you don't mind," he offers, and I shrug. "These are written reports from friends. Well, more like spies. And then there are some transcriptions of events told me by a few refugees now working for me. Some items have dates, others do not."

"Go ahead," I encourage, and he opens one of the notebooks and turns a few pages until he finds the page he wants.

"One August, nineteen sixty-five," he reads, rather slowly. "'Chairman Mao has written a letter of warm support for the Red Guards at Qinghua University Middle School, where the movement started, as a signal for Red Guard organizations to spread throughout China. Until now, they' (the Red Guards) 'have been confined to Beijing.'

"Fourteen August. 'At least a million Red Guards from as far away as Sichuan and Guangdong', (Guangdong Province includes Canton/Guangzhou) 'are converging on Beijing for rallies in Tiananmen Square.'

"Seventeen August. 'At midnight, battalions of college students and school children began marching along Changan dahie' (Avenue of Eternal Peace) 'toward Tiananmen Square. Carrying red silk banners and portraits of Mao, they sang revolutionary songs. Once in place, they waited for hours before Mao appeared, along with the rising sun. He and the rest of the Politburo were dressed in People's Liberation Army uniforms. It is the first time I can remember, since nineteen-fifty, when he sent forces to Korea. Mao said nothing, but Chen Boda and Lin Biao spoke until the crowded square was hysterical. When a girl student pinned a Red Guard armband to the Chairman's sleeve, the square erupted. See the attached copy of a letter written by one of the young participants.'"

Tommy turns a page and continues reading from a piece of paper that gently flaps in a brief gust of wind.

"'Let me tell you news greater than heaven. I saw our most, most, most dearly beloved Chairman Mao! Today my heart could burst with happiness. I was jumping! Everyone was jumping! I was singing! Everyone was singing! After seeing the Red Sun in Our Hearts, we ran like crazy all over Beijing. I could see him ever so clearly, and he was so impressive. Comrades, how can I possibly describe to you what the moment was like? I cannot possibly go to sleep tonight. I have decided to make this day my birthday. Today I start a new life!'

"Nineteen August. 'Lao She, author of *Rickshaw Boy* and *Teahouse*, and about thirty other cultural types were taken to the courtyard of the old Confucian Temple in Beijing, where they received yin–yang haircuts' (heads half shaved) 'black ink was poured on their faces, and signs saying ox demon or snake spirit were hung around their necks before the Red Guards beat them with stakes and leather belts until their clothing was drenched in blood.'

"Twenty August. 'Loa She drowned himself in a shallow lake not far from the Forbidden City.'

"Thirty-one August. 'Over the past few days, Red Guards have beaten at least one person to death in every housing block of Beijing. Three hundred twenty-five people are dead, including the baby of a reactionary family, that was only six weeks old. Fury of the idealistic young is now terrorizing their elders.'

"'The Security Minister, Xie Fuzhi, has told the police: Should Red Guards who kill people be punished? My view is that if people are killed, they are killed; it's no business of ours. If the masses hate bad people so much that we cannot stop them, then let us not try. The people's police should stand on the side of the Red Guards, liaise with them, sympathize with them, and provide them with information, especially about the five black categories: Landlords, Rich Peasants, Counter-Revolutionaries, Bad Elements and Rightists.'

"From a former Red Guard in Fujian, now an employee of mine: 'Teacher Chen was over sixty years of age and had high blood pressure when we dragged him to the second floor of a classroom building and beat him with our fists and some old broomsticks. He passed out several times but we splashed water on his face until he was awake. He could barely move his body. His feet were cut by glass and thorns. He kept yelling for us to kill him. When he lost control of his bowels someone forced a broomstick into his rectum and he collapsed and we could not get him awake.

When the doctor came, we told him the teacher's death was due to a sudden attack of high blood pressure, and that is what he put on the death certificate. We made his wife agree with the doctor before letting her take the body away. I had nightmares all night. After ten more days of watching this kind of torture and hearing the screams, I ran away.'

"A teacher, crippled by his students and now washing dishes for me, told me that teachers with any bourgeois connections—and Mei Liew is just such a connection—were important targets. He wrote down some of what he saw: 'On the athletic field, every few days, several teachers would be taken out and shot in public, while others were buried alive. Once, four teachers were ordered to sit on a pack of explosives and forced to light the pack. There was a horrible sound and then nobody could be seen. Legs and arms were in trees and hanging from roof edges. At least a hundred teachers were killed on that athletic field.'

"Eleven October. 'Red Guards are splitting along class lines. Children of workers, peasants and soldiers versus those from less desirable backgrounds. I believe they are being manipulated by competing provincial and national, political and military forces. Many Red Guard units are setting up reformatories and detention centers, where selected members are disciplined and punished. A boy of fifteen told me of finding friends tortured by schoolmates. Some were laying on the floor bound with ropes. Some were hanging from beams. His girlfriend was unconscious on the floor in a pool of blood. Her pants had been stripped off and her blouse was torn, exposing her breasts. Her body was purple from being beaten. The heavy bleeding was caused by dirty socks and twigs jammed into her vagina.'"

Tommy closes that notebook and opens the other. He turns pages until he apparently finds what he's looking for.

Then he gives some serious attention to a scotch & water that, until now, he's only been sipping. When it's empty, he pushes it aside and replaces it with mine.

"Twenty August, nineteen sixty-seven, just last summer. 'Investigations continue. In east Hebei, eighty-four thousand were arrested. Two thousand nine hundred and fifty-five were executed, tortured to death, or committed suicide. In Guangdong, seven thousand two hundred were interrogated. Eighty-five, including the provincial vice-governor, were beaten to death.'

"Twenty-nine September. Less than four months ago. 'While touring the provinces and viewing the chaos, Mao issued a directive requiring rival Red Guards and workers' factions to unite into "grand alliances". Violent strife continues among university Red Guards.'"

Tommy closes the notebook, and puts it down on the deck next to the first one.

"Enough?" Tommy sighs, and I nod in agreement.

"Then I'll join you," he idles, "in this Canton conspiracy. That has a nice ring, don't ya think? You be the boss. You make the plans and I'll take care of the details. All expenses are yours. If it fails, it'll be *your* failure. If it succeeds, I'll take over the operation. Start the whispering. We will split profits fifty-fifty."

"Nay! That's like asking me to bet I can spit with my mouth closed. They'll be your men under your orders. Your spies will be providing the intelligence. And it all happens in your part of the world, where I don't even speak the language.

"Of course, I'll cover the expenses. And I've some ideas that'll make the operation even more expensive. If it fails, we both fail. I lose money. Other people lose their lives, and Mei Liew will have instigated the death of her two brothers; her five nieces and nephews; along with one sister-in-law."

"Good enough," he rumbles. "So what are your expensive ideas?"

"My throat's so parched," I croak, "I'm not sure I can talk."

"I will not apologize for drinking your drink," he grins. "But if you wish, I will call the doctor …"

I shake my head. "Though time's a factor, we should bring in some Japanese to kidnap two dozen local Communist Party officials. I'll bare-boat charter a coastal freighter to hide 'em on, providing you can come up with a crew for the vessel. You see, should any of your men get caught, we can use the kidnapped comrades for, well, negotiations. Trading. You know what I mean."

Tommy nods.

"Until the freighter's ready, they can stay under guard at the Trader. It's closed. But your people will have to take care of 'em. At least well enough to keep them alive. No uncooked rice with whole boiled rats."

He nods, again.

"And I've been greatly concerned about the excessive free time these guests will have, so I'm going to find a copy of Karl Marx and Fredrick Engels' *Communist Manifesto*, as well as Marx's *Contribution to a Critique of Political Economy* and his *Capital Volume 1*. It's important these fellas understand something of their ideology. Therefore, the books will be read to them in Cantonese, though they will, no doubt, be written in English. Guess I'll need a translator. But I'll personally prepare tests to make sure they're paying attention. Anyone flunking a test will miss a day's worth of meals."

Tommy not only nods, he smiles.

"They won't be turned loose until your for-profit

kidnapping scheme has run its course. Then we'll sail them north, staying in international waters, and put 'em in a small seaworthy boat with a compass and a heading for Vladivostok. The Soviets won't believe a word they say. Especially if it's the truth. So they'll be taken to Moscow for who knows how many years."

Tommy nods, and *the ever present* arrives with two glasses. Mine's a cola. Observant man, *the ever present*.

"Separated from the comrades, I also suggest the Canton kidnappees be confined on the freighter. To give *us* time for passports and any other documents they'll need, to be forged; as well as giving *them* time to adjust to a new life. We certainly don't want the Canton kidnappees wandering round Hong Kong. In and out of the Chinese Embassy. That sort of thing. Seems we must protect ourselves and those who are happy about leaving China, from any who are not, or come to wish they were back in Canton."

"Very good. Very good, indeed. I hadn't thought of that."

"By the way," I disparage, "if we provided American passports, US Customs and Immigration will be suspicious of supposedly native-born Chinese-Americans who don't speak, read or write a word of English. The kidnappees should go to Malaysia. It's spread-out and under-populated with a sizable Chinese community. And it doesn't border China. When you're in the for-profit mode, it'll be the sponsors' problem what to do with kidnappees once they're safely delivered to Malaysia."

"Yes. Surprisingly, that makes a bit of sense."

"You made a good point, a while ago …"

"I don't believe it," he quips.

"Regarding the sister-in-law's possible un-willingness to leave. Since we have no way of guaranteeing the behavior of the kidnappees …"

141

"Are you sure *kidnappee* is actually a word?" Tommy frowns.

"Certainly. If there's a kidnapper there must be a kidnappee, or the equation's out of balance."

"But of course," Tommy sighs.

"We're going to need some pills or injections to knockout the people we're kidnapping, and keep them out until they get to your junk; perhaps eight to ten hours."

"Injections work faster than pills. I'll talk to my surgeon. If that's what he recommends. And if he doesn't have enough. We'll *requisition* what we need."

When I'm sure he has nothing more to say on the subject of drugs, I light another proverbial candle:

"I think we need two kidnappers for each person being kidnapped. The kidnappers should be dressed like Red Guards, complete with proper armbands. Neighbors might cringe at the sight of them, but they won't be surprised when *your* Red Guards break into a house and terrorize a family. And that's what they should do, terrorize the families until they can be drugged and taken away like they're suspects of the worst kind. I'm not an expert on Chinese behavior, or anyone else's for that matter, but I believe fear for their own lives will keep neighbors from rushing to aid the family, or from even showing curiosity."

By way of agreement, Tommy raises his glass of scotch and I clunk it with my humble glass of cola, before lighting the last candle:

"You should also bribe a local doctor to file a death certificate for each kidnappee. It wouldn't do for friends and family members still in Canton to make too many inquiries regarding the disappearance of those we've taken away."

I'm done, but there's neither applause nor a drumroll; nor have the twinkling lights of Hong Kong reorganized themselves to form the letters: L U K E.

"*Ayeeyah*," Tommy booms, then gets up and walks round the table. "You have more imagination than an eagle of opportunity; you have the imagination of an evil spirit; possibly a minor god." Grinning, he pulls me from my chair and gives me a solid hug.

It seems he caught my wobbly pass and we're on the scoreboard: six to nothing.

11.

Whether one's cold-sober or warmly-inebriated, fumbling with a room key attached to a big hunk of un-pocketable plastic can be a tyrannical hindrance, even to the most inviting of accommodations. The obvious moments-old solution: never touch another room key. Wife or companion uses room key. Bellman uses room key, and gets tipped for his trouble.

Inside our suite, the lights are on and the bedroom door's closed. A darkened bathroom suggests vacancy, unless there's a corpse floating in the tub, as they will if they can, providing there's adequate water at an appropriate temperature … and I have no idea what a corpse might do if the amount of water and its temperature are not to its liking.

A half-finished scotch clutters the sideboard. The mini-fridge still has five … yes they're cold, bottles of Coca-Cola. I open one, and take a swig before setting it down so I can use both hands to get undressed. Suitcoat, vest, pants, shirt and necktie onto one hanger in the tiny closet by the entrance; socks dropped on top of shoes.

I remove a bra and panties from the sofa cushions, note the drapes are closed, and put them on top of a sleeveless, pink-to-red iridescent Thai-silk dress that's lolling over the back of the sofa. Assuming they're acquainted, I don't bother with introductions.

Lights off, I retrieve my bottle of coke before sprawling on the sofa. With more to think about than talk about, there's no unselfish reason to wake Martha.

As always, sleep will come to me when she's in the mood, and sometime thereafter the sun will rise. And when it does, I pray it will not be shinning over the shoulders of Mao Zedong to help him blind another million kids.

"I've never spent an evening with so many charming and gracious people," M brightens, and ML nods her agreement as we sit in the suite waiting for Room Service to deliver lunch. "They talked. They listened. They smiled. They responded to everything I said. Never once was I asked a personal question. Oh, and the food, my goodness, it was absolutely divine. Pork that was moist and tender. Stir-fried vegetables so crispy-fresh and delicious I momentarily thought of becoming a vegetarian. And the shrimp!" she squeals. "*Three* different sizes, prepared *three* different ways. Even one of the cocktail hors d'oeuvres was shrimp. Headless peeled de-veined and cooked, Mei Liew explained, with the tip of the tail still on, for holding. Somehow, it was held in a tight coil so you didn't lose any of the caviar piled on top. When I wanted another, they were all gone. Instantly devoured. You're right, honey, people *do* love shrimp."

(Having deserted the sofa before Martha awoke, I've been swimming all morning. A small caliber coke bottle not far away, hidden in my bathrobe pocket. When I got back to the suite, M had left a message that she had gone to ML's room, so I showered, dressed, and ordered cheddar cheese sandwiches with extra mayonnaise, chocolate cookies, and Coca-Colas for everyone; before phoning the ladies.)

"Luke," ML injects, so M can grab some oxygen, "the women were beautifully dressed; nothing floor length or sequined; only dark, perfectly tailored wool. It's winter here, and Martha and I were the only women without fur coats.

"I explained that fur coats were going out of style in the U.S. They were shocked. But I assured them. And Martha's right, everyone was perfectly charming. So much so I felt like I was back in San Francisco, in some secret British enclave. There wasn't a man at the party I wouldn't marry just for his elegant manners. Sir Gordon has an extremely high opinion of you, by the way," – her smile as proud as a mother's and equally irrepressible – "he thinks you're the smartest American he's ever met. And he's *terribly* pleased you went to London for a *real* education."

"Did you have fun with the boys?" M prods, having caught her breath.

I nod, get up to answer the door, let Room Service in and explain to the server how I want things done. To use while we are eating, I take the yellow lined notepad and pencil I had requested, from the serving cart. When the server departs, I seat the ladies at the game table, where the sandwiches await on plates covered by silver domes.

"Does Sir Gordon have a nice home?" I ask, seating myself and believing the more they talk the less complaining they'll do about lunch.

"Precious," Martha twinkles. "It's on the side of a hill overlooking the harbour. A grand driveway loops under a portico supported by fluted columns of green marble. There's a matching green marble entry that changes to checkered green and white marble, then becomes an all-white marble floor with strategically placed Turkish rugs of various sizes, once you're inside the house. Nothing modern, only period pieces whose periods I can't identify," – she looks at ML, who shakes her head while chewing – "I was too intrigued by the people, and the view, and the food; and the conversation. I didn't pay very close attention to anything else.

"There must be more to the house than we saw; other levels could be creeping down the hillside. If you feel the need to give me an extremely sentimental present for our first anniversary, a house and view like they have would be scrumptious."

"I'll keep that in mind," I mumble, and watch as M uncovers her plate without comment.

"To have so many shrimp dishes," says ML, "was most unusual. Perhaps they know of your plans, and were honoring your new venture."

"Most likely. Any disparaging remarks regarding my absence?"

"Not really," M grins. "I told Elizabeth Beasley—that's Sir Gordon's wife—that you were unavoidable detained, and offered your regrets. With a straight face, she said, 'My goodness, if he's busy that's okay. But if he's been arrested, we absolutely *must* do something.' When she grinned I started laughing, and I couldn't stop until she introduced me to a witty gentleman from Singapore, named Redrup. He's a lawyer."

"Any news?" ML asks, as casually as possible.

Yes," I say, and since my sandwich is finished and the cookies are untouchable until the ladies finish their sandwiches, there's no reason to delay a response. "Mei Foo and Mei Han are still in Canton. Mei Foo's wife died recently, and neither he nor his children are getting enough to eat, because he's not allowed to work. Mei Han also cannot work, but his wife's family has been smuggling food to them, at considerable danger to themselves, and it isn't known how long that can or will continue. Mei Han has been placed on a watch list. Those who're discovered to have bourgeois connections are being targeted for torture, and often beaten to death. *You*, Mei Liew, are a *bourgeois connection*. So *you*, will not be going to Canton, for that reason and several others."

"How about me?" M whirrs.

"What about you?"

"I can go, right?"

"Go where?"

"To Canton, of course," M frustrates, and puts down the uneaten portion of her last half-sandwich. The better to stare at me.

"Certainly," I shrug, "as soon as you get permission from the People's Republic of China, and make sure your passport won't be revoked by the United States of America the minute you re-enter Hong Kong; otherwise, you'll be deported."

"No, no!" she angers. "I meant *sneaking* into Canton with Tommy's guys."

"Oh, *that*. Sorry!" And because it sounded good when I heard it in my head, earlier this morning, I lie: "The surgeon and nurses are going to Canton, and Tommy wants you to takeover surgery while they're gone. The doctor told him you were fearless, and quite skillful."

"Okay," she pseudo-disappoints. "If I must."

"Last night," I idle, to change the subject, "Tommy gave me access to firsthand reports and accounts of activities dating from August nineteen sixty-five—the beginning of the Cultural Revolution—through October of last year, when Mao issued a national directive that his latest and most monstrous revolution was getting out of control. Currently, China's the devil's playground. And the devil hasn't had so much unadulterated evil to smile about since the purges of Stalin, and Hitler's holocaust. However, the chaos may be to our advantage."

I'm surprised ML is smiling, as I push away from the table so I can cross my legs, which I do, and Martha follows suit.

"Good lawyers don't ask questions of their own witnesses, unless they know how the witnesses will answer," I solemnize, "and that's our first problem. Hundreds of millions of Chinese *do not* want to be rescued. They trust Chairman Mao; or have unbreakable family ties; or fill in the blank however you wish, but we can't possibly know who wants to be rescued and who doesn't, until it's too late.

"Case in point, the wife and children of Mei Han. We're not positive that his wife wants to be rescued. And if she does, she can change her mind for any reason including a sudden realization that her relatives might be tortured and killed, because of her disappearance. Then add to the equation, children who are old enough to have minds of their own. At a critical moment, if even one child gets scared or doesn't want to leave friends, and starts to scream and yell … everything fails. There's capture and death. The devil grins. He might even laugh."

"Then we can't be rescuers," M states, as sure of herself as if she's bidding a bridge hand of thirteen spades. "We must be kidnappers."

"Precisely! And that creates more problems."

"But …" ML injects, and pauses, her eyes narrowing. "I should go to Canton ahead and make sure that …"

"What if," M turns to her, "Mei Foo and his daughter want to leave but his son wants to stay?"

There's silence. Not contrived to pressure ML to agree with acts of kidnapping, rather because each of us, it seems, wonders if forcing her brothers' families from their homes, regardless of our good intentions, can be justified. In the future, when it's happening to earn the funds paid by relatives not in China (sort of ransoms paid in advance), it's simply a business issue: the violation of a few government codes for profit; the responsibility, arguably, resting with the payers.

"What will happen to them," ML seeks, "when the families get to Hong Kong?"

"They must be confined on a ship anchored in the harbour, for a while."

"Like prisoners?" ML groans, eyebrows rising.

"Without complete freedom of activity? Yes."

"What happens next?"

"They can't stay in Hong Kong, Mei Liew," I regret, "it's too close to Canton, and too much a part of China. So, they'll be taken to Malaysia to start a new life."

ML bows her head and shrugs her shoulders. M gives her a gentle sideways Martha-hug, and I want to do something similar.

"Perhaps you're wishing you hadn't bought the Hong Kong Trader," I guess aloud, and her bowed head bobs up and down a few times. "I'll buy it from you for what you paid, plus any expenses you've had. And you can keep a fifteen percent interest – for your trouble."

She looks up at me with moist eyes, but her lower lip no longer quivers. "That be good," she whispers. "Then I can help nieces and nephews."

"Oh no, no, no," I gruff. "The fifteen percent isn't so you

can become a fairy godmother in the form of a rich aunt, it's so you can continue to assist me *and* remain a mother substitute for Martha … and me, too, I guess."

"Thank you," she chokes. "Excuse, please. I go my room."

"Sure," M whispers, and stands as ML stands, but doesn't slow her flight. "If you want us, we'll be down by the pool."

"I only need hour. Maybe two," Mei Liew manages to say, while closing the door.

"If we're going down to the pool," I casual, when we are alone, "do you want help getting into your new swimming suit?"

"I don't know," she smirks, "do I?"

"It's either here or by the pool. Your choice."

"By the pool sounds like fun," she coos. "Then again, you'll be racing around, frustrated you can't close all the drapes and blinds."

We're sitting at a little round table made of wood and wrought-iron. The top's fashioned after a pizza, with slices of wood converging at the center. There's space between each slice so rainwater can drain away. It's rather contrived, but the table's as far away as one can get from the two doors opening to the pool area.

With two empty coke bottles nearby, still dressed in blazer, slacks, etc., I'm sitting across from Martha with my back to the main building. In deference to an afternoon winter-wind blowing off the mainland, Martha's keeping her white terrycloth robe tightly wrapped. Her less-than-perfectly-tanned legs are crossed, their skin changing from smooth to bumpy to smooth with variations in wind velocity.

"Let's not forget," she idles, "JJ will be here, late afternoon next Wednesday."

I nod in response, then remind her it's only Thursday of the week before.

"I know," she disparages, and reaches down to rub away the latest crop of goose bumps. "But I'll need to spend all day, every day from tomorrow until Tommy's people leave for Canton, with Tommy's surgeon and his nurses. I don't know his name. Do you know his name?" – I shake my head – "So I won't have much time to get ready for JJ."

"Your petulance seems out of character, my dear adorable wife, what ails thee?" says I, brow furrowed and distracted by an urgent need to meet with Tommy to cover a giant lie that I've already told.

Martha shrugs. It's a beautifully shrug, of course, and I could fritter away hours with caring questions of discovery regarding the why of the shrug that would profit us not a whit. When I ask if she still wants to swim, there's a non-verbal reply in the negative. When I suggest we go back to the suite she looks at me as a girl might after being told there are bathrooms and fireplaces to clean, clothes to iron, floors to sweep, and homework to do. With the reluctance of the condemned, she stands up, and shuffles away, her head bowed. I follow in silence, until we're inside and waiting for an elevator. She doesn't react when I tell her I have an errand to run, and will be back in a few hours.

When a bellman reflexively smiles at me, as I'm walking toward the main entrance, I can't remember if Martha was carrying a room key. I give him twenty HK and ask him to let the lady wearing a towel into the Bridal Suite, if she doesn't have a key. His smile becomes a leer, but he takes the money and starts for the lifts. Though it's not my problem, I'm sure there's not a Chinaman in Hong Kong who believes he's getting *enough*.

Parked prominently outside the door as if waiting for no one less than an ambassador, Tommy's car doesn't go unseen. It's being driven by Hu Feng, a bright English-speaking young fella, who's attentive and dresses well. Today he's wearing a black v-neck sweater over a white shirt, gray slacks and polished black shoes. I request that he take me to Tommy, wherever he might be, and we're quickly on our way.

After dark, the floating restaurants of Aberdeen are a stationary light show, reminiscent of fireworks frozen in the sky. In daylight, the restaurants are rather tawdry with limitless analogies. Sans the pleasant distraction of Martha as a traveling companion, I note the enormous community of families housed on sampans, for what's rumored to be a lifetime. Actually, moored sampans are an economical solution to the local housing shortage, and suggest a more practical use of Seattle's Lake Union than preserving it for landing the occasional seaplane.

At Tommy's, I'm silently greeted by *the ever present*, then follow him upstairs and into a room with a rosewood floor, paneled in Philippine mahogany, empty wooden chairs round the perimeter and a closed wooden door at the end opposite from my entry. He mimes me toward one of two chairs nearest the door. So, I go to one that's three chairs away, unbutton my suit coat and sit with my right ankle resting on my left knee.

I look at my watch. Three forty-three, local time. Right-foot in shoe suspended in air begins to agitate, but stops after receiving stern look of disapproval. There's a clause in right-foot's union contract banning such juvenile behavior without prior written consent, and right-foot knows it.

At four seventeen, sounds from the other side begin to penetrate the closed door. Either a brawl's starting or a meeting's ending. When the door opens, seven senior, possibly venerable, Chinese gentlemen come out. They're dressed in a variety of western suits, short subdued circa nineteen-forty neckties with white shirts, pants, and unpolished shoes. It seems my presence wasn't expected, for they look at me and gather together for safety but they don't point, though they spew high-pitched Cantonese. Before any of the gentlemen pulls out a meat cleaver, stubby gun, or starts flashing a knife, Tommy appears. I probably look relieved, as I stand and button my coat.

"*Ayeeyah*," booms the honorable Tommy Tang, then wraps an arm around my shoulders, as if declaring me approved. Combined with what he tells the seven possibly venerables, the gentlemen smile, nod, and reach out to shake my hand, while talking to each other like I'm one of the most delectable, perfectly-cooked whole fish they've ever seen. Another statement by Tommy ends the love fest and the seven depart, muttering as they go.

Tommy's smile wanes, lips begin to hide perfect teeth, his eyebrows arch. All together his face becomes a question mark.

"Sorry to barge in," I sashay, "but I need a few minutes."

"Let's go downstairs and have a drink," he suggests, "I've been talking for hours."

Side-by-side we saunter down the stairs while he explains the seven gentlemen are his partners in different activities; rather like a board of directors. He'd been telling them about the new kidnapping enterprise, which had caused concerns until he shared my suggestions of last night. Apparently, they too believe I have the useful imagination of an evil spirit or minor god. They're now supportive, and hope to participate in any future schemes that might originate from this *unique source*. While listening, I'm less worried about living up to a disputable reputation than whether I want the reputation at all. Then again, one never knows. It might be useful, and Martha would love it to death. Figuratively speaking, of course.

"What would you like?" he solicits, after we're seated.

"Two ounces of scotch in a tall glass and a cold bottle of soda."

Tommy translates my request. When the waiter leaves, I begin supplicating:

"This morning, I talked to Martha and Mei Liew. Mei Liew accepted her not going to Guangzhou, but was extremely disappointed that her brothers' families would be taken to Malaysia rather than staying in Hong Kong. So much so, I told her I would buy back her interest in the hotel, which seemed to make her feel better. Later, to avoid a nuclear argument, I lied and told Martha you were sending your doctor and nurses up river with the kidnappers, and that on the doctor's recommendation, you wanted her to stay in the hospital and handle any emergency while they were gone. Like a moth to a flame, Martha's attracted to adventure. The more dangerous, the more she's attracted."

Our drinks are served. We sit in silence. Tommy looks so gloomy, I pour less soda into my glass than planned. When the foaming stops, I swallow half. When Tommy bows his head and looks at the table, I swallow the other half, and then, while looking out the window, consider throwing the empty glass over my shoulder.

"Strange," he exhales, and waits for me to look at him, and when I do, he looks pensive then inquisitive. "Were you listening at the door?"

"Of course not! Besides, you ol' fool, I don't speak Cantonese."

Tommy nods once and then shakes his head. "It was the only way I could think of," he considers aloud, "that you'd know we discussed that very possibility. Fearless Martha, my surgeon calls her."

"And you were supposed to ask me if she'd help out?"

"Yes. Now you see why I was so shocked when you said, what you said."

"Indeed I do, and you'll be happy to know she'll be at the quay in the morning. Plans to train with your good surgeon until he goes up river. And please," I add a bit hotly, "explain to your frolicking physician that I *am* the jealous type, part American Indian and enjoy scalping my enemies."

"*Really*?" he astonishes.

"Absolutely! But I can't show you my knife, I didn't think I'd need it this afternoon."

"Scalp anybody you want," he chuckles, and leans back in his chair. "Are you really part American Indian?"

"One eighth. My great-grandmother, Summer Moon, was a full-blooded Shoshone."

"That explains *everything*!" he muses, nods and grins. "I had been in San Francisco for less than a year. Wandered into Portsmouth Square, where I usually met a few other Chinese boys, and there he was. A big dark-skinned man wearing animal skins with feathers on his head and paint on his face. I just stared. I couldn't help it. He didn't move. Just looked up at the sky and chanted in a language I'd never heard. He scared me so much I could hardly breathe. I *knew* he was an evil spirit – perhaps the leader of all evil spirits. In school, the next year, I learned he was an American Indian. If you're related to him, that really does explains everything."

"If you say so," I resign, to a member of a very superstitious race. Then I pause so he can tell me he was only kidding.

But he doesn't. So I continue: "Because you know what's happening locally, much better than I, I want you to buy thirty-four percent of the Hong Kong Trader. Help plan the remodeling and run the hotel as a classy *legitimate* business. A longtime employee of the Whitaker family, John James Scott, JJ to his friends, and he's a bit light on his feet, will be here next week. The two of you can work together on the remodeling. I want this hotel to be different from other hotels in Southeast Asia. Better, actually, and much, much more fun for the guests. A place people talk about— flatteringly, of course—because they had loads of fun, not because the lobby chandeliers are impressive. Do you have the time to be involved?"

"Yes!" he booms with pleasure. "I'll damn well make the time. You knew that before you asked!" He stands, almost upsetting the table, and offers his hand to seal the deal. "And you will spend time with me, while we're getting ready for Guangzhou?"

12.

Happy are the eyes beholding a dear friend in a foreign land. While Martha squeaks and trembles with glee, I give silent thanks for the brave and skillful pilots of Pan American Airways, along with those of every other airline safely flying JJ from Seattle to Hong Kong, via San Francisco, Honolulu, and Tokyo. Mind you, I'm not forgetting Almighty God's role in keeping JJ's various aircrafts aloft, as science has yet to garner my allegiance.

JJ—a parent-type since my mother died when I was seven—frowns while he waits, on the other side of a glass barrier, for his turn to have his passport stamped. If entering Hong Kong during the steamship era, JJ would be resplendent in his rumpled white linen suit, his natural straw-colored Panama hat (Monte Carlo style with hat band of Havana Brown), his white shoes, white shirt, and well-trimmed white hair and mustache. A pale-yellow necktie almost matches his hat, and from where I'm standing and smiling, the tie has a small design, that I can't identify, in a dark color.

It's an accomplishment for a man born in nineteen-thirteen to travel so far and look so good, following a recent cholecystectomy. If JJ's less than his normal one hundred fifty pounds, it doesn't show. Indeed, all five-feet eight-inches appear athletic and fit enough to be romping about on the courts of *his* Seattle Tennis Club.

Martha's moving into position for a hugging-attack. I'm following at a safe distance. JJ's five bags, there's rarely less than four, are barely glanced at by Customs before being reloaded onto a cart pushed by a young Chinese porter, while I'm biting the inside of my cheek and hoping pain will keep lachrymal fluids where they belong.

He's embracing Martha, and though this will continue for a minimum of two minutes, he manages to look over her shoulder to give me a wink through round wire glasses. Then he smiles ever so slightly, closes his eyes, and nods just a little.

I turn away to politely blow my nose with the handkerchief from my chest pocket; which, of course, I don't return to its proper place, and start for Tommy's car and driver. Within a few steps I'm chuckling over the needling I'll receive from JJ, regarding the funerealness of Tommy's Cadillac, while recalling that I'd done the same to JJ on the day Martha and I were married.

"As disrespectfully critical as you tend to be," JJ glowers at me, as we wait by the curb for Martha to finish supervising the loading of his bags, "I suppose you think I appear too rumpled, too seedy, and *much* too dated to be seen in your esteemed presence on this, of all things, a late Wednesday afternoon?"

The cutups on my Executive Committee are hushed so I can maintain a straight face and nod, since I don't want to disagree with something so true, in the presence of a champion—winner of gold medals, year after year against all challengers—for getting-in-the-last-word.

"I'll admit," he scorns, and waves at the Caddie, "I'm not dressed appropriately for the *funeral* we must be attending. But then, neither are you. Your necktie is so loud there's no need for a horn. If we place you on the hood, traffic will part like the Red Sea before Moses."

"What about Martha?" I parry.

"*Beautiful* women may wear anything … to anything! All other women must follow the rules of good-taste and proper etiquette, or stay at home."

Having uttered the last-word, JJ climbs into the backseat and sits next to Martha. I think of sitting cross-legged on the hood but settle for the front passenger seat, where I wonder, as we pull into the traffic exiting Kai-Tak, when did *bright* become *loud*?

My tie belongs to the Fourth Battalion York & Lancaster Regiment, founded in eighteen fifty-nine at Sheffield Town Hall. Known as the Hallamshire Battalion, it served with distinction in the Boer War; had the questionable honor of being subjected to the first use of mustard gas during World War One; defended Iceland against Germany in the next war before being part of the Normandy invasion, and later capturing one thousand and five prisoners, three Dornier flying boats and a German submarine at Le Havre. The tie, well, it's new-red with half-inch diagonal stripes of bright-white bisected by a one-sixteenth inch stripe of new-red, every inch and a half. Bright and colorful? To be sure, but certainly not *loud*.

"How are things?" JJ innocently idles, now we're seated next to a big window at my favorite French restaurant high above Connaught Road, with a glorious view of the harbour and boat traffic accented by red, green, and white running lights; sunset being at six o'clock, seven minutes from now. Drinks have been ordered with no reaction, voiced or animated, to my request for a unopened bottle of Coca-Cola. Extraordinarily tall menus have been propped in our laps. Perchance, the menu designer also created the business cards being carried by all the fellows from India, listing every enterprise or project ever participated in by the company they represent. When folded in half, these business cards are three inches wide by six inches tall.

"Fine," Martha casuals, which's the expected response and allows JJ's attention to bury itself in his menu.

I glance at Martha, who's looking at me and smirking. She's clearly pleased at knowing the rule, so to speak, that declares neither of us need open and suffer the pain of perusing the menu, as JJ will order the same for all for us. It's become a tradition of our gathering together, that one self-appointed individual orders the same for everyone. It makes the event more like a dinner party in a private home. The first time was in a San Francisco restaurant. On that occasion Martha was the *appointed*, it being her city, after all, and on her wedding night. She'd made a menu proposal subject to a vote. The motion had passed unanimously, and that was also how the meal was relished.

Adolf had been present. Tomorrow, he'll be back from India, having accomplished all I wished: the purchase of a big steel barge, high-powered pumps and firefighting monitors. Oh, yes, we no longer vote. Whoever heard of going to someone's home for dinner and then voting on what's to be served.

"Are you going to tell us?" she asks JJ, so sweetly I wonder if her next inquiry will be about *her* inclusion in *his* will.

"*Bouillon du pot-au-fen,*" JJ nasally garbles, sounding very French. "*Haricots verts frais à l' ail. Nids de pommes de terre. Pommes frites. Poulet fricassee. Tuiles aux noix* for dessert. I'll discuss wines with the steward." He looks at Martha for objections, then at me.

"I didn't hear the word broccoli," I comment, non-accusatively, "or any reference to salt-dried anchovies, but I also don't speak French."

"Neither is an ingredient, my boy," JJ assures, with a patronizing smile, then turns slightly and repeats the dinner order to our waiter. But JJ fails to call for the man in charge of expensive bottles, so there's no conferring about pricey grape juice.

"Now then," he smiles, his attention back to business, "when can I have a look at the Hong Kong Trader? We don't want the hotel closed any longer than necessary, and I am bristling with ideas. But it's been years since …"

"The prisoners should be out by Friday," Martha assures.

"Yes," I clamor on her heels, without giving JJ a chance to react. "The new crew has boarded the coastal freighter I chartered. The cots and bedding have been delivered. We're waiting on chairs, provisions, fuel, and proper locks. And we decided it'll be better if the ship's underway rather than swinging from a buoy."

JJ, of course, frowns. Fearful, no doubt, that he's about to be the butt of an unfunny joke. His good spirits having been depleted by endless siting on airplanes, sleeping in strange beds, time changes, and food not coming from his own hands in his own kitchen. Then there's the weather of January. Dry and only warm in Hong Kong. Cold and wet in Seattle. He finishes his gin & tonic—what else could he possibly drink while wearing all that white, since we didn't give him time to change.

"I hate to ask," he sighs, and looks at Martha, seated to his right, "but who are these *prisoners*? Guests failing to pay their bill?"

"No," Martha leans closer to him and whispers. "They're mostly communist leaders of local labor unions. Twenty-three. Nineteen men and four women. We're holding them so we have something to trade if any of Tommy's people get caught in Canton, while kidnapping Mei Liew's two brothers and their families. Sort of insurance. One of Luke's better ideas. To perform the abductions, Tommy imported a dozen Japanese World War Two veterans—part of a gang that didn't adjust well to peace—and their wives, so they appeared to be tourists. It went very well, after the first night.

"You see," she continues quietly, after pausing to take a long sip of her own gin & cold tonic without ice, "we had only identified four of the leaders we wanted, and needed them to give up the names and whereabouts of some other local communist big shots."

When I see our waiter approaching with a tray of soup, I frown and shake my head. He puts the tray down on an empty table and comes to me smiling. I ask for another round of gin & tonics, and two ounces of scotch in a tall glass along with a cold bottle of soda."

"*Oui, monsieur.* Shall I slow your dinner order?"

"Please."

"Waiter," says JJ.

"*Oui, monsieur*?"

"Ask the wine steward to choose something *very* expensive to compliment the *poulet fricassee*, if we're ever allowed to eat. And while we're drinking, some warm French bread and softened unsalted butter, would be nice."

"*Oui, monsieur.*"

163

"I'm sorry, Martha," JJ croons, "please continue."

"Well of course, they didn't want to betray their comrades. But one of the Japanese wives, the only one of the whole group speaking Cantonese, had a unique way of getting information. I wish I could remember her name. Oh well, I will. Anyway, it was four o'clock in the morning, and there was no traffic on Queens Road. Luke and I were in the shadows so we couldn't be seen, and the four men were gagged with their hands and feet tied to bamboo poles that were long enough to go from their shoe tops, under their belts and almost to their chins, so they couldn't walk. The kidnappees, as Luke believes they should be called, were laid in the street on their stomachs, and their arms were extended above their heads. Then the Japanese woman had them dragged into positions like this," – Martha holds out her hands, palms down, fingers one and two in opposition, one inch from touching, to represent the four men lying face down in the street. "The Japanese men held them, while she got a car lined up."

Drinks, bread and butter arrive. A quieted Martha takes the opportunity to sip a quarter of her fresh gin & tonic. When she comes up for air, she smiles at JJ and continues:

"The Japanese had four cars driven by four of Tommy's men. I'll tell you about Tommy in a minute, or Luke can. Anyway, our heroine went to the car nearest the kidnappees and talked to the driver, who got out of the car and let some air out of each of the car's tires. How much I don't know, but enough so that when he drove where she directed him and stopped, each pair of tied hands (two on the right, two on the left) were pinned under a soft tire, without breaking any bones.

"The kidnappees couldn't move, and remained perpendicular to the car in the middle of Queens Road, where they were covered up to their necks with old tarps. In less than an hour, pre-dawn traffic wouldn't know there was anything but a stalled car in the middle of the road, with dirty, lumpy tarps on either side. Drivers hurrying to work would swerve to avoid the stalled vehicle … and likely run over some part of the lumpy tarps.

"Of course they might not die, which I later learned was explained to them, but having their feet, ankles, and legs mashed into pulp would be excruciatingly painful … as well as unfixable."

We all take a swallow. JJ does so without taking his eyes from Martha.

"Well," she continues, rather too gleefully, "Luke saw that a kidnappee might be run over prematurely, and jogged to a point behind the stopped car, where he could direct traffic. Within a few minutes, Luke motioned a nosy lorry to go wide around the stopped car. As soon as the lorry passed by, one kidnappee, and then another, indicated—I'm not sure how, I wasn't close enough—that they wanted to talk. Gages were removed, one at a time, and it wasn't long before the Japanese woman had more than enough information.

"So," Martha shrugs and smiles in conclusion, "the Japanese finished their kidnapping and went home. This morning, several newspapers reported sketchy sightings of old Japanese soldiers dragging hooded victims into cars. One Chinese language paper, known for its sensationalism, conjectured the Japanese were remnants of the occupation, and their victims were certain labor union leaders who've been mysteriously disappearing. Another, more reputable English language newspaper, put the sightings on a par with those of flying saucers.

"Now you know why we have prisoners at the hotel, until tomorrow.

165

"Luke," Martha wisps, after a brief wait for some reaction from a speechless JJ, "We should get the name of that Japanese lady, along with her address, so we can send her a Christmas card, next year."

I nod to Martha, then turn and nod to the waiter. Presently, I discover a proper use for Australian beef. Roast selected portions. When done, remove the bones. Gently boil the bones for several hours, save the liquid and discard the bones. Season the liquid with subtle magic. Chill, degrease and serve. Delicately finessed by talented hands, our chilled beef bouillon must be labeled: excellent.

"Someone was going to tell me about this Tommy fellow," JJ reminds, between silent sips from the side of his spoon.

"He's our guy getting things done," Martha says with pride, between not so quiet sips. It seems there's something about soup that induces her to talk. "He's outrageously tall for a Chinese man. As a kid, he was sent to San Francisco just before the Japanese invaded Hong Kong. He graduated from the University of San Francisco, in the early fifties. Very friendly. Very polite. Very important. He runs the most successful Triad in Hong Kong. Has a complete hospital type operating room on his junk, including a surgeon and several nurses. Last week I helped with an emergency operation. One of his men was knifed while breaking a picket line, or something like that. When Tommy's doctor and nurses accompany his men going after Mei Liew's families, I'll be in charge.

"For the past five and a half days, I've been working with them. Doing everything. Using the electric cautery's foot control was tricky at first. I tie sutures as well as the surgeon. Scalpels, clamps and retractors aren't a problem. It's doubtful that I'll have to operate on anyone, however, since we only work on battle wounds, and no battles are scheduled."

"Good grief," JJ excites, his soup finished, "don't you realize these men are criminals. This Tommy person is a mobster!"

"I suppose," Martha considers, as she slowly puts her soup spoon to rest, "but Tommy's not yucky and crude. He's a *Chinese* criminal. They're much different."

"*They are not!*" JJ scorns, shaking his head. "And *we* are not criminals!"

"Aren't we now?" I sneer. "That's not what the bloody FBI said last summer, when they were extorting our cooperation, which they'll try to do again, whenever their black hearts are so inclined. You know precisely why we've moved out of the U.S. And where *I am*, JJ, the operation *will be*."

"Luke," he grumps, "you needn't lecture me. *I*, of all people, know what it's like to be on the *outside*. But that doesn't mean I condone murder and kidnapping, drug smuggling and prostitution."

"Neither do I. Helping Mei Liew requires more than writing letters and holding protest rallies. She tried to do it by herself. Threw away money by the handfuls *and* got herself abducted. If I hadn't slugged one of her abductors— on a Star Ferry, no less—she might still be missing. Though he was extremely reluctantly, Sir Gordon Beasley came up with Tommy Tang.

"JJ, Triads are part of Hong Kong's economy and its very existence. There have been nasty men here from the beginning. And by no means were all those nasty guys members of a Triad. Regardless how we might wish the world to be, a *rose bush* has *thorns*."

JJ looks away. Uses his napkin to pat-dry his mouth and mustache. Our waiter clears the soup service and asks if anyone wants another cocktail before dinner, and I do.

Wine steward sallies forth, bottle of wine in one hand, bucket of ice in the other, a big medallion hangs from a wide ribbon round his neck and bounces off his chest. Conducts silly-ass ritual in French, with JJ. Martha appears impressed. JJ smells the cork and nods, then smiles. The steward dribbles some clear-ish liquid into a glass. JJ swirls it, takes a sip, smiles and nods. Steward partially fills two glasses, before working the bottle into ice cubes and making a show of a white napkin becoming a collar round the neck of the bottle. Though he's Chinese, the steward removes my inverted wine glass with Gallic disdain, and I resolve to have my nose surgical removed if I'm ever overwhelmed by a compulsion to sniff a cork or cap from a bottle of scotch.

"Luke," JJ patronizes, too paternally, "I'm well aware of the current situation in China."

"*Situation*? I'd hardly call it a *situation*," I anger. "Try: *massive homicidal chaos* – Mao Zedong style."

"I'm well aware of China's Cultural Revolution," he calmly advises. "Once a month I dine with a professor from the University of Washington's Far East & Russian Studies Department. His sources are excellent. And he is extremely candid. He describes the current events not as a counter-revolution, but rather as a post-revolution, revolution. Reminiscent of the Bolsheviks cleaning out the Mensheviks. But he says China isn't Russia.

"Mao has few other choices, my professor friend tells me, if he's going to change China's traditional culture of self-serving bureaucrats, wickedly abusing a poor and overpopulated country. He says it's terribly creative to use children as terrorists, and he predicts the strategy will be copied in the future. Somewhere else, of course. He strongly admonished all who would judge Chairman Mao, to wait for the ultimate success or failure of his programs."

"And how should we define *success*?" I challenge. "Confucius offered a definition. He said: 'Good government obtains when those who are near are made happy, and those who are far off are attracted.' I guess we will have to wait and see if a time comes when the world's population wants to immigrate to China, and much of the Chinese population no longer wishes to flee."

With no sign of an objection, I continue:

"For generations to come," I hunch forward and forcefully predict, "the Chinese population will be tethered to their place of birth. They will be modern serfs; a last vestige of a feudal society controlled by new masters calling themselves enlightened socialists, when they are nothing more than a red-tinged oligarchy too poorly educated to realize their ideas are a few hundred years too late. The People's Republic of China, which isn't a *republic* and doesn't belong to the *people*, will have many layers and *own* almost everything; at every level, governing will be done by an *ever growing group* of 'self-serving bureaucrats', who will enrich themselves by participating in the profits of both public and private enterprises, while creatively stealing as much as they can hide … mostly in Hong Kong.

"As the world becomes more prosperous, so will China and China's population; not due to state capitalism, but due to the sweat and resourcefulness of the Chinese people. In addition to the enormous amount of funds that will be received from the sale of China's natural resources, the future capital required by the People's Republic of China for developing and modernizing China, will have come from the profits produced by cheap Chinese labor.

"Always remember the inspired words of Abraham Lincoln: 'Labor is prior to, and independent of, capital. Capital is only the fruit of labor, and could never have existed if labor had not first existed. Labor is superior of capital, and deserves much the higher consideration.'

"Nevertheless, the Chinese people will be happier when the civil wars cease and they have enough to eat. But, dear friends, it's quite possible to have enough to eat, a safe place to sleep, and even a car to drive, while being a slave; albeit a prosperous slave.

"And if Hong Kong eventually reverts back to China, it will appear to be autonomous, because mainland government officials will continue to need a place to stash their loot—their stolen treasure—where it won't be taxed."

"I must say," JJ groans, after a long, perhaps respectful but definitely pensive, silence, "I wish you hadn't gotten involved in Mei Liew's personal problems, though it's understandable. Before she left Seattle for Hong Kong, we had some wonderful chats and she confided that her son is in a North Vietnamese prison camp. By now, I'm sure she's told you the same, and that he's your half-brother."

Martha looks shocked, but smiles quickly since she's familiar with her own cataclysmic family discoveries. For me, the intellectualization of this new information requires time that's not immediately available. My Executive Committee adjourns itself, though the more earthy Brotherhood of Digestive Components notifies me of an impending strike unless there's some badly needed distraction.

"If you don't mind," JJ humbles, now he's proven possession of the bigger bomb, "tell me about your preparations for the rescue."

"They're almost done," Martha calmly rehearses, and I give her my thought-dominating attention. "We have the drugs, syringes, tanks of oxygen, blood-pressure cuffs and other medical equipment. A doctor in Canton, Guangzhou, has been bribed to complete and file death certificates for each kidnappee. Two lorries with local Guangzhou drivers have been hired. As I mentioned, Tommy's surgeon and his three nurses are going. The hospital junk will be waiting for their return, just inside Hong Kong waters. Luke has observed the training of the young men selected to go. They have official armbands to wear that belong to a real Guangzhou Red Guard unit."

To keep my mind from potentially painful pondering of putrid jungle prisons, I'm trying to calculate the surface of our table in square centimeters.

Lovely plates of golden chicken fricassee, cooked in white wine with tarragon, mushrooms, and pearl onions, all bathed in a rich sauce of cream, butter, vermouth, and a hint of lemon, are put before us. It's a favorite of mine, and one reason I often dine here. On the side, are smaller plates of tender green beans sautéed in olive oil and finely minced garlic with breadcrumbs added toward the end for a gentle crustiness. Each of us has a nest made of grated potatoes, cleverly deep-fried and then filled with a handful of French fries. Though ill-mannered, I'll be tearing off chunks of French bread to mop up any sauce remaining on my plate. Dessert, no doubt, will be anticlimactic.

"I'm told," Martha skillfully manages to enunciate while eating, "it will take them ten hours to go from Kowloon to Guangzhou; eight hours coming back to the junk. That's a long time to hide in an old riverboat that smells bad and probably doesn't have a bathroom or even a toilet. There won't be food as good as this, and I haven't been able to find any American candy bars for them to take along."

Abruptly, JJ raises a hand, apparently to stop Martha from speaking until he finishes masticating. Then he pats his face dry and takes a sip of wine.

"You're quite right," he grins, "there are few chocolate bars for sale in Southeast Asia. However, most of my smallest suitcase is filled with the objects of your desire. They were for Luke—and I have no idea as to their condition—but you may help yourself. And don't be surprised if your Chinese friends don't share your enthusiasm for American candy."

"Martha," I inject, "the boat's crew makes that trip *all* the time. They'll be cooking something in some kind of wok, over some kind of a fire …"

"Sure," she scorns, "fish heads and rice in river water."

"How long were your Japanese friends in Hong Kong?" JJ queries, to change the subject.

"They arrived Saturday night," Martha answers, "and went home last night."

"And when is the *excursion* to Guangzhou supposed to begin?"

"Soon, is all I can say," she confides. "The kidnapers will be wrapped in burlap and carried aboard like cargo. They should arrive in Guangzhou around nine o'clock at night, so it'll be dark with little traffic on the streets. They've allowed ninety minutes for traveling to the homes of the two families, getting them sedated, and back to the boat. Rendezvousing with the junk is planned for sunrise, around seven. After unloading, the river boat will continue to Kowloon, along with the rest of the day's traffic coming down the Pearl."

"Will the … the kidnappees," JJ whispers, as the restaurant's filling with unescorted Chinese ladies in fur coats, "be taken to Hong Kong?"

"No. Luke won't allow it. They'll be kept as prisoners on the same coastal freighter confining the comrades."

"But separated," I inject.

"Not chained and fed gruel," Martha shrugs, adding her own interpretation.

"Considering her son is in a prison camp," JJ mumbles, "I can't image Mei Liew is very happy about that. I suppose you don't know for how long."

Other people chew or masticate, I savor. So while savoring the final morsel of sauce-drenched French bread, I shake my head to indicate that I don't know for how long. Plates are cleared. Wine glasses are refilled and I accept the offer of coffee.

While hoping my half-brother's older than I am, some walnut wafers shaped like mini rounded roof tiles are served, and JJ asks if we want to hear his ideas for the hotel. I don't, but Martha nods. Before he begins, I ask if he's changed his mind, and now plans to leave his friends, his Madison Park house, his tennis club, and move to Hong Kong. He shakes his deadpan-face that needs a shave.

"Yesterday, I signed papers forming a Hong Kong corporation, which is the new owner of the Hong Kong Trader. I've given Mei Liew fifteen percent of the stock, and, at my invitation, Tommy Tang bought a thirty-four percent interest, with the understanding that he'll be responsible for the profitable *and* lawful operation of the hotel. I've told him you and Martha will be representing my controlling interest. He's looking forward to working with you, JJ, beginning with lunch tomorrow on his junk. Martha will be there, but I'll be collecting Adolf at the airport."

"Very well," JJ casuals, "then I'll save my ideas for tomorrow's … junk-lunch. Who, may I ask, is on the board of directors?"

"You," I smile, "Martha, Mei Liew, Tommy and Sir Gordon."

13.

Summer Moon claimed the dawn of each day arrives without our sins from the day before. Great-grandmothers, I suspect, say all kinds of things to please their great-grandchildren; things they wish, perhaps, they had said to their own children.

Of course, I was young and loved her very much, for she was humorous as well as profound, and told hair-raising tales that ended happily for whomever she liked at the time: mostly Indians; never politicians. Now, I find it hard to believe our sins disappear overnight. Nevertheless, I'm fond of concentrating on *today* and *tomorrow* versus worrying about *yesterday* and *the day before*.

Though the dawn of this particular Thursday, January eighteen, nineteen sixty-eight, has faded, all of its possibilities remain. Even before the sun rose, Martha began celebrating the day with soft kisses and cuddling; our depleted energy restored by hot coffee, boiled eggs, and buttered toast; my mood so elevated I'd have eaten fish heads and rice seasoned with rat poison. We showered. She dressed in new black woolen slacks, a black long-sleeved cashmere sweater and old black loafers; before kissing me goodbye on her way out the door at sunrise—which for the entire month of January happens between three and six minutes after seven, local time.

It's five minutes before eleven o'clock, and I'm not alone on this concrete quay in Kowloon. Adolf stands to my left; picked up at Kai-Tak in Tommy's funereal Cadillac; his plane having arrived in time for him to clear Customs by nine forty-seven. To my right stands Mei Liew, who in polite silence rode with me from hotel to airport to where we are. Men have just finished cleaning the quay with fire hoses using water pumped from the harbour. Clean, therefore, is a relative term, but fish guts and other garbage have disappeared.

A dozen similar boats are tied to the quay, while being unloaded and reloaded. These are crafts of burden not pleasure, made of scuffed wood, including teak, protected by worn-out vehicle tires and looking like big shoes. About fifty feet long or longer, wide amidships and not tapering much before terminating in a blunt up-turning bow, with an elevated stern that ends abruptly and supports a small cabin doubling as a wheelhouse, out of which a humble exhaust stack smokes lazily. I doubt they draw much water, so they're rarely snagged by the Pearl River's shifting sandbars.

We're forty-five yards from the boat of interest. I'm dressed as if conducting serious business: camel hair overcoat, dark-blue suit, etc., and a brown fedora borrowed from JJ. Also in disguise, Mei Liew wears heels, stockings, a black raincoat, sunglasses, and a red silk scarf. Without time to change clothes, not that it would make any difference, Adolf sports a baggy tweed suit with a red vest, white shirt, dark bow tie, his large head adorned by a red wool Cuffley.

175

It's important no one think we're involved in quay activities, and we must be succeeding for we're being ignored.

Even my binoculars are going unnoticed. But thanks to their lenses, I'm only fifteen feet from said boat that's being loaded by pairs of coolies carrying shoulder-poles supporting irregular burlap bundles hanging from ropes. It's unlikely the coolies care what they're carting from the back-ends of two lorries. Sixteen young men, four nurses, a doctor, candy bars, oxygen bottles, medical equipment, weapons I suppose, and drugs for sure—twenty-four bundles of varying weight. Loading completed, I lower the glasses. Mei Liew puts her small hand inside mine. Perhaps to share her anxieties, thus adding them to my own.

Adolf, our expert on inhuman behavior, walks behind me, puts a big arm round her shoulders and turns Mei Liew toward the car. I follow at a respectful distance, wondering how he divined the implications of an event about which nothing had been said during our trip from the airport. While entering the backseat to sandwich a petite woman between two men, I note the sun sliding behind black clouds; the day's gloominess momentarily complete.

In route to the Hilton, Mei Liew seems to gain mastery over disturbing thoughts by controlling car-talk: asking Adolf about India, and generally pulling any conversational string he offers. Realizing I'll hear nothing about his current weapons stash, etc., I tune out. With twenty-three angry comrades imprisoned in our Hong Kong hotel, JJ and Tommy meeting for the first time over lunch, the kidnappers on their way to Guangzhou, Martha playing doctor, Bill Stuart having taken off this morning from Dutch Harbor on his way to Sapporo in an old but, hopefully, perfect DC-3 with an extended range, Captain Mackey and crew currently braving winter in the North

176

Pacific as they drive my tug from Anchorage to Sapporo, I feel somewhat as though I'm standing in front of a pinball machine that's simultaneously playing six steel balls, while I can only watch as they weave, bob, stall, stutter and bounce their way to a conclusion.

Since it's too much to worry about before lunch, I casually look out the window and start counting beautiful Chinese women walking west. To count those walking in all directions would be impossible.

"Look!" Mei Liew startles and then halts, as we walk into the Hilton behind Adolf and a bellman carrying his one suitcase, a humbly masculine amount of luggage. "*Ayeeyah*!" she shrieks with alarm. "Luke, your name on every sign!"

"Yes, it is," I say, after looking from Lobby Porter to Lobby Porter. "Must be a joke."

"*Oh, no!*" she worries, loudly enough for heads to turn, "Something bad!"

"Mr. Whitaker! Mr. Whitaker!" yells a desk clerk, approaching on the run with her arm and hand stretched out as if ready to pass a baton in a relay race. "Urgent message! Urgent message, sir!"

I can see something tiny and white in her hand, and brace for a collision. Thankfully, she manages to stop, and though panting, stand still. With Mei Liew almost in tears and everyone watching—expecting, I suppose, that I'll open the envelope and trumpet the contents to a hundred and thirty-nine of Hong Kong's most idly curious—the moment's rather embarrassing. Even worse, I normally don't *fumble* for tip money, but with all the screaming, yelling and running about …

LUKE WHITAKER, reads the card I take out, CALL HOLLY STUART REGARDING A MATTER OF CONSIDERABLE IMPORTANCE.

Perfectly stuffy. Just the way a message should be written when it involves a possible panic. It's not what Holly actually said, of course, but, in someone's alert-mind, it's what she should have said. With no hint of death nor the immediate need of my personal presence to avert a nuclear war, I hand the card to Mei Liew and begin ambling toward the Front Desk to make certain they're taking righteous care of Adolf. In Seattle, it's nine o'clock last night.

"Mr. Whitaker's office. This is Mrs. Stuart," Holly sighs, with unusual formality.

"It's Luke. Are you okay?"

"I'm a little tired," she seems to exhale. "Liam is asleep. As far as I know, Bill is still in the air and the Captain is still afloat, but I have some bad news from South America."

"You sound so terrible, you must actually be human. We've all been wondering about that, you know," I tease, attempting to lighten the moment.

"I'm sorry, Luke," she brightens a bit, "It's just that I've been on the phone for hours, in the hope that when you called I would be able to give you some good reasons why four of our hotels burned down. Today. It's childish, I know, but I so like impressing you by doing the nearly impossible …"

"Holly!" I surge, to comfort her, "they're insured! Over insured, probably. It's not the end of the world, my dear."

"You're right."

"Which hotels, and when? And was anyone hurt, or killed?"

"The authorities aren't giving me straight answers about injuries, or fatalities, or much else, for that matter. Our hotels in San Salvador, Panama City, Lima, and Valparaiso all caught fire about the same time. It has to be arson."

"Yes, of course" I agree, after a quick unsuccessful search for some other reason, "it must be arson."

"Who would do that?" she moans, reading my mind. "And why?"

"Damned if I know."

All silences are circumstantial. Some connote rejection. Others produce frustration or irritation, sleep or boredom, disappointment or worry, and, of course, there's always anger. Silence, I've just learned, can also unlock dark closets filled with fear.

"This'll rob sleep, for which I apologize, but as soon as I hang up, I want you to call the hotels in Anchorage, Vancouver, Portland, Oakland, San Pedro and Mazatlan. The GMs will likely be at home. But find them, and tell them what happened, and that I suggest they have fire drills in the morning, and triple their security, tonight; that you'll keep them informed of developments. Tell them where I am, if they want to know, and how to call me.

"In the morning," I say, trying to sound relaxed, "get all the files and paperwork together for the properties that burned. Call our lawyer, Sally Evans. Explain to her what's happened, where I am, and that I need an appointment."

"Anything else?"

"Yes. Keep your doors locked. Don't send Liam to school or let him play outside until Monday. Continue trying to get more information. Talk to the lead owner of each hotel that burned down. Somebody must know something, but don't make any promises. Just between you and I, Holly, I don't want any more involvement with those properties. Times have changed and their locations vary from undesirable to awful."

"I understand, Luke, and I want you to know I'll be ready to move by month's end, and …"

"Someone's at the door. We'll talk about it tomorrow. I'll call you at nine in the morning, your time. Good night, Holly."

"Good night, Luke."

"Can I come in?" Mei Liew humbles, when I open the door.

"Sure," I smile, "but would you rather go to lunch?

"I told Adolf we would meet him in the lobby bar at one. He wanted to take a shower and put on clean clothes. Could we talk for a few minutes?"

"Sit down, sit down," I friendly. "Want a coke?"

"Beer and bourbon would be better," she teases, while walking to the sofa, "but a coke will do."

When I hand her a bottle of coke with a straw that's being expelled by effervescence, her smile's gone.

"You are doing so much for me," she breathes softly, while crossing her legs and shifting her weight to one side, not un-provocatively, "I feel there are things I should tell you."

"Happy things?"

"Perhaps. Yes, I think so. Mostly."

"Good," I enthuse, then smile, then wait.

"Your father has two sons. I named your brother, John. John Whitaker is five months and three days older than you are. When I realized I was pregnant, your father had already married your mother. By the time I was brave enough to tell him, your mother was pregnant with you.

"Married or not, I was honored to have his baby. I had been in love with your father for a longtime. He was tall, and handsome, and kind, and made me laugh, and he was Caucasian American. Before he married your mother, I dreamed of becoming an American wife. When John was born, your father was with me and put his name on the birth certificate as John's father.

"I went to live with Summer Moon near San Rafael. I took care of her, and she helped me with the baby. If you came to visit, John and I would disappear. When John turned four, Peter moved us back to the city, so John could attend what your father thought were better schools. We lived in the Francesca. The same apartment where you and Martha had dinner with me. Though I missed Peter, and I still do, John was a wonderful boy. Nothing escaped his attention. And he rarely got in trouble, though he was easily bored.

"We didn't see Peter after your mother died. He was spending time with you in Seattle, and traveling, of course. At first, I thought he was avoiding us in fear I would try to rekindle an old romance. In time I became certain he never stopped loving your mom, and spent the rest of his life mourning her death. Nevertheless, he was very kind to us, and I was lucky with the money he gave me.

"From age thirteen, your brother dreamed of going to West Point. He thought the army would be an adventure. Nothing would change his mind. He studied hard, was very athletic, and received an appointment to the academy. In the photograph you saw, he was wearing his West Point uniform. He graduated in nineteen sixty-one, the top third of his class, and chose the infantry. Then he maneuvered his way to Vietnam.

"Intoxicated by adventure and excitement, I have no doubt he did the most dangerous things he could find to do. He's been listed as missing in action for almost three years. No one tells me anything official, but unofficially they seem to think he's in a prison camp.

"I still pray for him to come home, but my hope is waning."

I nod and wish somehow I could smile.

"Naturally, Luke, you remind me of John. Even Martha can see the resemblance, and *I* can actually feel it."

Mei Liew puts the coke bottle on a lamp table, gracefully gets up and glides to the window where she stands with her back to me, arms folded. It's easy to wait in this silence with my heart hammering, for I don't have a single coherent thought, and we're not looking at each other.

"Here in Hong Kong," she muses, without moving, "good and bad are so close I can almost touch them; ghosts and evil spirits cannot be ignored. It was easier in San Francisco; my family was far away, in a different world, where I could not help them. I felt pain but no guilt. Now, I am close enough to my family that I feel guilty, and guilt is worse than pain, and the pain has not gone away."

She turns and looks at me. Her face inscrutable, quintessentially Chinese. Her demands, if any, undefined. Protests unexpressed. *Love* and *hate* silenced by their marriage of convenience. Her respiration provides the only sign of life.

"Please forgive me," she whispers, after a labored quiet, "if this truth makes you uncomfortable, but I had to tell you."

Fearing any words I speak will be wrong; I borrow Martha's proclivity for hugging. With her head on my chest, my brother's mother starts to sob. And I feel better, for there's nothing inscrutable about crying.

As we approach, Adolf smiles and stands. He's been drinking from a bottle sporting a yellow label. San Miguel beer from the Philippines; at its best without bourbon.

"Adolf," I gladden and grin, as he pulls a chair from under a little table for four, and though he and Mei Liew know each other from this morning, I say: "let me introduce Mei Liew, the honorable mother of my brother."

His surprise disappears faster than a casino chip. "Nice to meet you, ma'am," he says with affectionate formality and she smiles with satisfaction; possible the result of being officially recognized as an almost-American-wife. "You look strangely familiar," the old flirt adds, and Mei Liew turns toward him, and perhaps it's just as well I can't see how she's looking at him.

When asked, I order an Irish coffee. Mei Liew follows suit. Adolf requests two more San Miguels, and I start negotiating for some cheddar cheese sandwiches with extra mayonnaise. Thanks to the one of us being fluent in Cantonese, and in spite of her giggling, the sandwiches will be served in a lobby bar that doesn't serve food.

"What's so funny?" I query, desiring any and all levity.

"Peter and I always stayed inside and ate dinner in his apartment in the Francesca. In those days it was my job to take care of the apartment. Anyway, one rainy night—the same day he met your mother, as a matter of fact—he insisted we go out for dinner. I was thrilled, of course. We went to the Top of The Mark. After I had a few gin fizzies and was ready to dance on the table, he wanted to order dinner. In those days, the Top of The Mark didn't serve food. Not easily defeated, Peter asked for a telephone to be brought to our window-table. He planned to call Room Service and have them deliver dinner. But, wise as he was, he figured the department was run by Cantonese. So he told me what to order, it was very fancy, and he handed me the telephone. It took forever for me to find someone in Room Service, who was related to someone related to me. Over the objection of the maître d', we got our dinner. The Chinese gentleman who took and served our order, was fired. When I found out and told Peter, Peter hired him to manage the Room Service Department at the Oakland Trader; he was there until he died of old age. Sorry."

I believe my chuckle, smile and head shaking tells her there's *nothing* to be sorry about. If not, the way Adolf's patting her hand certainly tells her of his, well, appreciation. The two are whispering, and our drinks haven't even been served.

Given the current unpredictability of events, they will be running for the elevators before lunch arrives. Seems I've gone from confidante to odd-man-out. "So what's the big deal?" hails my Executive Committee. "Happiness doesn't have a schedule. We've been trying to tell you that for years. If you'd pay more attention you might learn something; what, we're not too sure, but something."

Without provocation, Mei Liew tells me she has written a story of how my parents met, along with some things that happened about the same time. Apparently, she has pieced together a collection of items remembered by herself, her aunt, who was my father's secretary, and a Chinese man, who was my father's driver and companion when in San Francisco, before he was married. She wonders if I'd like to read what she wrote. Adolf, of course, is eager to 'peek under the bed', and I assure her of my interest.

14.

Just as I'm leaving the hotel suite, Bill Stuart calls from Sapporo. He's safely on the ground. He's tired but proud of the plane's performance, the performance of his crew and, by implication, his own contribution. I congratulate him, suggest a night's sleep, and then I give silent and sincere thanks to He who owns the Heavens … and everything else.

There's a knock on the door. I willingly take delivery of an inch high notebook sized package wrapped in red cotton shirting. It's from Mei Liew, probably her story.

The hospital junk rests, smartly secured to her wooden quay with engines rumbling comfortably and producing diesel fumes adding to Hong Kong's pervasive aroma. Climbing the gangway, I cautiously hold onto the railings and feel the subtle throbbing of two hearts in a wooden body.

When Martha waves from the poop deck, it's exactly two thirty-three, local time. My adorable doctor-for-a-day wears green surgical scrubs and looks so boldly medical that Tommy would not be pleased with how easily she can be seen. I wave back while wondering if Tommy and JJ are somewhere below decks, locked in mortal combat or convivially discussing the future. I'll know soon enough.

Another climb and I'm within reach of Martha, and her delightful hug justifies every calorie I've burned to get here, and her kiss suggests the availability of a deserted operating room.

"You smell nice," she coos.

"Not like wood smoke?"

"Why would you smell like wood smoke?" she asks, and pulls her head slightly off my chest to look up through a seductive tangle of eyelashes.

"When old hotels burn down, they create wood smoke."

"Not" – she pulls further away – "the one housing our comrades?"

"No, no. That hotel isn't built of wood, but our aging hotels in Chile, Peru, Panama, and El Salvador are wood frame. And according to Holly, who I talked to a while ago, they all burned to the ground last night. At about the same time."

"No … I don't believe it."

"Believe it, my dear. Obviously, you have more enemies than you realize."

"ME! What about YOU?"

"Yes, well, one or both of us."

"How can you be sure the fires weren't accidents? Of course, they weren't," she corrects herself, "that's ridiculous. What are you going to do?"

"Collect the insurance."

"And then what?"

"And then … I don't know."

"Was any one hurt or killed?"

"Holly's making inquiries. Eventually, we'll know."

"Yes. I suppose so. Have you told JJ?"

"I sent a carrier pigeon. But unless you've seen it walking the deck, it got lost."

"Don't be silly."

"Okay. Since I found out, JJ's been here and I've been somewhere else."

"Will he be upset?"

"Certainly not! His new passion's here in Hong Kong. And JJ tends to be passionate about one thing at a time. Not for very long, of course, but …"

"You're awfully chipper, considering everything," Martha interrupts, and lets her words hang in the air to be used in some torturous way if I wrongly respond.

"There's more news. But, my dear, don't you have lives to save and patients needing attention?"

"No," she frowns. "None. Not one. There's been nothing all day. I'm so frustrated I may have to cut my own leg just to have a wound to stitch closed. So," she smiles, "start talking or volunteer a limb for me to operate on."

"Bill has landed in Sapporo. Everything's fine. Holly will be ready to move here by month's end. So I need a permanent place for her and Liam …"

"And for us!"

"And for us," I echo. "That means flying to Singapore next week, to find something; unless I have to go to Seattle and meet with Judge Evans about the hotel fires."

"If you go to Seattle, *I'll* go to Singapore."

"Mei Liew told me about my brother," I intimate, to change the subject, because I don't want to argue about who's going to Singapore. "So, JJ told the truth, and you were correct …"

"I always am. And what made you think JJ wasn't telling the truth?

187

"… about my resembling that West Point photograph in Mei Liew's apartment. She named him John Whitaker, and he's slightly older than I am. Sometimes, JJ will do or say anything to gain the advantage."

"Where is he? Is he really in a North Vietnam prison?

Unable to find the proper euphemism or a brightly colored paint that will hide the truth with a single coat, I tell her exactly what Mei Liew told me. Martha scowls and walks away. If the sun was shining, which it's not, it would be scurrying behind a cloud or perhaps encouraging the moon to get between it and Martha.

Because we're alone, Martha paces without impediment. She finally halts a foot from my face and gives me, what I believe she believes to be her most intimidating mother-reproves–child stare.

"We must do something!" she proclaims.

"What?"

"Get him out of prison, of course. Out of some filthy bamboo cage. The situation *cannot* be ignored!"

I nod in wonder *and* dismay.

"I'm extremely good with people. I can usually get them to do what I want. Just get me to that prison. I'll get him out!" declares the world's newest neophytic zealot, displaying the group's usual naiveté.

"The people you'd be dealing with are not humans, as you know them. Get a grip on your hallucinations. There'll be no parachuting into the night from an old DC-3 while it's flying through anti-aircraft fire and missiles over North Vietnam, so you can waltz through jungles and hug deranged prison guards after disarming them with your charming smile."

"That's what John would do for you; *or* me," she bludgeons with her club of tempered guilt. "And you damn well know it!"

"I know nothing of the sort, and neither do you. But if you're right, John suffers from severe, perhaps fatal, overexposure to comic book heroes. *Of course,* I'd love to bust him out. But if there's a way," – I shake my head – "it's different than what you are proposing. He may not be in prison. He may, in fact, be dead. The consideration of various alternatives and scenarios must wait until we're finished with the business at hand."

"You're a *stuffy* bastard!" she stabs.

"Indeed I am!"

"The *stuffiest*!" she sneers, and I expect her to stamp one perfect foot forcefully on the deck to make her point. But if that's her intention, she's distracted by the unexpected appearance of JJ's white hair and round steel glass as he climbs to the poop deck.

"Ah, my friends," he puffs, and pauses to catch his breath. "I must say, you were right. About Tommy. Suggesting things to him is rather like praying. When he agrees, you have every confidence that it's going to happen. And when he disagrees, his reasons are perfectly convincing. For the future growth of our many enterprises, I suggest we treat him like a treasure, and give serious thought to selecting young Chinese boys to live and be educated in San Francisco. Orphans, of course. From Hong Kong, naturally"

I nod, momentarily grateful for the shift of subjects from jungle-prisons to orphans bound for San Francisco. Martha looks skeptical. Then she starts to glow; sings of John with emphasis on his distinguished lineage; points to how he was raised and educated in San Francisco (which isn't completely true). Concludes—to make her previous argument for heroic rescue—with remarks regarding his potentially enormous value to the family during the extended time it will take JJ to implement the cultivation of his transplanted Hong Kong children-without-parents. She never offers to birth all needed males. Apparently, I'm genetically flawed by a stuffy-gene and have been demoted from breeder to entertainer.

JJ wisely nods, and he's about to speak but I hold up my hand to stop him. "Did Tommy happen to mention when the freighter will be ready for the comrades?"

"It's ready," JJ states. "Tommy says they'll be moved aboard after dark."

"Excellent. That's all I wanted to know. Obviously, you had a productive lunch. Martha can fill you in on recent events. I'm scheduled to call Holly at midnight. I'll be back with Mei Liew and Adolf about one o'clock in the morning. That should leave plenty of time for us to get on station for the rendezvous."

While JJ nods in agreement, and to avoid further unwanted conversation, I quickly back down the ladder from *ye o'd* poop deck onto the main deck, where a big hand gently grabs my shoulder.

"Going to a fire?" Tommy teases.

"Nope, gettin' away from one," I sigh, and he motions with his head for me to follow him, as he goes toward the side of the junk opposite the quay. When we get there, he swings open a gate in the junk's railing to expose a substantial rope ladder falling to an empty Garwood.

"You drive," he smiles. "I never do."

Delighted with his offer, I begin to lower myself, one-tedious-step-at-a-time.

Hong Kong Harbour belongs to the South China Sea, which belongs to the Pacific Ocean. There's enough surge and wakes from other boats to require timing my last step from the rope ladder onto a rising and falling float—that has been lashed to the junk—with the speedboat, bumpers out to protect its highly varnished hull, tied thereto. I take a moment to get the rhythm and then get aboard without an embarrassing incident requiring a trip to Martha's surgery. While Tommy scrambles down the ladder and into the boat, I check the gear selection, push the start button, and idle in neutral. Tommy casts off mooring lines and takes in the bumpers. When he settles in the passenger seat, I turn the wheel slightly to starboard then ease the throttle forward so we're plowing more quickly away from the junk, with the sound of our Garwood's throaty engine taking me back to Lake Washington and a few thrilling childhood memories.

Tommy leans over and asks if I want to visit the freighter.

"From a distance," I answer. "This speedboat's much too conspicuous for us to be climbing up a bloody rope ladder."

"The *Matilda* has a boom and a cargo net," Tommy advises. And when I look at him, he's grinning without malice. "She can lift all the comrades in one load," he adds, "though the women won't be able to breathe for all the men piled on top of 'em. Try some throttle," he encourages.

Quickly, the boat's on a plane rushing over small swells and boat wakes coming from every direction, aggressively slapping the water, throwing spray port and starboard. At thirty-three something an hour I stop accelerating. There's more speed but there's also traffic, and I haven't done this for a very long time. Driving a car can't compare to the primal thrill of skippering a speedboat. No lanes, no traffic signals, no speed limit (I think), and no brakes or civilized paved surfaces. In spite of the windshield there's a wonderful speed-produced wind that smells of salt; bits of spray blow into the cockpit, from one side or the other depending which way I turn; gradually, of course, as sharp turns are only recommended for skippers who prefer swimming.

Uneven water makes the Garwood a lunging animal, whose fur coat resembles Philippine mahogany. *Bounces, dives, twists,* and *slides* arrive in disquieting combinations until patterns become recognizable. I'm having fun. I wasn't sure I could without my playmate; though I'll miss her in less than an hour.

Tommy taps my left shoulder. I look at him and he points to a smallish freighter riding low in the stern with a light-blue and white hull that badly needs to be cleaned and painted. He taps me again, and this time draws a circle in the air with his index finger, which I take to mean I should circle round the floating pile of dirty iron.

Our inspection starts as we roar past the stern, where faded red paint spells *Matilda.* I slow down, so we can safely turn to starboard without going too far beyond our target. The freighter's nothing to look at, but she blends well with the others of her ilk. Careful not to get between her bow and her mooring buoy, I again turn to starboard and we're halfway down the last side when Tommy taps me hard, and motions with a hand as though he's cutting his throat with his fingers. I pull the throttle all the way back, and turn to port. The engine goes quiet and we mush to a stop with the Garwood rolling from side to side.

"What's the matter?" I alarm, and Tommy points to *Matilda.*

Twenty feet above the water, a seaman stands by the rail. He's frantically waving a soiled yellow rag, and appears to be looking at us. Believing he has our attention, he drops the cloth in the harbour and starts hollering in angry Cantonese. To me, excited Cantonese always sounds angry.

"One of the crew," Tommy thunders, "has fallen and cut the hell out his shoulder. The man wants us to take him to hospital. He doesn't know who we are."

Tommy yells something back to the man, who then waves his arms over his head and vanishes.

"They'll lower him in the cargo net," Tommy advises.

Having driven near and parallel to *Matilda*, I'm waiting for the net, with Tommy stationed in the stern. As it's lowered, I keep adjusting our position so the injured fella will end up in the boat and not in the harbour. Tommy does the rest. He gets the fellow loose from the net, and quiets him down. When Tommy's sitting on the stern seat with the sailor's head in his lap, I push the throttle to its limit. On a straight course we're only minutes from *Martha Memorial Hospital*.

A hundred yards from Tommy's junk, I grab the can of compressed air with a horn on top, and start pulling its trigger to blast a warning of our arrival. At twenty-five yards, I start decelerating, and three men are scrambling down to the float. More are looking over the side. In a few seconds the Garwood's at the float. There's a cacophony of Cantonese as young men grab the Garwood, and Tommy yells orders before picking up the unconscious sailor, putting him over his shoulder and scrambling up the rope ladder with three men in pursuit. I check the mooring lines and then carefully straighten my tie before cautiously following. By the time I get aboard, there's no one in sight.

"Luke!" yells a woman. "Get down here!"

I think of asking why, but I don't. I descend, and receive orders, muffled by her surgical mask to: "take off your damn coat and tie, roll up your shirt sleeves, put on a mask, sit where I'm pointing, and don't touch *anything* I don't put in your hand." Had I been ordered to unbutton my shirt's collar button, I'd be out the door. Such an act exposes too much bare throat in a place with sharp blades, long needles, and poisonous anesthesia for keeping victims from getting up and running away.

The patient lies on the operating table. Tommy's cutting away blood-soaked clothing. Like Martha, he's gowned and wears a funny floral hat, rubber gloves, and a mask.

If I should ever become an armed robber, I'm going to dress just as they are, but with long false eyelashes, so the robbees might believe I'm a tall woman with a deep voice.

"Have you ever had," Martha challenges, "syphilis, malaria, infectious hepatitis, any chronic allergic disease or sensitivity to drugs?"

"Of course, not!" I answer.

"Hold out your arm," she commands, once I'm in her elevated chair, "if I touch you I will be contaminated, so *you* will have to insert this needle into a vein. I'll show you where and tell you how."

"Why?" I retort, "I didn't do anything!"

"Your blood type is O negative," she rather accuses, again proving she never forgets anything I've ever told to her. "*You*, my dear, are a universal donor, and I need your blood for the patient. I don't have time … "

"All of it?"

"Just a little. And I'll …"

"Shouldn't I lay down?"

"You have to be higher than the patient. Now, please shut up, and pay attention. And for heaven's sake, don't faint."

I follow her directions, even though the needle looks large enough to be a weapon of war, and even though there's a length of clear plastic tubing leading from the needle in the general direction of a nameless man, who didn't ask for my blood and may, Lord help him, somehow become infected with my stuffy-gene.

When the tube starts becoming blood-red, I look away. A minute later I hear Martha reciting—and wish I couldn't—

what she's read and remembered: "The basic steps in management of lacerations are: debridement, irrigation, and wound closure, usually under local procaine anesthesia. Always examine for damage to nerves and tendons, and for the presence of foreign material. Tetanus Prophylaxis is advisable, if soil contamination is suspected. When in doubt, administer antitoxin or toxoid, as indicated."

After each buzzing of the cautery there's the smell of burning flesh. Martha asks for sutures. Tells Tommy the size needle she wants and the gauge of silk thread to attach. Martha and Tommy are communicating little enough to give the impression they know what they're doing. When the patient starts to groan, I assume he's returning to consciousness. That's confirmed by Martha ordering me to remove the transfusion needle from the patient, and then from my own arm. *And* to keep both ends elevated so blood won't drain all over the floor.

By the time the sailor's being bandaged, he's snoring.

"Thank you Tommy" Martha smiles, without her mask and while pulling off her gloves.

"It was my pleasure," Tommy smiles back at her, while I head for the door with coat and tie over an arm.

Once again, I climb to the poop deck. "How's the injured man?" JJ greets, his brows furrowed.

"Short of an infection he'll be fine. Doctors Whitaker and Tang took good care of him."

"Excellent!" JJ ordains, smiling widely. "A good omen for the rest of our nerve-racking day."

"It could be," I nod. "Who knows, of course. Hope you're right, though."

15.

It's a humbling experience to walk the streets of Hong Kong. Perhaps not as humbling as walking the streets of Cairo or Calcutta but a reminder, nevertheless, that I'm but one of millions of people—billions, I suppose—and if we're all God's children, then He has a large family and I have living relatives who are not POWs.

With all of the *pinballs* still in play, my anxieties have destroyed the calm required for a worthy consideration of JJ's hotel plans or Mei Liew's literary submission. Nor is there a justifiable reason to rush back to the Hilton and burst in on either Mei Liew or Adolf, or the two of 'em together, so I'm sauntering towards Sir Gordon's office— and the always amiable welcome offered by Judy Chen— while wondering if humans are allotted a finite number of breaths. And if so, should I be taking large breaths and holding them for as long as possible? How about people who get in a panic and hyperventilate? If they didn't get so excited, would they live longer? Eventually, medical science will pretend to have the answers.

At four twenty-one, local time, I enter a certain stylishly

modern law office, high above Connaught Road, and announce myself.

"Good afternoon, Mr. Whitaker," beams the lovely but rather plastic receptionist, whose clean desk suggests she's ready to go home. "I'll tell Judy Chen you're here."

She picks up the phone, speaks in Cantonese, nods several times while listening, then replaces the receiver and escorts me to the desk guarding Sir Gordon's private office. Judy's on the phone but hangs up quickly, and motions me to a chair reserved for subordinates, which I find to be consistent with the conclusion I've come to while walking. When Judy leans toward me, I reflexively lean toward her, and note she's not facing me, but rather looking up and sideways through fine black eyelashes, as Martha does on occasion. Indeed, if Martha was Chinese and petite, she'd be wearing a miniskirt and heels just like Judy, and she would be equally as coy and smart, not at all as I've been imagining Martha while I've been waking. In my imagination she was dressed in a floor length khaki skirt and a soiled white cotton blouse buttoned up to her neck, with lace at the top; long sleeves buttoned at her wrists, with more lace; holding a dainty white lace handkerchief and wearing a wide-brimmed straw hat with mosquito netting bunched on top of its brim; perspiration evident on her prominent cheeks, her royal nose and her furrowed brow; daubing her hanky in a mixture of ice water and wood alcohol then onto the forehead of a Chinese gentleman lying silently before her with his eyes closed.

"I told Sir Gordon you're here," Judy whispers. "He was pleased. We have a bit of a situation he's hoping you might help with." She looks me in the eye and smiles, as women do when sharing a secret they don't want repeated.

"Your wish's my command." I gallant.

"Thank you," she says softly, and looks away.

"But only yours," I add, while shaking my head, "not his."

She looks back in surprise, with eyelids fluttering, and I think she's blushing, not the least bit inscrutably.

The door opens. Sir Gordon slips out, quickly closes the door behind him and approaches with his hand outstretched, his serious face trying to smile.

"Luke, old chap," he greets, "your timing is impeccable. I didn't expect you, but you might be perfect."

Without standing, I twist and take his hand. We shake briefly before he squats next to my chair.

"Luke, I have a bit of a situation," he intimates. "I can't share details with you, but I need a favor. You see, old boy, I'm the Chairman of the Hong Kong Safety Committee, and one of my unofficial duties is to … well … talk to people, you might say, who are causing problems. People the Hong Kong government and the police can't talk to for a variety of reasons … if that makes some sense."

I nod and squirm.

"Good," he says, and pats my knee. "Then perhaps you won't mind talking to the fellow in my office. He's Chinese and doesn't speak a word of English, and my Cantonese is primitive at best … "

"I don't speak a syllable …"

"Oh, I know that. Judy will translate."

"What, pray tell, am I supposed to talk to him about?"

"Oh, that!" Sir Gordon sighs, and looks away. When our eyes meet again he's not smiling. "I want you to scare him …"

"Then you need Tommy Tang. Not me"

"Mr. Tang is too well known. Mr. Wu, the gentleman in there," – he hooks his thumb toward the office door –

"would never believe Mr. Tang was doing me a favor. He'd suspect something straight away, and continue clamming up. I want *you* to pretend you're a secret agent of the American government, and if he doesn't tell me what I want to know … you will fly him away somewhere and do unspeakable things to him."

"You're joking," I grin, suspicious that he and Judy have concocted this nonsense for the first sucker arriving without an appointment.

"Not in the least," Sir Gordon grumps, "and there's no time to write you a script. So either you'll try to help … or you won't."

I look at Judy. Clearly, she's questioning my status as a white knight.

"Okay," I concede. "Has Mr. Wu ever been in the United States? And if you'll tell me what he's mixed up in, I can at least sound informed."

They shake their collective heads. Sir Gordon stands, and seems to be waiting for me to do the same.

"A matter of extraordinary importance, right? I don't want to make a fool of myself over some puny issue."

They nod. I stand and start for the door. Judy rushes ahead, opens the door, steps aside and bows, so Mr. Wu can see her as I pass by. Sir Gordon, looking fierce, motions for Judy to enter the room. He closes the door and walks to his chair behind the desk, where he settles himself with solemn deliberateness.

Mr. Wu has been seated on a sofa against a wall opposite the view windows. He's older than I presumed. Perhaps venerable, though probably not. As if stalking a prey, only his eyes move. His mouth's shut, but not relaxed. Nor are his hands, with fingers intertwining while on his lap. His brown suit isn't stylish but it's clean and pressed. White shirt buttoned at the neck, no tie. Brown sox and shoes, scuffed, of course, and there's a brown fedora hat next to him on the sofa. Gray hair combed away from his wrinkled face and cemented down with something shinny. He's fit enough to sit up straight, and doesn't seem about to jump and run, or about to attack.

Declining a face to face performance, I stroll to the window and look out.

"Mr. Wu, my name is Randolph Blackfeather," I say, as relaxed and as casually as would any career sadist who enjoys his work, and I remind myself to pause frequently so Judy Chen can translate. "Randolph was my father's name. My mother was an American Indian. A single black feather was the first thing she saw after I was born. She was a wonderful Indian mother. Taught me to kill rattlesnakes with my bare hands before I could walk."

I stare out the window. Judy speaks.

"I'm here with an offer, as a favor to Sir Gordon Beasley, because I am married to one of his wife's cousins, a hot-blooded young woman, whom I adore."

While Judy finds the proper words, I twist and look at Sir Gordon. He's maintaining a very serious composure, though perhaps his eyes are laughing.

"I'm employed by the United States government, though officially I don't exist, and you'll have a longer happier life if you *never* tell anyone we met."

I stare out the window. Judy speaks.

"Because America won the war with Japan, Japan made certain concessions. Near Sapporo, Japan, my government was given a lovely old estate, that's cool in the summer and cold in the winter. A place where people are taken while we patiently wait for them to tell us their secrets."

I stare out the window. Judy speaks.

"Perhaps due to my fame as a snake killer, I'm in charge of this very private estate. We can only accommodate eleven guests at a time, and there are a great many people waiting to tell us their secrets. One of my responsibilities involves … no one waiting for too long."

I stare. Judy speaks.

"When we're crowded, as we are now, I have some of our guests—the most senior, those that have been with us the longest—taken outside so they can enjoy fresh air, while they're tied to bamboo poles and laid on the wet driveway, where small trucks are driven back and forth over their feet and ankles. They scream, of course, but they also breathe in lots of fresh air … which is good for their health."

While Judy speaks, I slowly turn to stare at Mr. Wu.

"Naturally, we untie these nice people from the poles, and help them into the house, where they're given some medicine to keep them awake, so they can fully enjoy their pain."

I stare, smiling just at the corners of my mouth. Judy speaks.

"After dinner, the staff and guests, the ones who were not lying in the driveway, gather round a wide dirt pit in the basement. One at a time, those who played in the driveway, are tied to a chair, unclothed, with their slowly bleeding, mangled feet and ankles, resting gently on the dirt floor."

Judy speaks. I look at the floor and pace while keeping the hint of a smile.

"When I left the estate last week, we had fifteen flesh eating rats, and about a hundred jumbo cockroaches. But, Mr. Wu, you know how cockroaches are. There're probably two hundred of the buggers by now. Anyway, the rats and cockroaches are loosed into the pit, and wagers are made as to how long the guest on the chair will scream, before he or she passes out."

I stop pacing and smile at Mr. Wu. Judy speaks.

"It's good clean fun, actually. The wagers are small and no one drinks too much. Best of all we hear lots of secrets. Unfortunately, a few guests, those with weak hearts, have died. But we have a unique funeral service. We take the deceased up in the same old bomber we use for flying our guests to Sapporo. The staff pretends they're bombing some fishing boat in the ocean far below, using a corpse rather than a bomb. To keep the event festive, we usually take along a few live guests, and, of course, there's wagering and drinking; done respectfully, you understand."

I turn and look out the window. Judy speaks.

"Now, Mr. Wu, that same airplane's waiting for me at Kai–Tak. I have to leave in an hour. My short holiday, already over. As a favor to Sir Gordon, I'm inviting you to come with me. It would be great fun to have you as a guest. I'm sure you would enjoy the wagering, and you would feel much better once you tell us your secrets. Snow covers Sapporo at this time of year. It's quite lovely. I'll wait outside while you make up your mind."

When Judy finishes speaking, I turn round, smile a crooked smile and offer my hand to Mr. Wu. When he takes it, I note his hand's quite slippery.

"I have a car waiting, Mr. Wu," I announce in farewell, "so please, don't take too long."

Even before Judy starts translating, Sir Gordon's coming from behind his desk. With an arm round my shoulders he ushers me from the room. While Judy begins speaking, the door closes.

"Thank you, Luke," Sir Gordon delights, "However did you come up with … with all that? It's not true is it?"

Without smiling I look at him and shake my head, once.

"Well, old chap, it certainly made my skin crawl. It was rather like watching Humphrey Bogart play a role written for Peter Lorre; ever think of the stage?"

I can't help but smile at his absurdity, and I nearly chuckle.

"That's my boy," Sir Gordon grins. "Welcome back to reality. Why don't you and Martha join Lizabeth and I for lunch? Tomorrow, about one? If you say no … well, I'll resign from the hotel board."

"Only," I negotiate, "if we can mix in a bit of business."

"Certainly, certainly. Lizabeth thinks you're fascinating as you are, after I tell her of this … well, you can talk of anything you wish."

"It was nothing."

"By Jove, you only say that because you don't know who that man is," he disputes. "Though there are more serious issues that I can't discuss, we suspect he may be involved in the disappearance of several dozen union leaders. See you tomorrow," he jollies, while moving toward his office door.

Reception area and elevator are empty, as I exit the high-rise world of momentary make-believe.

"Hello?" Holly greets, with a slight question mark.

"Hi, it's Luke. I'm calling an hour early, but I can call back."

"That's all right, we've been up for a while. Liam's had breakfast, and he's watching television. He doesn't understand why he can't go to school, but I've told him that's what you want, so he isn't complaining."

"You're a good mother."

"Thanks. But don't ask Liam for *his* opinion, right now."

"Did you make a connection with Sally Evans?"

"No. She's somewhere in Europe. Her firm's trying to find her and they're offering other lawyers. Since the hotels are not in the U.S., maybe your attorney in Hong Kong could handle things just as well. What daya think?"

"Good point. Excellent, in fact. Tell her office that we'll call again, if we need her. What else?"

"The police told the Valparaiso owners they caught the man who burned down their hotel and killed seven guests. He was buying drinks for everyone in some bar, bragging about what he did and paying with greenbacks …"

"Great!"

"No, not great. Supposedly, he told the police that Luke Whitaker paid him to do it, because the land and building were worth less than the mortgage, and he (you) wanted to collect on the insurance."

"Not great!"

"Yeah," she says, and pauses. "They want a recent picture of you for identification purposes. What should I do?"

"Do the police know where I am?"

"I told the owners. I don't know if the police know or not."

"I've been in Hong Kong the whole time, so I have an alibi," I reason aloud, "and I don't know if there're any recent photo's … other than a few wedding pictures. The man's lying, of course. Put up to it by somebody who wants to cause me a ton of trouble. I'll talk to Sir Gordon Beasley. He's our lawyer here. But I can't do it tonight."

"I have all the papers together," she surges. "I can drive them to SeaTac, and put 'em on flights to Hong Kong."

"Did you reach those GMs I wanted you to warn?"

"I did. They were, well, startled. I'm not sure they believed me. They asked for you or JJ to call them … when there's time."

"This morning, call them back. Explain I'm on a ship in the South China Sea with JJ and Martha until the day after tomorrow. Tell 'em that I wanted you to remind them this isn't a joke, and that I have options. They'll know what you're talking about."

"I'll start calling when we hang up."

"How would you and Liam like to go for an airplane ride?"

"Sure."

"Did JJ get you an American Express card?"

"He did."

"Is your passport up to date?"

"Yeah."

"Then pack a few bags for you and Liam, put the papers you've collected in a briefcase that you promise not to let out of your sight, and try to get two seats on tonight's Northwest Orient flight to Tokyo. You'll arrive in the middle of *tomorrow* night, so make reservations at a hotel near the airport, and you'll need reservations on a flight from Tokyo to Hong Kong. Call here and leave the flight information with the operator."

"Are we coming back to Seattle?"

"Oh, sure. I just need your help a little sooner than I thought. Are you okay with this?"

"Perfectly."

"Oh, yes. Buy some comic books for Liam to read on the plane."

"Great idea. I will. Goodbye, Luke."

16.

Concerned only for the survival of union members they represent, my Executive Committee called an emergency meeting and passed one motion after another without discussion or unanimity:

1. *Don't leave the suite until you are ready to board a direct flight to Moscow!*

2. *Change into casual clothing and wear rubber soled shoes for sailing on the junk!*

3. *Go as you are but wear your overcoat and don't leave the room until you've had a few drinks!*

4. *Sit on the toilet to avoid an embarrassing accident in less than an hour!*

5. *Get in bed and go to sleep. In the morning bleach your hair, put on lipstick and change your name!*

6. *Whatever you do, don't walk very far!*

7. *Whatever you do, don't eat or drink anything!*

8. *Whatever you do, don't tell anybody what you know!*

9. *Whatever you do, please don't commit suicide!*

10. *Call Holly and tell her to send a picture of JJ to Valparaiso!*

11. *Call Mike what's-his-name, the FBI guy you despise, and find out if the FBI's doing this to pressure you into more cooperation, and if not, find out if they know what's going on!*

12. *Read a good book; you always feel better after you've read a good book, and it will give us time to get properly organized!*

13. *If you sail on the junk, stay below decks. The way your luck's running there will be shooting and union members will be injured!*

14. *Somehow this situation can be turned to your advantage, but we haven't figured out how!*

15. *A motion to adjourn has passed. Goodnight!*

I call Mei Liew and tell her I'll be leaving for the junk in half an hour; ask her to meet me at the car; suggest she call Adolf; thus demonstrating the full extent of my sensitivities.

Similar to the blazing guns of a randomly attacking fighter plane, my Executive Committee—like most committees—has accidentally hit a target or two. So I visit the bathroom then don my camelhair overcoat and into one of its pockets I slip a fifth of Cutty Sark.

Under the Hilton's portico and standing next to our car, I'm feeling particularly appreciative of real friends. Enough so, that I greet Mei Liew with a gentle hug then take Adolf's right hand in both of mine. He smiles back, but the smile's accompanied by something of an unasked question, which he allows me to ignore as we get in the car; me up front next to the drive, who's wished each of us a good evening and sits behind a steering wheel that's on the left side of the old Cadillac, the wrong side for Hong King traffic.

On our way to the waterfront, we discuss the night's sedate weather, who had what for dinner, then I mention that Holly and Liam will be out in a few days. This turns the conversation to the joys of sharing one's world with children; my participation becomes one of nods and chuckles as seem appropriate. A solemn silence descends as we leave the main road for the quay where the junk's moored. We get out unassisted and the big car moves into the shadows, where its lights are extinguished.

I'm last aboard. Heading for the companionway and Martha, I pass JJ introducing Mei Liew and Adolf to Tommy, who's offering a tour of the boat, which only Adolf accepts. Going below, I can hear the gangway being removed along with the increasing throb of diesel engines. We've six hours to go about twenty-five miles. Ghosting seems an appropriate speed.

I find Martha behind a door next to the operating room. Her sleeping patient looks comfy in a berth big enough for two, while she sits on a hard metal chair at a dimly lit desk and reads a book. Her welcoming smile seems fatigued, and she doesn't jump up to give me a hug.

"Hi," I solo, with enthusiasm. "Are you practicing to become one of those interns who never sleeps?"

"Hi, yourself," she tries to cheer. "Not really. This afternoon, I did consider going to medical school, but two hours later I changed my mind."

"Why? Not because of me, I hope."

"No, dear. Not because of you. At least that wasn't the biggest reason."

I pull the Cutty from my pocket and begin a hunt for two glasses. Scotch isn't a proper substitute for sleep, though with good fortune it'll make her less reluctant to take a nap in one of the room's five empty berths. Thus justified, I pour two fingers of scotch into a clean-looking glass and hand it to Martha. She takes it and waits while I pour the same into a glass for myself. We smile at each other and clunk glasses. I sip. Doctor-for-a-day throws her's back, makes a face, gasps a couple times, and soon smiles with decidedly less care and woe.

"You see," Martha whirrs, "I was impressed with my hands doing things with severed blood vessels and nerves … like they had a mind of their own and I was only an observer.

"That's part of what a scrub nurse does, ya know. During a surgery they watch the surgeons hands so they can anticipate what's next. And I think that's why I wasn't freaking out at the time. I was used to watching *hands* operate."

She pauses while I pour another two fingers of scotch into her glass.

"For a while afterwards, I was so impressed with myself—and don't you dare laugh—I thought I shouldn't deny mankind the benefit of my medical genius. My magical hands."

Eyebrows, mine, arch all by themselves and as soon as I stop nodding, I sip more scotch.

"Well, Luke, that was easier to believe than no explanation at all."

"I suppose."

"Of course, it doesn't fly. I know what I can do. And what I can't do. And I can't do, what I did!"

"But with training and practice, you …"

"Nope," she disputes. "*Those* hands weren't just trained, they were talented. After you left, even Tommy commented on my remarkable *talent*—that's the word he used—before he suggested Providence may have intervened, or something like that."

Martha sips some scotch then licks her lips. "What daya think?"

"I'm always an empiricist when it comes to making assumptions that don't have to be made without tallying observed experiences."

"So?"

"So I don't believe there's a God – I *know* there's a God! Other than my own, personal experiences, I spent time with Summer Moon. There was no choice, she was continually thanking God, complimenting His wisdom, and making flattering remarks regarding *His* amazing and beautiful world. I suppose," I sigh, "you should thank Him."

"I have," Martha admits. "But I don't think that's quite enough."

"If it'll make you feel better," I grin, "we can have a ceremony on the poop deck. Sacrifice a vestal virgin or two, if we can find any."

I respectfully wait through a period of silence that's without the expected giggling or laughter. Then I suggest she take a nap; that I'll recruit Mei Liew to watch the patient. Martha agrees, and adds the sailor would benefit from being fed a warm clear soup. I suggest rum and Coca-Cola rather than soup, and she advises—while slipping out of her scrubs, and I never argue with Martha when she's undressing—that my brand of healing should be confined to the recently deceased.

Eager for something to do other than courting anxieties while she waits for us to meet the riverboat, Mei Liew delights at the opportunity to help the wounded sailor, and disappears with the easy grace given to purposeful women. I look at Adolf, now alone. His eyes are shinning and a repressed smile's barely being contained.

"Have you toured the boat?" he asks, as he leans closer to whispers like one child would to another when standing before a pile of beautifully wrapped presents on Christmas morning.

"No," I humble, like a deprived orphan.

"Then you haven't seen the gun?"

Speechless, I shake my head.

"It's an old Oerlikon. A single-barreled twenty millimeter cannon with a large spring coil surrounding the barrel, mounted on a fixed pedestal in a space under the poop deck. The stern windows conceal it but they're rigged to fall away so it can fire."

I twist and look at him. My frown signaling disbelief, disapproval, and a lack of understanding.

"Versions were used by all sides during World War Two as naval anti-aircraft weapons," Adolf quietly enthuses. "This one has a sixty-round magazine on top. And it's free-swinging with armored shields on either side, with shoulder supports for the gunner. It'll fire four hundred rounds per minute, with a trained crew, and has a range of two thousand meters against aerial targets. The muzzle velocity is eight hundred and twenty meters per second."

"Why's Tommy worried about being attacked by aircraft?"

"He isn't," Adolf confides, "it would have to be topside to be used against aircraft. I was told the boat's previous owner was once in the smuggling business, and occasionally used the cannon against Japanese patrol boats."

"Does it still work?"

"Oh, yes!" Adolf grins. "When the weather permits, Tommy takes the junk fifty or sixty miles into the South

China Sea, so the crew can practice. You know the guy dressed like a waiter, who's always hanging around Tommy?"

"Sure, I call him *the ever present*. Not to his face, of course, that would be rude, just in my mind. I actually don't know his name."

"Neither do I," admits Adolf, "but he's the gunner. Surface to surface, the gun's range is shorter than if shooting at aircraft. Tommy says his man is quite deadly up to a distance of three hundred meters."

"Way beyond the range of our water cannons," I sigh.

"True," Adolf also sighs, "but the water cannons are legal. And neither the crew of the shrimp processing barge nor the crew of the tugboat would have any idea how to use a gun like Tommy's. However, guns like Tommy's have been mounted through the fuselage on DC-3s for use against the Vietcong and North Vietnamese Regulars."

"Whatever you do," I surge, forgetting to be quiet, and while grabbing his forearm, "*don't* tell Martha about that. She's determined we should rescue my half-brother from his prison camp."

"I won't," he whispers. "Her rescue plan really wouldn't work. Though if the pirate situation is worse than we think, having a couple of those guns mounted on your DC-3 might be handy."

"Why?" I flash, quietly. "So it can fly air cover for the shrimp barge? I'm certain that's also terribly illegal, as well as expensive …"

"Luke," he interrupts, "we'd only have to do it a few times and the pirates would stay away from the barge forever."

"They'd only stay away if they heard the plane flying at night, or saw it in the daytime. And it wouldn't be long before they'd bribe some Indonesian General to send up a few jets and shoot the old lady to pieces."

"Only as a last resort, then," Adolf mumbles, in disappointment. When I look at him, at least in the present lighting, I'm struck by how much his appearance resembles that of the villainous Auric Goldfinger.

"Before that," I whisper and smile, which gets the attention of his arching eyebrows, "as a *last* resort, you'll have to come up with a submarine, complete with torpedoes and crew."

He nods and grins. When we climb up to the poop deck, Tommy waves for us to join him while he's addressing eight men. All are standing at their equivalent of attention. The language, Cantonese.

After a few moments, Adolf leans sideways and mumbles, "He's saying something about guns and prisoners. Mei Liew's been teaching me some Cantonese."

It seems strange to me that Mei Liew has been teaching him words like *guns* and *prisoners* as pillow talk. But what do I know, lonely lamb in the wilderness that I am.

Soon, pistols and rifles are being distributed by two more men, who have arrived with plenty of both. Adolf takes one of each. I accept the forty-five semi-automatic pistol when offered and—preferring a coke bottle at close range or ducking for cover if there's time—hand it to Adolf, who stuffs it into his waistband along with a piece of his vest, then moves a little closer to me. Me, the kid he's watched out for … for so many years.

Hearing the junk's engines go quiet then rev in reverse to stop our forward progress, I look round to see where we are, and right away recognize the dirty blue and white hull of *Matilda* less than ten feet to starboard. The junk isn't wallowing as the speedboat had yesterday afternoon. It's very early Friday morning. No other boats are about, so there're no wakes. Only the long ocean swells gradually move the big junk, while nothing seems to move *Matilda*.

Eight armed Chinese men make a fast, forward-facing decent of the ladder from poop deck to main deck, using only their hands, no feet. Then six of the eight tromp down the companionway and disappear. One of the two men left on the main deck opens the door in the railing, that yesterday led down to the Garwood. I hear Adolf chamber a shell into his short-barreled rifle and note he's holding it in such a way it can be fired quickly. Tommy has a forty-five automatic in his hand hanging next to his leg, muzzle pointing at the deck. At the same readiness as Adolf, *the ever present* stands next to Tommy. Only the helmsman and I are unarmed.

When there's a noise from overhead, Tommy's big flashlight swings up to illuminate a large bamboo cage that's slowly being lowered from the freighter's boom. It stops with the bottom of the cage just below the level of the main deck, an opening in the cage aligns with the gate in the junk's railing. For holding the cage in position, there are two ropes; one tied to either side, each being held by one of the men who didn't go below. Because of the junk's two sailing masts, the cage can't be lowered onto the main deck.

The planning, preparation and execution are impressive but seem a bit much for putting an injured sailor—who probably ought not be moved—back aboard his freighter. And unless the issuing of firearms constitutes a ceremonial show of respect, some sort of Triad tradition, it's a silly thing to do under the circumstances ... which I clearly didn't understand now that I see three of the men that went below, come backing up the companionway with their various weapons aimed at a group of blindfolded men and women, who are stumbling their way up to the main deck, hands tied behind their backs—twenty-three *comrades* in all—herded from behind by three men using rifles as prods.

Doubtless, I'm the only person on the whole damn boat who didn't know the comrades were here. And I declare to myself, that since I first met Martha, I've spend much too much time on one dangerous boat after another.

Tommy Tang, most honorable leader of most honorable Triad, bellows orders with the authority of a lead baritone in a grand opera. Nearly shaking the big junk, they're not to be disobeyed by anyone capable of understanding. Some non-violent assistance forms the comrades into a single file that faces the nine-foot-square cage. The men who were backing up the stairs enter first. One by one, the comrades are helped in. The two rope holders weave the steadying ropes across the opening. The cage begins to rise. Our engines are put in gear. Their rumbling acceleration almost obscures the collective moans of those who are being hauled somewhat closer to heaven.

Now that what I assumed was done earlier and differently, has been accomplished, I walk over to Adolf and ask the whereabouts of JJ.

"He was going below to do some sketches for a nightclub he said was going to be part of the remodeled hotel.

"Tommy's tough," he continues icily, "I like him. He's not sadistic. Never would have qualified for the Nazi SS of my era. Those bastards would have shot two or three of these prisoners in the legs and thrown 'em in the water so their blood would attract sharks. *Everyone* would have been made to watch while the wounded swimmers were ripped apart. Then a few more prisoners would've been shoved into the water so the rest would wait in terror for their turn. Luke, the SS was so gratified by suffering they were disappointed by death."

I sigh, pat him on the shoulder and turn away knowing he intended to compliment Tommy, but wishing he'd be a bit more cheerful while we're negotiating our way to an unseen line, the other side of which the water belongs to The People's Republic of China, and there to wait alone in the dark unable to rewrite whatever has happened in Guangzhou.

To be sure, these are plans of my own making: the ransom fodder being hoisted aboard a coastal freighter; kidnappers and kidnappees—some or all—now going down the Pearl River toward detection or escape. *Plans*, it seems, are simplistic when envisioned, brightly colored when proposed, get complicated when translated into orders to be executed and directions to be followed, and generate considerable anxiety for planners while being performed.

Light from the helmsman's binnacle helps me find the fancy round table and one of the deck chairs. From my overcoat, the bottle of Cutty Sark goes on the table, as I seat myself and sigh yet again. Like a shuffling shadow, Tommy comes from the dark and sits next to me, takes the bottle, unscrews the cap and gives it a long embrace before passing it to me. Since there'll be no service from *the ever present*, I do likewise, then pass it back. The cap's replaced, and Tommy tenderly rests the bottle on the table. We're silent. Neither of us wanting to speak on any issue, and to Hegel's disappointment, neither of us needs the other to validate his existence.

"Thanks for including me in the hotel ownership, and its operation," he sinceres after a while, as though I'd given him a gift, when he had paid a fair price.

"You're welcome," I casual. "Glad you're involved."

When a six foot, five inch male Chinese squirms it's extremely hard not to notice. So I turn to see why, and then offer my handkerchief that's only been used for decorative purposes. It's accepted, and used to mop up bits of lachrymal fluid before blowing a nose. It's nice to know I'm not the only male with that particularly *circumstantial affliction*.

"Sorry," he says, "sometimes scotch does that to me."

"Me, too."

"Well," he says, and of course I'm anticipating a change of subject. "I hear a lady named Holly, and her young son, will be arriving in a few days. If I remember correctly, she is the wife of your pilot."

"Right on both counts."

"Good. It's nice to have children around."

"So I'm told."

"I'm known to get emotional when I'm tired and things are going well; new and dangerous things that I haven't done before. I'm also very happy—proud too, I suppose—to have you and Martha and your friends, your family, along with me."

"But Tommy, you have an entire Triad for a …"

"It is not the same," he flashes, "we are not a family. Our bond is not affection but the shared risk of death, injury and prison … all for money … money spent on gambling, lots of gambling, drinking, sexy women and frivolous things whose value fads like the night before the sun. A few of my men have families, those who run my legitimate businesses. A few others give money to aging parents. Most save nothing, but what I short them. My men will be loyal only as long as I'm successful, and they share in that success."

"Pass me the bottle, please. Thanks. What you describe, well, it's the same in every business everywhere. Maybe not the issues of death, injury and prison, but everything else. Your activities have a rather high risk compared to their rewards. Nevertheless," I sigh, "I'm sure they fit the nature of your men."

I pass the bottle back. He unscrews the cap. When he puts the bottle back on the table, there's too little light to see how much remains.

"Yes," he disparages, "my young men would be soldiers if there was an attractive war for 'em, so they're soldiers in skirmishes I invent. For profit, of course."

After waiting respectfully, I realize he's finished.

"I have a personal question," I yawn, "if you don't mind." He nods. "Why don't you have a wife and children?"

Slowly, and seemingly without thought, Tommy unscrews the cap but leaves the bottle on the table. He stares at the bottle for a minute or so, and then replaces the cap, and looks away to survey the night and a few distant lights.

"I did," he chills. "She was Chinese. And a delight to the eye. A tender and very intelligent woman, who gave meaning to more than the bedroom. Our three daughters were gifts of joy and happiness, and they were as gentle as butterflies. Eleven years, one month and three days ago, they were all killed. An enemy of mine, not theirs, cut their throats while they slept." He twists in his chair and looks me in the eye. "Unfortunately," he steels, "I still have enemies."

"I'm sorry. I can't even imagine your loss, but they wouldn't want ..."

"I cannot have another family," he clangs. "Not while I'm churning up the world and uncovering maggots. I hope, my young friend, you'll *never* understand."

It's not a strange remark, when considered in the light of recent hotel fires. "Perhaps," I humbly solicit, "you're not too tired or too sad to share your wisdom; regarding a personal matter."

"Of course," he suddenly seems to shine. "There's nothing so refreshing as other people's problems. They are always a most marvelous distraction."

I nod, because I agree.

"Before you begin would you like something to nibble on? We mustn't get too drunk," he offers and admonishes, as the perfect host.

"Indeed, something to nibble would be welcome, so long as it isn't salt-dried anchovy filets."

"Fresh out!" he assures. "Won't be a minute," he states, and waves me back to my chair when I rise to help.

Not quite as quickly as promised, the aging minor god's coming up the ladder, awkwardly using one hand, his other long arm surrounding four cereal-like boxes that are passed round: one to Adolf; one to the helmsman; one to *the ever present*; the last box unceremoniously placed next to what's left of the Cutty Sark, which must have been pleading for a friend, as Tommy casually takes a fifth of Dewar's (just what we don't need) from a bulging pocket and places it alongside the Cutty.

No iridescent suit for Tommy, tonight. Black shoes, khaki pants, a khaki military-style shirt with epaulets and pleated button-through pockets, over a black turtleneck, both tucked into his pants.

I wait for the box to be opened and passed. Gingersnaps. First cousins, if not siblings, to those served a few days ago. Not on a royal plate, but tasting almost the same.

"I checked around while I was below," he chuckles. "Mei Liew waved and grinned when I stuck my head in the door, so everything's okay, or the patient died quietly and she doesn't know it yet. JJ … JJ has fallen asleep at the desk he was using. I didn't have the heart to wake him though he's drooling on his sketches. Now," he says, with real or craftily manufactured cheer, and while handing me the nearly empty bottle of Cutty, "have a swig and seek my wisdom."

I'm surprised how good gingersnaps are with scotch.

Rather better than with tea. Green *or* black.

With reserve, I summarize my adventures with Martha. Our introduction. Our reunion, including Bill the pilot and Holly the hotel telephone operator. The disappearance of Martha's father. Our coercive meeting with the FBI in Seattle, and our "fishing expedition" in San Francisco with Martha as spy-bait.

Tommy's such a good audience, and asks so few easily answered questions, that I tell him about Tina and what Adolf found in her apartment, the FBI's plan for the spying Congressman, and how they reneged on their offer of immunity from prosecution. He's still shaking his head in disgust, when I mention the fiery death of *Tropicana*.

Intentionally presented as an afterthought, I speak to the very recent and simultaneous burning of four hotels in Central and South America; then add that I've been identified, by name only, as the man paying the fellow who torched the hotel in Valparaiso, killing seven people. Tommy shrugs. Either because he knows where I was at the time of the fires, or because he doesn't see why it's such a big deal. As I've finished off the Cutty, he opens the Dewar's, and takes a sizable sample along with a single gingersnap.

"Welcome to the club," he smirks. "It seems you've made a powerful enemy. Most likely it's the sleazy Congressman. Whose girlfriend you killed. And whose life you ruined. I'm guessing your FBI friends are also part of the Congressman's arson frame."

"Why?" I startle, the hair on my arms standing in alarm.

"Because, sometimes a mouse successfully threatens an elephant. The FBI needs the Congressman to continue doing whatever he's doing for them … and they can't be completely sure he won't tell his former employers about his relationship with the FBI. So, you see, when the mouse wants something so it can hurt 'that damn Luke Whitaker' … well, what's a mere morsel of information to an elephant; to the FBI?"

Indeed! The Congressman's more a rat than a mouse and Tommy's conjectured connection seems frighteningly plausible. Probable, even. Perfect, actually.

"I'm without an informer within the FBI," he bemoans, as if reading my mind, then unscrews the Dewar's and pushes it in front of me. "But, I know someone who might have one … should have one."

"Yes, well," I pretend to idle, as a crescendo of thoughts reminiscent of Tchaikovsky's Fifth become so alluring that I permanently disband my Pacifist Committee.

"I'll pay one million Hong Kong," I casual, as if buying a sack of oranges, "to know the Congressman's *previous* employer. With specifics, of course."

"*Ayeeyah*," Tommy delights, in gleeful Cantonese, "Evil spirits come close. Pay attention!"

"There'll be another one million, Hong Kong, when you load the Congressman safely aboard *Matilda*. And four additional million, Hong Kong, of course, should you help me succeed with, well, a *wee bit* of trading."

"*Six million!*" he voices, with long arms stretched to the sky and the stars beyond. "How much time to do this?" he sobers.

"The sooner the better."

"May I use your plane … and her pilots?"

"There'll be conditions, but yes."

17.

Lacking anguish and guilt previously provided by my Pacifist Committee, the earliest hours of Friday, January nineteenth, nineteen-hundred and sixty-eight, have been painlessly devoured by the Dragon of Life, never to be experienced again.

Local time per an impeccably accurate watch: thirty one minutes after five AM. An hour and thirty five minutes prior to the sun's official appearance. Too soon, it seems, for rendezvousing with our riverboat from Guangzhou, and a thin slice of new moon illuminates almost nothing.

Tommy, Adolf, and *the ever present* have been absent the poop deck for hours. From the occasional sound of metal-on-metal, I'm guessing the *boys* have been playing with the cannon. No doubt, fondling it with awe and adolescent pleasure.

A canvas deck chair can only be tipped back and forth so many times before it falls apart. Since mine's about due, I attempt to stand, which I can only accomplish after granting new retirement benefits to the Amalgamated Brotherhood of Leg Muscles. Once erect I keep moving, toward and then down the ladder from poop deck to main deck. Realizing, as I do so, another reason why explorers of the Spanish galleon days were so happy to find land. Spanish galleons had towering poop decks. After a long voyage their crews must have been nearly crippled from climbing up and down hundreds of times each day.

It's dark at the bottom of the companionway. Navigating by light escaping under closed doors, I find the recovery room and enter into gloom provided by a single low-wattage desk lamp. Mei Liew looks up from a book. Squints to focus, then stands. Presumably, she's relieved to be relieved.

"Everything okay?" she whispers, smiling weakly.

"We're floating," I whisper back. "And I've potentially solved some problems. Yeah, everything's okay." I pause, until she's no longer using the desk edge to keep her balance. "I'll baby-sit if you want to go topside and breathe real air."

Mei Liew nods, but her weak smile dies. Perhaps she's thinking about what's to come. As she leaves, she gives my arm a lingering touch. When the door closes, I remove my overcoat, toss it onto the back of the only chair, and go to the upper bunk of she-who-slumbers.

Martha looks so angelic it would be a sin to fondle her until she wakes. Besides, she's not a cannon; a pistol, maybe, but certainly not a cannon. Then again, tickling her into consciousness would be worse. Neither's necessary. The nearness of my overwhelming presence opens her eyes.

"Hi," she quietly says, and pulls the sheet and blanket up to her chin to prove my presence isn't overwhelming in the least. "How's the patient?"

"Should I wake him and ask?"

"Nooo," she croons while yawning, and then stretches under the covers. "Mei Liew and I helped him to the bathroom and back, about an hour ago. He'll sleep a few more hours and wake up hungry."

"Hope he likes gingersnaps," I cheery. "We're positively awash in gingersnaps. Maybe gingersnaps and green tea?"

"Gad, a menu planner you're not."

"What daya mean? I've been drinking scotch and eating gingersnaps for hours."

"Well," she disparages, "*you* aren't normal. I remember when you ordered raw liver, at its natural body temperature."

"Yes, well …"

"Yes, well, yourself," she grins. "How about going next door and getting my street clothes. They're folded. On a shelf. Near the autoclave. Just look around, you'll find 'em."

"Yes, dear."

"What happened to: 'Yes, my ladyship,' or 'Yes, my worship,' followed by a modest, groveling bow? And why haven't you given me my now-terribly-tardy-birthday-present; the one you promised about two weeks ago? "

"The rule book quite clearly states that treating you as royalty may only be done while flying in First Class sections of American air carriers, so fellow passengers wonder who the hell you are. As to the birthday present, it's shameful, of course, but I haven't been able to choose between giving you Macau or the New Territories. Sorry."

"You should be! And though I haven't been to either place, had you asked, which would have been the polite thing to do, I would have told you Macau."

"I was leaning in that direction, but it requires haggling with Portugal; could take quite a while and I wasn't sure you'd be willing to wait. I'll get your clothes while you give it some thought?"

She nods. As I leave, she's throwing back the blanket and sheet, preparing to extricate herself from a cozy bunk

224

with scant headroom. Chinese sailor's dead to the world, so to speak.

With left arm cradling black loafers, black wool slacks and a black long-sleeved cashmere sweater that smells tantalizingly of Martha: Gucci, maybe Channel, maybe both, I leave the operating room. Take seven steps. Open the door to ye old recovery room, which I quickly close behind me, as Martha's standing partially in the shadows, hands on hips, adorable feet and trim ankles fifteen inches apart.

"Put 'em on the desk," she decrees, imperiously, "and come hither. I don't want Macau or the new Territories. I want a *slave*."

"As you wish, your worship," I grovel, bow and go to the desk expecting her to wait … definitely not expecting her arms to be going round my neck when I turn about, or the little hop she does to put magnificent legs round my waist. Royalty, I've noticed, bloody well does whatever it wants; thank heavens.

My recovery's a bit languid. Martha dresses rather quickly, considering, and she's going out the door when the engines stop throbbing. Suddenly, someone's striking the gong loud enough to raise the dead, along my blood pressure.

Rushing to pull on clothes in their proper order, I hear running feet pounding by and streams of excited Cantonese. While straightening my tie, I hear a throat being cleared. I glance at the patient, who, having been *royally* entertained, now grins with improved health.

There's a distant explosion, as I reach the main deck, and the gong's still gonging and I can't use the ladder up to the poop because Adolf and *the ever present* are coming down, almost dropping. They say nothing as they rush to and through a little door going under the poop deck and slam it closed behind them.

Before climbing, I glance round. Martha's nowhere in sight. The gonging has stopped but the engines are revving and the junk's heeling and twisting to port as she maneuvers to reverses her direction, probably with the wheel hard to port, the port engine in reverse, the starboard engine full ahead.

Top of the ladder I'm met by Mei Liew, and she's shaking so hard she's about to fall. I help her sit on the deck and think of joining her, but *Adrenaline* says stand for fight or flight. On a ship, big or small, there's nowhere to run and—unless you're being boarded by pirates—there's no one to smash with a coke bottle or kick in the groin.

Tommy's next to the helmsman. Probably giving maneuvering orders. Martha's behind the round table leaning against and gripping the stern rail. As she looks ready to jump overboard, I stride to her side and grab her arm.

"What's happening?" I yell in her ear.

"Some boat," she yells back, "Tommy says it's a Red patrol boat, and it's firing on another boat."

"Not firing at us?"

"No. The other boat looks like our riverboat. Here," – she's handing me binoculars – "take these and look were I'm pointing."

It's dark as hell, but after adjusting the focus and because of the boat's bow wave, I find the target. "Yeah, I see it. Where's the patrol boat?"

Before Martha can answer, I see a flash of white and orange about two football fields behind the riverboat, and about four hundred yards just to the left of our stern, as we complete our turn. Both boats are going from our left to our right, toward Hong Kong. As the speed of light is greater than the speed of sound, the sound of the explosion arrives just as a shell from the patrol boat makes a big splash, barely missing the riverboat.

The patrol boat's a fast predator chasing a slower prey. If the gunner can't hit his target, providing he's not just trying to make the riverboat heave-to, it won't be long before ramming's an option.

"What's the plan?"

"How the *hell* do I know," she blasts. "Ask Tommy! All I know is I saw a flash just as I got to the top of the ladder. Then I heard an explosion. Tommy was beating the gong and yelling at the helmsman. Suddenly, Adolf and the other guy took off."

Swallowing a speculative prediction, I run the few yards to Tommy and must pull on his sleeve to get his attention. He twists round. His almond shaped eyes squeezed to narrow slits.

"What?" he shouts.

"Are you going to shoot before we know what's going on?"

"The bastards are shelling my men. Of course I'm going to shoot! And get Martha away from that rail!"

I think of hitting him in the face to slow him down, but that won't stop our cannon, and Martha's standing too close to its muzzle only a yard below her. I run, then start dragging her and her protests away from the rail…

BOOM, BOOM, BOOM, BOOM, BOOM … our cannon growls like a grouchy dragon, firing its first magazine of sixty twenty-millimeter shells at the rate of several hundred a minute. There's another flash from the patrol boat's gun followed by an enormous explosion and fireball in the vicinity of the riverboat. Seconds later, and thanks to *the ever present*, the patrol boat blazes and then explodes.

We stopped firing. With two vessels burning the dawn's less black, but we're too far from either vessel to hear crackling flames or screams from the injured and dying.

Martha sinks to the deck, wraps her arms round Mei Liew. In shock, I stumble over to Tommy.

"You and your damn plan," he screams, and spits in my face; so I smash a fist into his stomach, doubling him over and releasing a flood of guttural Cantonese.

"You fool," I yell, so he'll hear me over his own voice, "that riverboat wasn't ours, unless you had it smuggling high explosives. Fruits and vegetables don't explode. Start looking for survivors."

"*Ayeeyah*," he trumpets, and—gripped by a spirit more evil than mine—smiles a nasty smile. "Yes, yes, you're right! We cannot leave witnesses!"

Tommy bellows orders to the helmsman and then more orders to men on the main deck, who run below as we heel and twist to starboard. The men reappear with rifles and big flashlights, and run to the bow, as we stop twisting and head toward the burning riverboat.

If I had the gun I gave to Adolf, mutiny would be an option, but Tommy's not likely to let me get close enough to attack by hand. Not a second time. Not while he's armed. Not while he's desperately trying to save himself.

"Mei Liew!" I shout, kneeling on the deck in front of the two women. "Mei Liew! Pay attention! I need your help!"

She looks up, numbly staring at me.

"The riverboat was NOT; I repeat NOT our boat from Guangzhou!"

She nods.

"There must have been a signal to identify us to our riverboat. And another signal that identifies the riverboat to us."

Both women nod.

"I have to know those signals. I can't ask Tommy. No one else but you speaks English and Chinese. Will you help me?"

Again, both women nod, and Martha helps Mei Liew to her feet.

"We must go down to the main deck. I'll go first. Then you. Then Martha. Mei Liew, I know you don't feel good, but it's not very far … and, my little butterfly, I'll catch you if you fall. Okay?"

When she nods, I start down the ladder dropping past the last three steps to stand on the deck and look up with my arms out and bent for catching. Very cautiously, Mei Liew puts one foot down one rung. When the other foot joins it on the same rung, she puts the one foot down again. With five steps still to negotiate, I reach up and pluck her off the ladder. She stands on the deck, almost paralyzed by fear. I take her by the hand and lead her to the cannon room's little door.

"What I do?" she groans.

"I will open the door," I command, our three heads are only inches apart, "go inside with a happy face. Martha will go with you and close the door. Martha will stay by the door while you explain we are looking for survivors. The riverboat wasn't the one with our people. Give Adolf a hug, and ask him if he knows the recognition signal. Then ask the other man if he knows the recognition signal. Ask as nicely and as seriously as you can. If he wants to know why, tell him Tommy told you the signal and assigned you to be the starboard lookout. Tell him you got scared. Dropped your flashlight and forgot the code. Tommy's so busy you don't want to bother him. If Adolf or the other man has a flashlight, ask to borrow it. Martha, if the other man won't give the code to Mei Liew, you step outside and I'll go in.

Then Adolf and I will beat it out of him! Okay?"

They nod. I stand aside so I won't be seen as they enter. Martha closes the door. Involuntarily my hands become fists and I wish for a coke bottle, or a gun, and wonder if I can recreate that sadistic bastard I pretended to be in Sir Gordon's office.

Three minutes have passed. I was prepared for one minute. Only my trust in Adolf and the automatically renewing assumption the door will open in a few more seconds, keeps me from bursting in.

The door opens.

"Hi, honey," Martha breezes. "We waited for Adolf and Wang Fu to finish throwing out used shell casing and load a new magazine. Did you know the ammunition, oops, the shells, are greased before going into the magazine?"

"What's the code?"

"We flash two long dashes," sings Mei Liew, as we're joined by Adolf and Wang Fu, "and they flash a dot, a dash and a dot."

"Morse code," I grin. "They're flashing R, for river, and we're flashing TT, for Tommy Tang. Did ya get a flashlight?"

Martha, Adolf and Mei Liew each hold one up. I nod, tell Martha to take Adolf and Mei Liew to the bow, start flashing two long dashes, slowly cover an arch of a hundred eighty degrees. I tell Adolf to fire his gun in the air if they see a dot, dash, dot.

When I explain we're looking for survivors and Tommy may have told his men to shoot anybody they find, I order Adolf to interfere with any man aiming a gun. With smoke in the air, I add my guess we're getting close to where the riverboat exploded but little will still be floating. I ask Mei Liew to translate what I said, to Wang Fu, and to ask his opinion. She does, as far as I know.

"He doesn't think we should kill survivors," she reports, "and he believes Tommy will change his mind. He wants to know if he should stay with us or go with you."

"Tell him to come with me."

Apparently she did, as Wang Fu smiles and nods at me.

"What the hell's going on?" JJ detonates from behind me, having just come up the companionway. "I doze briefly and all hell breaks loose!"

I turn. "You go with Martha," I glare.

"I'll do nothing of the sort, dear boy," he blusters. "This, this, whatever it is, seems like a low budget movie shot in black and white with non-English speaking actors, no subtitles, no background music; a rather laughable attempt at film noir done for drive-in audiences to watch on rainy nights. If you'll excuse me," – his chin now tilting upward to demonstrate his superiority – "I'm going up and talk to Tommy."

"SHUT UP!" I hiss, loudly. "DO WHAT I TELL YOU OR GO BELLOW!"

"*Well!*" JJ huffs, and stamps a foot.

Without waiting for JJ's next act, I take Wang Fu by the arm and urge him to the ladder. He ascends on his own and I follow. Tommy's where I left him, standing beside the helmsman, peering through binoculars. Wang Fu's walks to Tommy. I go to the round table, shuffle deck chairs to get one I haven't teetered to death, and pick up the badly depleted bottle of Dewar's.

Wang and Tommy talk with animation and a few *Ayeeyahs*. Normal for a polite Cantonese disagreement. In a minute or less, they look in my direction. Wang waves me over. I take the Dewar's with me, nervously screwing and unscrewing the cap on the way. I offer it to Tommy—rather like a peace pipe—and he takes it. Swigs greedily, then hands it to Wang Fu, who does the same. Bloody thing's empty when I get it back.

Wang Fu's heading for the ladder when Tommy says: "My honorable associate has convinced me that survivors might be worth something, if kept alive … to put them on *Matilda*. Keep them away from the others. He's gone to tell everyone assistance must be given; not to shoot."

"Wise fellow, Mr. Wang Fu," I congratulate.

"Sometimes," he grunts, and walks away.

The junk slows as we enter a scattering of burning wood. I move to the port rail and run the beam of the flashlight over the water. Shark fins are absent; pieces of broken hull float past, none big enough to keep someone afloat. When we start circling, I'm reminded of Martha's description of unsuccessfully hunting for her father somewhere in the North Pacific. After circling three times, we increase our speed and head for where the patrol boat might be, or was.

Within a few minutes there's excitement forward. The junk slows, then revs in reverse to stop. Yelling's followed by several splashes and more yelling. Regardless of the language expressing excitement, there's life and several lifesavers have jumped into the water, with Martha doubtlessly among the swimmers.

Tommy concentrates on the action and I offer a silent tearful prayer of gratitude, while slowly turning to look across the poop deck and over our starboard rail into the night.

In the distance there's a short flash of light … followed by a long flash … followed by a short flash. Heart beating like a war drum, I rush to the starboard rail and reply with two long flashes.

"TOMMY!" I trumpet and point. "OVER THERE!"

18.

In a fetal position, partially on me and partially on a pile of red apples, Martha sleeps with her badly wrenched right ankle slightly elevated atop my left leg. To conserve body heat, she's covered by a disgustingly soiled and soon to be discarded camelhair overcoat. I too, am stretched out on my back upon the same pile of apples destined for Kowloon. They're heaped so high to port, starboard and astern that I can't see the horizon.

After the kidnappees, doctor, nurses, and Tommy's gang of young men were transferred to the junk's comparative elegance, we hitched a ride on this heroic riverboat for the balance of its morning journey. During the aforementioned transfer, I didn't see any bandages or bleeding, but everyone was either too tired or too drugged to smile or shake hands, or to be hugged.

It will take hours for the junk to reach *Matilda* and offload the kidnappees, plus the two Chinese men blown from their patrol boat and pulled out of the water with only minor injuries plus the forever-grinning sailor belonging to *Matilda*'s crew, along with some medical personnel, supplies and equipment.

We had the choice of being late for lunch with Sir Gordon or opting to ride back with the apples … on a boat who's transom should read *La Wretched* but doesn't. Our arrival at Kowloon's concrete-quay-of-yesterday should be about half-past ten. From there we can catch a cab to the Hilton for several showers (one each being insufficient) and a complete change of clothing.

Before leaving the junk, Martha—humbly dressed in baggy surgical scrubs she donned when I'd insisted her wet and polluted *swimming attire* must be thrown away, discarded, burned or chucked overboard—had giggled at what she said was my surprising concern for social niceties such as being on time. I'd patiently explained that it had nothing whatsoever to do with good manners, but rather had everything to do with my being accused of arson and murder.

A thinnish layer of these red apples had been used to cover old tarps hiding everyone on their return from Guangzhou, and the smell of this useful fruit is nearly masking the boat's odorous bilge, while a brisk wind from the southwest carries diesel fumes away from our location in this decidedly-less-than-a-yacht and also dilutes the sun's needed warmth.

I've repeatedly told myself to sleep. Each proposal vociferously ridiculed and loudly jeered by grumpy members of various unions. With my Pacifists scattered and suffering from exhaustion, my current period of consciousness can be dedicated to the contemplation of Martha's belated birthday present. Had the gift been given when due, its precise nature wouldn't be so important. Within days of being a month tardy, it must now be perfect. Absolutely, unequivocally perfect; from Martha's point of view, of course, not mine. From my point of view, it should say: I LOVE YOU! Something I've rarely expressed since we were married, as one doesn't promise or vow to say it, just to do it.

Regrettably ponderous, my cognitive processes often take dialogue as a form. Yes, I talk to myself. Usually in silence. Though under the present circumstances, which are more than a tad lonely, I'm tempted to pick up and sincerely address an apple—they're all round me and known to be excellent listeners—but if Martha catches me talking to an apple, she'll be certain I'm as balmy as she believes I am.

I could give her Hong Kong currency in small bills that total a million U.S. Carefully packed in boxes of assorted sizes wrapped in beautiful red paper—as celebrations to greet the Chinese Year of the Monkey begin the end of this month—yet money's only a commodity representing other commodities, so said Karl Marx, and it seems rather impersonal. Perhaps adding a hand written note saying it's a small token of my appreciation and there'll be a million for every future birthday might make the currency, well, more personal.

Of course, there's the matter of inflation. Perhaps next year her birthday-million won't have as much purchasing power as this year's. Martha's no fool. She'll think I'm planning to love her less each year, hedging funds to be used for mistresses; concubines as they're called in China and Hong Kong. I'll have to add a caveat to the hand written note saying that each year her birthday-million will be adjusted for inflation and possibly referencing the Consumer Price Index or some other standardized measurement of inflation being used wherever we're living … and throw in a paragraph or two regarding deflation … and a page about what happens to future birthday-millions if she divorces me ... particularly if I've done nothing wrong ... and the required pages to define *wrong*, and who, if not a court, will make that determination, and if a court, what court will have jurisdiction. Sir Gordon will have to draft the document and encourage Martha to seek her own legal counsel before she signs it in the presence of proper witnesses.

Not entirely romantic. Actually, it doesn't seem romantic in the least. Not since Martha doesn't give a hoot about money. Indeed, it could even be a bit dicey. Martha might interpret the cash as payment for services rendered. And if she doesn't do that, she's bound to believe I was too lazy to go shopping. And I certainly can't claim I don't know her well enough to know what she'd like; besides, I think she's told me.

Last summer's spontaneous trust fund might have said: I LOVE YOU! But I fear a copious quantity of money has lost its novelty value, much like overdoing an erotic act of cuddling.

A year ago, I was alone; had been for years. Too busy, I suppose, to be lonely. Oh, I missed my father ... and the *idea* of my mother, because memories of her only come from photographs. JJ was my only friend, and I'd yet to meet and fall in love with Martha, which were simultaneous events. Since then, I've missed Martha if I haven't seen or talked to her for more than forty-one minutes. If I wake up in the middle of the night, I'll sit in a chair and look at her. Savoring her companionship. Finding peace in her innocent slumber. Wanting so much to believe she'll always be with me, I shed a few tiny tears of joy when I finally convince myself it's true.

Being one of the world's wealthiest women, it's understandable that Martha doesn't care about money. Her wealth comes from love. In varying denominations she gives it away … and always gets back more than she gave. With more to give, she gives more … and gets more … and so on. It's rather like compounding at an extraordinarily high rate with the principal and interest guaranteed by Almighty God, not some minor deity. I've watched; understand how it works; can't do it myself; believe it's something women and children do, and it may be why men love them.

Perhaps jewelry! Hong Kong overfloweth with jewelry made with twenty-four carat pink gold. The Chinese buy it to show off, and to hoard as a hedge against worthless currencies. It won't burn or rot, so it's safe to bury or hid when next invaded and, in the form of slinky necklaces and bracelets, it travels well in the hems of warm garments if one needs to flee in the cold of winter. In hot weather, pearls are better. They weigh less and hot weather garments are of a thinner material. To me, pearls are more feminine than gold. Small pearls, of course. Not ones the size of golf balls, or *apples*. It's equally true of wearable gemstones; bigger isn't better. If not true, then Martha would be exponentially more beautiful if thirty feet tall, rather than five feet, six inches. At ninety feet, she'd be too ravishing to be looked upon by mere humans.

However, there's no evidence that Martha covets jewelry. She wears her wedding and engagement rings, the Double Happiness necklace from Mei Liew … and nothing else. Never even slows when passing a jewelry store; has never verbally admired some piece of jewelry worn by another woman. Seems Martha would rather show off her figure and smile to sharing attention with a gaudy babble.

No, no jewels or jewelry for Martha. If I gave her something of that nature she'd feel she had to wear it … and won't want to … and wouldn't that be a fine *How Da Ya Do* when I'm trying to say: I LOVE YOU!

There's always the gift of something practical. Martha loses or destroys sunglasses and wristwatches at an alarming rate. If I give her a dozen each, they'll be gone before she's a year older. But it seems a bit fatherly. Any message of I LOVE YOU would be understood to include IN SPITE OF YOUR IMPERFECTIONS, which isn't true.

Maybe two or three dozen hats. Martha loves trying on hats but never buys one. She had a well-loved straw hat on *Tropicana*, until it blew into the straits and we didn't give chase. Nope. I'm certain women prefer buying their own hats after testing for appearance and size.

A car! Martha adores driving. She has a marvelous aptitude for handling any vehicle at any speed in any congestion. A convertible, of course. Something sporty. A Jaguar XKE would be *perfect* … "if slightly less phallic" adds my stuffy-gene. With a top speed nearing one hundred fifty miles an hour, Martha would find the Jag … well, exhilarating. British Racing Green, I should think. Though Martha might like red. I'll take whatever's available, wrap it with a giant ribbon … and have it painted if she doesn't like the color. Yes, yes! What fun!

Oh no … no, no, no … not a car. Martha knows I don't have a driver's license, and that I wouldn't drive a car, her car or any other car, unless it was a matter of life or death, which it would quickly become. She might think I gave her a car so she can chauffeur me about to save money, as then I wouldn't need to hire a car and driver. With the Jag's limited seating, everyone else we're always transporting would have to run alongside … and Martha couldn't go very fast, so driving wouldn't be any fun at all, and, unless I'm somehow arrested for arson and murder, we'll soon be living in Singapore. Her beautiful Jaguar would have to be loaded onto the deck of some freighter of the *Matilda* class and delivered to Singapore, where they'd completely disassemble the vehicle searching for illicit drugs.

To promise somebody they'll get something in the future, even an XKE, as a present for a birthday that happened weeks ago, seems in poor form … and the only way I can be sure the Jag will say: I LOVE YOU is to get a horn rigged to somehow honk I LOVE YOU rather than beep, beep, and I can't imagine Martha driving round Singapore using a horn like that. And truthfully, I don't want her to.

By Jove! How about a beautiful house? Martha *did say* she wanted a house like Sir Gordon's. Of course, Singapore's much too flat for a cliffhanger with a splendid view, but Martha's reasonable. It wouldn't be hard to find a house that's a major improvement over living in a hotel suite. A house, of course, doesn't exactly say: I LOVE YOU!

An estate, on the other hand, can be named. At the entrance to an imposing drive that leisurely winds its way through palm trees as it wanders to the main house, there must be a sizable plaque. Bronze, I should think, and properly weathered to a tasteful patina that reads: I LOVE YOU! But that's somewhere in the future; which's neither today *nor* tomorrow.

I can't very well, as a birthday present, give Martha permission to start a family. And to present her with some other woman's baby, certainly doesn't say: I LOVE YOU!

A box, no matter how refined the box, filled with salacious negligées doesn't say: I LOVE YOU! Rather, I fear, it suggests I'd prefer being married to a prostitute, when that's neither a desire nor one of my many imperfections.

Perhaps a piece of investment-grade fine art along with several first editions. They possess intrinsic human warmth and generally appreciate in value …

"You awake?" Martha whispers, so she won't disturb me if I'm sleeping.

"Yeah," I reply, sans enthusiasm and with a bit of frustration.

"Oh my. You haven't been sleeping, have you?" she worries.

"Are you kidding? This bed of apples belongs in The Book of Job, right next to Satan smotting poor old Job 'with sore boils from the sole of his foot unto his crown'; Chapter two, verse seven."

"Which version?"

"King James."

"You haven't memorized the bible, I hope."

"Of course not. Why would I do something like that?"

"You do weird things; know weird things. What *have* you been doing? And how close are we to Kowloon?"

I look at my watch. "It's nine fifty-seven, which makes us close enough to arriving that we should get off these apples with as much decorum as we can mustered. Providing *mustering* off apples isn't a mixed metaphor."

"I don't care about mixed metaphors. You get up and then you can help me."

"Okay," says I, and start to move.

"But first, while you're right where you are, and I can still make you lose some of your precious decorum, I'll tell you about *my* dream, and you'll tell me what you have been worrying about? And don't tell me you haven't been worrying, because you're covered with *worry*."

"I am?"

"You are!"

"If you must know, I've been trying to think of a birthday present that says: I LOVE YOU."

"Do you mean one of those little dolls with a string in the back, a chatty something?"

"No, no, no. Some present, that by its very nature speaks silently to the fact that I love you very much. There. That's it; nearly three hours' worth."

"Well, I *have been* suspicious. There were signs, you know. Little things. Why not just give me money? I can always use more money."

"Nope. I rejected that idea. Not personal enough."

"I see," she says, and pauses. "A car then. I love to drive."

"Thought of that, too. Rejected it as well. Believed you would think you had to drive me everywhere. And besides, there's only room for two people in a XKE convertible, and I didn't know what color you'd like, and it would eventually have to be shipped to Singapore, and Singapore would inspect it for drugs by taking it apart, and it would never get put back together correctly."

"I see. What a pity. British Racing Green would have been my first choice. Not too flashy. Well, hmmm. We need a house somewhere, but that would be for both of us, and it's too complicated for a birthday present. I don't collect things, and don't really want to. If you promise never to forget my birthday again I'll let you off easy."

"Cross my heart and hope to die from hiccups."

"No. Say:'cross my heart and hope to *suffer* from hiccups'. *Dying* lets you off, way too easily."

"Okay, I cross my heart and hope to suffer from hiccups, forever."

"That's better," she satisfies. "For my Birthday … you can take me dancing, and when we get home you can give me a lovely red box containing a sexy nightie with an absolutely gushy birthday card."

"Are you sure? I'm a terrible dancer."

"True, but it'll be fun when we get home. Want to hear about my dream?"

I nod, my smile weakening with apprehension.

"You and I were in the Garden of Eden. I suppose it was all these apples. You were Adam. I was Eve."

"So far, so good," I cheery. "Was I as handsome as ever?"

"Even more," she smiles.

"I wouldn't have thought that possible."

"And there were no serpents," she continues, "but you were growing restless from boredom, and soon picked an apple, took a bite, said it was delicious and that I should do the same, which I did. Then you started chasing me, and I was giggling and we got thrown out for making a disturbance."

"Sorry about that."

"That's okay. I was the silly one doing all the giggling."

"Yes, but I was the one that started it all … makes sense, though. Anything else?"

"No. That was it. I dreamt it over and over again. And if you want something to worry about, don't worry about my knowing that you love me, worry about what we're gunna give Adolf and Mei Liew for a wedding present."

"*You're kidding!* When?"

"Sunday. They're very much in love, you know."

"No, I didn't know. Indeed, I'm always the last, the very last to know anything about anybody. The day after tomorrow?"

"Yes, dear. If the kidnapping hadn't worked out, they we're going to delay the ceremony. But everything worked out, didn't it?"

"I suppose. And by the way, dear wife, if you become pregnant I'd deeply appreciate being the *first* person you tell."

"Of course, dear. Now, please, be very careful getting up.

19.

I t's rather comedic, I suppose, holding Martha in my arms to save her ankle from unnecessary wear, while one of her hands fishes for passports lurking somewhere inside the chest pocket of the suit coat I'm wearing; the narrowed Chinese eyes of a Hong Kong Customs and Immigration officer watching her every suspicious move, with a hand on his service revolver. I doubt he's ever had two Americans arrive aboard a riverboat filled with apples. So he might be imagining Martha will pull out a deadly fountain pen and stick him in the eye. Even though we're tired, I shouldn't be snickering and Martha shouldn't be giggling as if we're stoned and/or getting away with something illegal. Thankfully, she hooks the passports.

Our documents are in order. Reluctantly, we're allowed to proceed *without* Mr. Uniform standing aside, which forces us to twist and squeeze through a narrow opening in the chain-link fence.

Apparently, the riverboat crowd doesn't hail taxis for lunch at the Peninsula Hotel, or anywhere else. After three blocks of looking for a hirable vehicle, the unions representing my arm muscles are ready to strike, and when we find one, the driver won't leave Kowloon but he will take us to the Star ferry terminal.

Grumbling arms carry Martha up the stairs and aboard the vessel. I put her on one of those slotted wooden benches and go to the men's room. When I return, Martha doesn't want me carrying her into the women's room, so I gently put her down at the entrance and she hops inside on a single foot.

Another taxi to the Hilton. Martha's loaded onto a baggage cart. On our way to the suite, we stop to collect a key and two messages from the Front Desk, then wait for an elevator.

"Good news?" Martha asks, regarding the messages, once we're ascending along with our cart-pushing, door-opening bellman.

"Actually," I idle. "Bill Stuart's in the air, or was, flying from Sapporo. He expects to land here about five o'clock this afternoon. And Holly called. She and Liam will be on a Cathay Pacific flight arriving noon tomorrow."

"Wonderful!" Martha squeals, "We'll need lots more rooms."

Even after a long hot shower and self-massaging her ankle, I'm surprised Martha yielded to vanity in the form of brown leather high heels matching her purse and going nicely with her camelhair suit—skirt, short and tight— white blouse and a silk scarf in a paisley pattern of blues and dark red. Walking with only the hint of a limp, she's ahead of me by a few steps as we approach Sir Gordon's front door.

Perhaps, I look as midday-debonair as Martha asserted. Yet I see nothing debonair about a light-gray flannel three-button suit with only the middle-button buttoned, well-shined black penny loafers, white button-down shirt and a regimental stripped tie of the Yorkshire Hussars. Her remark must have been motivated by the tie of alternating three-quarter inch stripes of Oxford-blue and silver-white, the latter bisected by an eighth inch strip of new-red. The Yorkshire Hussars trace their roots to seventeen ninety-four and the threat of Napoleon Bonaparte, when they were raised as the Northern Regiment of West Riding Yeomanry Cavalry. A volunteer force of small farmers not obliged to be used overseas without their individual consent; some were the tenants of the nobility who served as their officers.

We're arriving precisely on time—thanks to our riverboat return, my impeccably accurate watch and Martha's ability to dress faster than Superman can change clothes in a phone booth—and before I can knock, Sir Gordon himself opens the door.

It's never been my pleasure to see him in a venue other than his office, so I never noticed how much he looks like Ronald Colman. Thin mustache, perfectly groomed. Wavy hair combed back. Ample forehead hardly lined. Subtle dimples when smiling broadly, as now. Lips are narrow, ears to scale and close to his head. He's a handsome gentleman with vestiges of a rakish youth.

Behind him at a coy distance, Elizabeth Beasley—still a blond with a small red heart-shaped mouth à la Gloria Grahame—poses, profiled in a gray turtleneck sweater tucked behind a wide brown leather belt atop a full skirt of gray that goes to her knees; high heels to match her belt, of course. I'm guessing her whistle-at figure has caused more than one young wolf to suffer a rebuff. The first time we met, I was entering Sir Gordon's office and she was about to leave. A gracious woman who's not the least flirtatious, anymore.

Sir Gordon isn't quick enough to offer a welcoming hand, so he receives a Martha hug and tries not to smile but fails. "Terribly nice to see you both," he says, when allowed to breathe because Martha's now advancing on Elizabeth.

To Sir Gordon, I offer a hand that he shakes with nervous enthusiasm, then straightens his navy-blue blazer and, by the elbow, leads me to Elizabeth. During our brief trip I consider how best to respond to the welcome I assume she'll offer. When she does, I twist on the balls of my feet to loudly snap shoe heels together and bow in a quickly contrived Prussian/American fashion, and she giggles.

Their Chinese houseboy materializes. In a starched white tunic above baggy black pants and black shoes, he's smiling and standing at a proper distance waiting for Sir Gordon to advise him of our choice in beverages. Sir Gordon looks at us with eyebrows raised as his way of asking.

"Brandy and soda, no ice. If it's not too much trouble," says I.

"Me too," Martha echoes, "and if it's not too much trouble, could you put your view of the harbour," – she turns, looks at the windows, and opens her arms – "in a bag or a box, to go."

With chuckles all round, Sir Gordon requests four brandy and sodas, then tells the houseboy, who isn't a boy at all, to do what he can about the view; after lunch.

"Any recent adventures?" softly sings Elizabeth, while looking at us with ice blue eyes.

"Well …" Martha begins, but I cut her off.

"It depends," I grump, "if attorney client privilege extends to the attorney's wife."

"Oh my," Elizabeth groans, and turns to her husband. "Does it, dear?"

"Interesting question," he muses, "not only for what it implies," – he smiles hungrily – "but as a point of law and ethics. If she's in her husband's law office, and the time is being billed, I'm rather certain privilege would apply. Particularly if the attorney's wife understands the issue of privilege, and agrees to be bound."

"I do, and I do," chirps Elizabeth, "but must we go to your office?"

"No, we needn't go to my bloody office, but I will have to bill the time. So there's a record of legitimacy." I nod approval. "And you'll *do what*, my dear?" Sir Gordon urges.

"I'll keep my mouth shut about anything Luke or Martha say."

"OR?" he challenges, staring at her.

"OR … or you'll be disbarred," she stammers, "and we'll go broke, and the girls will have to marry for money, and I'll have to serve cocktails or take in laundry or disembowel myself."

"Yes, Lizabeth, I think you've about covered it," judges the barrister, and then takes the last tall elegantly thin glass containing brandy and soda from the silver tray being passed by his houseboy. "However," he adds, looking at Martha and I, "I cannot extend this confidentiality to the household help. Whatever they overhear they're free to repeat … and probably will, you understand."

I nod and so does Martha, before she raises her glass and sings:

"To secrets!"

Four glasses delicately ring out their pleasure at being touched by one another and I wonder if her toast and the ringing of glasses seals our mutual agreement well enough to hold up in court.

"Let the record show it's twelve-seventeen," I announce,

"and I have a small question."

"First, my good fellow, why don't we sit down over here," Sir Gordon invites, extending his arm in the direction of an intimate grouping of chairs to our left, near one of the big windows, and away from the dining room.

Elizabeth turns and walks, swaying ever so slightly, in the indicated direction. We follow, with Martha holding my hand so I won't follow too closely. Four big armchairs upholstered in the hides of ostriches are arranged in pigeon-toed pairs, each pair opposing the other and sharing a rosewood end table that's complete with two coasters, a large marble ashtray matching the floor, a clear crystal box containing cigarettes, and a small silver-plated tabletop lighter.

The chairs are sink-into soft. Perhaps, they were intentionally designed to retard physical confrontation, for if suddenly angered, getting to one's feet without assistance would take longer than most men can sustain a desire to attack. Ladies, of course, never have the desire to feel someone else's facial bones give way to their fist, preferring to throw whatever's handy, such as a potentially lethal marble ashtray.

"Luke, ol' boy, you had a question," Sir Gordon reminds me and then, in perfect concert with Elizabeth, reaches for and lights a cigarette.

"I was just wondering if this gathering has a time constraint."

"Not really," Sir Gordon smiles, while Elizabeth exhales smoke through her nose and then smiles. "Weekends tend to be a bit cluttered—what with social obligations and two daughters—so for some years I've reserved Friday afternoons as a time just for the two of us."

"We've even," Elizabeth smirks, and recrosses her legs, "given the servants the afternoon off and chased round the house."

"*Lizabeth*," her husband blushes, "Luke and Martha *really* would rather not know."

"*Indeed?*" she quips, looking at him with maternal patience. "I just want them to realize we're not as old as we might appear."

"I think it's delightful," enthuses Martha, as if she can't wait for the fun to begin, "and very good exercise."

"Yes, of course," Sir Gordon idles, before taking an extended drag from his cigarette. "Any other questions, Luke?"

"No, sir. And, well, for what remains of my life there may *never* be another question."

There's laughing, winking and sipping. Lots of sipping. A bit of looking at the floor, the ceiling and through the window. Then we're summoned to lunch, and I welcome the change of atmosphere.

"Luke," Elizabeth sings, once we're seated, she and Sir Gordon directly across the table from Martha and I, new brandy and sodas in place, "you promised to tell of your adventures."

I smile, nod and wait while a platter's being passed by one of the kitchen staff. It's piled with sandwiches. And I'm so wolfishly hungry that tasting trumps story telling.

Oh, my! They're aged cheddar cheese atop bean sprouts, thinly sliced water chestnuts and slivered pork that have been pan-fried in real butter before being mounded on bread. I look at Elizabeth and shake my head while smiling to silently conveying my pleasure and wonder. She grins. Clearly, she has sources of information in which she takes pleasure, ones heretofore unknown to the western world. If one loves hot melted cheddar cheese sandwiches, these are too spectacular to be moral.

"Elizabeth," I croon, knife and fork still in the air, "you must apply for a patent, so that each time these culinary miracles are served in the new hotel we'll have to pay you a royalty."

"My dear," Sir Gordon confides loudly, as he leans toward his wife, "Luke confers no higher compliment."

"That's true," Martha surges.

"Well," says I, mouth momentarily vacant, "since we've the time, and certainly won't be going hungry, I'd like Martha to rehearse some history I believe will help you understand a few current issues. Martha's not only entertaining and accurate, but she can do it while eating. Three things I've yet to prefect."

"Bravo!" Elizabeth applauds. "And, my dear, don't you dare leave out the good parts."

Editing with a form of care bordering on wild abandon, Martha has left out very little that my stuffy-gene considers titillating. Otherwise, her rendition supports the possibility she once assisted James Michener in writing a novel that began with the Book of Genesis. Thankfully, she ended as Tommy's junk departed Hong Kong, earlier this morning. The kidnapped labor leaders weren't mentioned, but she did, rather cheerfully, include the discovery of my half-brother and his believed whereabouts. The burning down of Central and South American hotels along with my being accused in the Valparaiso fire was presented with a touch of indignation, and more than a hint of irritation. Of course, what I hadn't told Martha she couldn't relate.

Except for the brandy and sodas, lunch concluded and the table was cleared long ago. Martha had paused whenever the ear-count, including two of her own, exceeded eight.

Sir Gordon had smiled with interest, as lawyers will do to stimulate testimony without asking questions. Though on several occasions he'd been so overwhelmed with the

251

appalling behavior of certain characters, he had bowed and then shaken his head with obvious remorse or disgust.

Elizabeth's reactions—a movie producer's dream—were as if she'd been invited to the private screening of a soon to be released film: she laughed, wept and groaned; exclaimed "Here, here!" whenever the heroine prevailed (which was rather often as that was how Martha told *her* story) and even I received one "Good Show!" for walking out on the FBI. It was clear that Elizabeth was perplexed by Tina. Perhaps she'd been thinking of her own daughters. However, the business about playing Ravel's *Bolero* on a grand piano, had elicited a giggle. And the way Martha told of seeing the newspaper headline that morning at San Francisco International, was so touching even I got a bit misty.

"*My word*!" Elizabeth emotes, looking at Martha. "What an exciting life! And you're still so young, and so beautiful. And shameful as it is, I can't wait to hear what happens next … though I'm *terribly* glad you're not one of my daughters. Good lord, I'd *never* sleep."

"I concur," smiles Sir Gordon, pushing away from the table. "May I suggest we try the window seating once more, and perhaps some coffee?"

"And a plate of chocolate cookies," purrs Elizabeth, actually winking at me.

"I could use some help," I remark, when we're settled and the smoke from two cigarettes floats toward an extraordinarily high ceiling.

"Yes, of course," he says reflexively, without a moment's hesitation, while some mild alarm seems to be tightening the mouth of his wife, who may fear I suddenly need money for a risky venture.

"I'd like you to represent me … everywhere. In Chile, to get charges dismissed. After all, you know I was in Hong Kong and couldn't possibly be in two places at once. Then there's settling with insurance companies in Chile, Panama, El Salvador and Peru. I hold the mortgages *and* I pay the fire insurance premiums. Also, I've no desire to rebuild. The locations have degenerated over the years.

"My office manager—Holly Stuart, wife of Bill Stuart the man who'll be landing my almost-new DC-3 in a few hours, that he'll have flown to Hong Kong from Seattle via Alaska and Sapporo—and her son are flying in from Seattle, with pounds and pounds of documents. They'll land at Kai-Tak, noon tomorrow.

"As soon as I heard about the fires, I had Holly call the general managers of the other hotels whose mortgages we hold, to tell them about the fires and to suggest they increase their security. Quite naturally, they're reported to be a bit jumpy. I'd like to take advantage of their possible discomfort, and would like you to negotiate a conversion of the remaining mortgages, to my ownership of the ground under the hotels, that I'll lease back to them for twenty years at a monthly payment equal to half whatever they're currently paying on their existing mortgage. Those hotels are in Anchorage, Alaska; Vancouver, Canada; Portland, Oregon; Oakland and San Pedro, California. There's also a hotel in Mazatlan, Mexico, but we might have to form a Mexican corporation to own the dirt under that property.

"I don't want my name or Martha's connected with any of this ownership, so it seems a Hong Kong or Singapore corporation, with you as the Managing Director, will be needed.

"It may be unfair, of course, but you'll find each mortgage includes an option allowing me to buy-back the hotel, using a formula based on the property's gross sales. It was a hedge against dreadful mismanagement. I want to exercise the buy-back options on the hotels in Manila and Singapore. The option can also be used, if necessary, to motivate conversion from mortgage to ground lease.

"Due to the circumstances, there's a considerable urgency and a substantial amount of traveling, if these matters are to be dealt with expeditiously. I'll pay you for eight hours, at your normal hourly rate, for each day you're not in Hong Kong. Plus, since Martha's a shameless romantic, I'll cover *all* travel expenses for yourself *and* Elizabeth, including an extra week in Seattle, San Francisco or Honolulu, going each way, for the purpose of, well, *acclimating*, shall we say."

"I see," he says, and pauses to light another cigarette while Elizabeth squirms, what I hope is a happy squirm.

"I do see a few problems," he idles. "And it wouldn't be the *least* expensive way of handling things, you understand. I don't suppose I can talk you out of it."

"Nope."

"There's my calendar. My associates, of course. The committees I'm on. At the moment I can't make a commitment other than …"

"Oh, dear, dear husband," Elizabeth pleads, "*do* make it work out. I've never been to Central America, or South America. I absolutely adore San Francisco. And Honolulu is so … so extremely romantic."

Sir Gordon reaches over, pats her hand, and looks at her with a loving, perhaps even a lusting smile.

"Luke," he disparages, "I believe you want for sleep, or less distraction. Your being in Hong Kong at the time of the fires does not defend against a charge that you paid someone to start the fire in Valparaiso. Indeed, if I understood Martha correctly, you were actually *in* Valparaiso before meeting

Martha in Seattle and flying to Hong Kong. Furthermore, to start aggressively trying to collect on the insurance … well, it would give your accuser greater credibility. And you shouldn't make any statements about not rebuilding."

I nod.

"I find nothing wrong with the rest of your agenda," he considers aloud. "Even as to its timing. However, I strongly recommend that you—we, I suppose—pursue the same program regarding the four destroyed hotels. To wit, the conversion of their mortgages into ground leases to counter, rather well I believe, any charges of burning them down for the insurance money and the resulting deaths; murders, if you will. Have you any idea who's behind these *dastardly* deeds?"

"Yes. I do, actually."

"And whom might that be?"

"Our spying Congressman. Tommy surmised as much, and he also believes the Congressman had help in the form of information from the FBI. Tommy guesses the Congressman threatened to quit being a double agent, unless the FBI provided him with some information about me, so he could retaliate. Martha and I did rather mess up his life. And parting with a little information doubtless means nothing to the FBI."

"Tommy Tang?" Sir Gordon blusters, none to happily.

"The one and only," I respond, a bit pridefully. "Do you know him well?"

"I do."

"They're distantly related," Elizabeth injects. "You might say they have skeletons in the same colonial closet."

"Life's wonderful," Martha elates, while setting her empty glass on a coaster to her left. "When I learned of *my* family skeletons I thought it was inexcusable, unforgivable, and surely made me subnormal; diseased in some way. Learning that Mei Liew is the mother of Luke's half-brother. Knowing that you, Sir Gordon, are related to the wonderful Tommy Tang ... well, it all makes me feel so much better."

We chuckle, raise our glasses and nod toward Martha in a silent toast to her feeling better about herself, and also to some unspoken truth regarding humans and human nature. Fresh un-requested brandy and sodas are served. I look at mine and doubt it's an antidote for anybody's fuzzy thinking. A shame the coffee got lost.

"Another thought on this fire business," Sir Gordon exhorts, struggling from his chair and beginning to pace; it's not exactly an act I find comforting. "Of course, the man who paid the arsonists wasn't Luke Whitaker, but he could very well have shown the arsonists a picture of Luke, which, I suppose, could have been provided by the FBI. And, in addition to paying for the fires, the man could have paid a bonus—or threatened in some way—so the arsonists would identify a likeness of Luke, or Luke himself, if he's presented in a line-up.

"I must say, I don't take comfort in such a scenario. But it's best to pose it as a *possibility*. And considering that Luke has been implicated in one fire, it's more likely a *probability*, if one considers the trouble that someone has gone to, that he'll be implicated in the other fires."

"Should I prepare to hang?"

"No, Luke," Sir Gordon glowers. "But what has *our* Tommy suggested?"

"His personal cooperation," I say, wondering if I should say more.

"Cooperation with what?"

"I've asked him to find out who the Congressman was spying for prior to becoming a double agent for the FBI."

"Why?"

"Because the FBI suggested he was stealing top-secret plans for the Vietnam War."

"And you assume that means the Congressman was working for the North Vietnamese, or the Chinese, or the Soviets?"

"No, sir. Just the Chinese or the Soviets."

"And if so …"

"Then I'll pay Tommy to have the Congressman kidnapped, and taken somewhere safe while we work out a trade."

"A trade? A trade for what?"

"My brother."

"I see. Interesting. A bit dangerous, of course. Have you considered trading the Congressman back to the FBI, on the condition they vouch for you having nothing to do with the fires?"

I glance at Martha. Her eyes are ablaze. "Do you *really* think that's a good idea?"

"No. I do not. It probably won't be necessary. And even if it was necessary, from what you've told me about your dealings with them, they can't be trusted, and they are unlikely to do anything that would help Luke Whitaker. It's just that since yesterday afternoon in my office, I've been wondering about how Luke's mind works."

"Tommy," I smile, "thinks I'm an evil spirit, if that helps."

"Well, yes. Hmmm," he rather mumbles to himself, while lighting another cigarette, and while Elizabeth appears to be taking mental notes.

"Luke is *not* an *evil* spirit," Martha flashes. "A bit of a *free* spirit, and lonely like every other man. He certainly has too much money for his own good, but he is definitely *not* an *evil* spirit!"

"Martha's absolutely right, dear," Elizabeth volunteers, "and you know it!"

"Yes, yes, of course," Sir Gordon ordains. "But remember, please, the Chinese imbue evil spirits with supernatural qualities enabling them to trick or fool or convince mere humans to do things they wouldn't otherwise do. I believe Tommy was alluding to Luke's ability to convince him, Tommy, to take actions he wouldn't ordinarily take."

He looks at me with eyebrows raised. I nod in agreement.

"There. You see, Elizabeth," Sir Gordon says, twisting to look at her, "Tommy didn't mean Luke was evil, just unusually convincing, combined with an unearthly freedom of thought—Tommy would use the term Soaring Eagle— that Martha identified as 'a bit of free spirit', which, in my humble opinion, Luke actually contracted from Martha as it *can be* rather contagious."

"Dear," sings Elizabeth, standing with fluidity and unsuspected grace, "you make Martha's sense of adventure sound like a communicable disease. And if it is, I'm hoping to become infected. Now then, who else would like more chocolate cookies? I'm finding them a perfect complement to brandy and soda. And since I'm still able to stand, I suggest more of both. And when I get back, I must hear about what went on in your office, yesterday. The part about Luke."

Without waiting for a cookie-confirming vote, Elizabeth moves away like a cloud in a gale. I ask Sir Gordon if he can arrange for a law firm to represent us in Singapore and Malaysia, and he suggests it won't be necessary, as he's licensed to practice in both countries; would consider it a privilege, and that Elizabeth adores Singapore, thinks it very romantic. Martha, who's been grinning like the Cheshire cat in *Alice and Wonderland*, solicits Sir Gordon's opinion regarding a wedding present for Mei Liew and Adolf, which are quickly narrowed down to a rubber plantation or a hotel in Malaysia. Sir Gordon asks her a few questions, lights a cigarette, and says he'll give the issue some overnight-thought.

"Here we are!" trumpets Elizabeth, gleeful at the head of a small troupe: two members of the kitchen staff, each carrying a plates of chocolate cookies, houseboy bearing a silver tray loaded with four glasses of brandy and soda.

"Now then," she smiles, sitting with the same practiced perfection used in rising, "I'm *dying* to know about yesterday."

Sir Gordon begins by saying he can't mention the man's name—Martha's listening as eagerly as Elizabeth—and he delivers an entertaining summary that relies heavily on analogies.

"So dear," Elizabeth cross-examines, "what did he tell you?"

"Did he confess?" Martha prods, while grinning.

"I wasn't seeking a confession, Martha, though he did cough up some useful information. You see, we suspected he was part of a gang stealing high explosives from Chinese armories and smuggling the awful stuff down the Pearl and into Hong Kong, at considerable risk to our local population, as it was being stockpiled in a local warehouse before being shipped to the world's highest bidders.

"With his information, I was able to tip off an old acquaintance—now a high-level prig in the PRC (People's Republic of China)—about a shipment scheduled to come down the Pearl, last night. I'm sure he alerted the boats on patrol, which made it a bad night for all smugglers. This morning I was told there were several explosions about where the smugglers would've entered Hong Kong waters.

Apparently, one was quite spectacular.

"Even though there's been no official confirmation, and there may never be any, for that matter, the Safety Committee is in your debt," he sighs, and nods once in my direction.

"Here, Here!" jollies Elizabeth smiling at me, her hero of the moment.

Silence emanates from Martha, much like it circulates in a cemetery.

On tarmac Kai-Tak allocates to air freight, among aircraft being loaded and unloaded, Martha and I stand shoulder to shoulder. *Lord* and *Lady Whitaker* (according to her bluff and my contemptuous frown), here to welcome her uncle, Sir William Stuart, her mother's older brother, the successful owner of Stuart Air Freight and innumerable other enterprises. Caught off guard, groveling authorities acquiesced to her every request.

It's five o'clock. Officially only three hundred and seventy-two seconds remain in the local tenure of today's pale winter sun. I'm covertly smiling. My Executive Committee has just advised me of Martha's reason for changing from her silk paisley scarf to a wool scarf whose tartan belongs to an unidentified clan, or no clan at all. "Apparently," saith their report, "Martha believes she's more of an *English Lady*, if wearing tartan versus paisley." Before handing the memo back to the messenger, I scribble "Brilliant!" at the bottom; again amazed at what a committee, any committee, finds worthy of its attention. Being but a simple man, I find the scarf's combination of green, yellow and red, pleasing to the eye.

Bill and crew will have flown the old DC-3 about six thousand eight hundred miles. This accomplishment, in addition to his nursing the plane back to full functionality, makes the aircraft more his than mine. I'm glad his name's on the fuselage, and the plane's painted in *his* family's ancient tartan. It's unique and a rather subtle camouflage.

"Do you see 'em?" Martha purrs, putting her hand inside mine.

"Not yet."

"Are they very late?"

"Not yet."

The DC-3's something of a tired growling angel with long outstretched arms, when we hear the distinctive low-pitched roar of her twelve-hundred horsepower Twin Wasp radial engines, and see the grayish aircraft descending with lights flashing, wings steady, wheels down.

A boyish mind wonders if his father might step off, once they've landed, as he's done so many times in the past.

"I love you," I sigh, feeling a bit lonely.

"Of course, you do," she smiles, "now hush, they're landing," and grips my hand with excitement.